Angel on Bakeoven Road

Sandy Cereghino

Angel on
Bakeoven Road

A Novel

Bakeoven Series
Book One

Sandy
Cereghino

Sandy Cereghino

© 2019 by Sandy Cereghino
Cover by Sandy Cereghino

Printed by Gorham Printing, Inc.
Centralia, WA 98531

Printed in the United States of America

ISBN 978-1-7342467-0-4

Angel on Bakeoven Road: a novel/ Sandy Cereghino

1.Title. 2. Fiction 3. Romance 4. Angels 5. Road

… always believe

Sandy Cereghino

Author's Note

Though this book is entirely a work of fiction, the inspiration behind Angel on Bakeoven Road was drawn from several real-life events. After I heard about the latest wreck and that the person survived, I thought, there must be an angel on this road and so, the story was born.

Located in Central Oregon, just two miles south of the historic town of Shaniko, Oregon off highway 97, Bakeoven Road is a twenty-six-mile country road, which has seen its fair share of wrecks. While doing research, far as I can tell, no one has died, though many should have.

The events and characters have been enhanced for the story. I do believe something, or someone is watching over those who travel Bakeoven Road. And, I hope this story will leave you, the reader, with a sense of hope and understanding that second chances are all around us.

I want to thank my friend Debra Holbrook for listening to me that day, and her continued support over the last six years as I worked to bring this story to life.

Sandy Cereghino

Acknowledgments

When I started to write this book, I thought I knew what I was doing but soon learned I didn't have a clue how to write. If not for my sister Janie Berry, an author in her own right, urging me to attend my first writers conference with her, I would never have had the courage to finish this book. Thank you for pushing me out of my comfort zone.

To all the coaches and new friends, I have met at Oregon Christian Writer's conference over the last six years, thank you for your constant support during this journey as I continue to learn the craft of writing.

I want to thank Mary Ann Hake for editing my book and teaching me so much along the way, and all my family and friends who have listened and read my early attempts. I hope you enjoy the final version.

A special thanks to my daughter April, who has listened to me tell the story so many times she knows it by heart.

Most of all, a heart-felt thank you to my husband Richard, who has encouraged me to follow my dreams wherever they make take me.

Angel on Bakeoven Road

Chapter One

April 1930

Kelly guided the truck back to the main road from the farmer's house, as dawn rolled over the high desert landscape. She had another 18 miles to drive before she reached the town of Maupin and prayed, they had what she needed to restock her supplies. Kelly still thanked God, that Mr. Ward happened to come by, when she had a flat tire halfway across Bakeoven Road. They were both in need of saving that day, but nursing school never prepared her for what she experienced this last week. It had tested her ability and her faith. The hardest part now, was saying goodbye. She glanced at the tiny yellow rose bush sitting next to her and smiled. Mr. Wards' little girl had given it to her as a goodbye gift. She promised Kelly it would bring sunshine where-ever she went. Kelly was still admiring the rose bush and didn't see the curve ahead until it was too late.

August 2018

Lou McClelland paced across the threadbare carpet of her editor's office, seething with anger.

"It's my story!"

"Calm down, Lou. I know it's yours." Brad shifted in his chair.

"Only, now, you'll have a partner."

Lou stopped in front of his desk and glared. "I don't want one. You said Chris, and I had to work alone. I've spent weeks setting up interviews with these people. Now you want me to share everything with a stranger. Who is this person?"

Brad flipped open the file folder on his desk. "I'm doing a favor for an old friend who runs the New York Post. From what I understand, Jason Peterson should arrive around one p.m. tomorrow."

Lou plopped into the chair next to Brad's desk and folded her arms as if doing so would help calm her pounding heart. So, this person was a man. "What's going on here Brad? Why don't you let this guy work with Chris? I'm sure he would rather collaborate with a man."

"Let it be, Lou. I have assigned Chris to a different project, but I expect each of you to produce an exciting, informative story. After I've read then, I'll make my conclusion about the position. Think of this as a learning experience. I'm serious, Lou. Pick this guy's brain or..."

"Or what?" she snapped at him.

Brad closed the file, clasped his hands, and placed them on top of it.

"I pull you from the piece, let Chris do his story, and assign you to something else. Your choice."

Lou dropped her arms, digging her nails into the palms of her hands. "You can't be serious."

Her mind raced. Could he do that? Would he do that? This was the story she needed to prove she could manage the job of an investigative reporter. The previous one retired, and the paper was looking to fill the spot.

"Yes, I am. Give the guy a chance. You might even make a new friend."

Lou didn't want to give the guy a chance or make a new friend. But if she kept protesting, Brad might take her story away or worse, she could lose her job. Bile rose to the back of her throat. For a moment she thought she might get sick.

She pushed herself up from the chair and faced the window to hide her frown. As she starred through the glass, the heat radiated against her face, causing a bead of perspiration to form on her upper lip. For nine in the morning, August promised to be a scorcher. She was about to turn away when a whirlwind caught her attention. Hypnotized, she watched it sweep along the street, picking up the parched maple leaves and debris that lay in the gutter. It swirled them high into the air, before disappearing behind the weathered brick building across the street. She felt her life was spinning out of control like the leaves.

"Fine, have it your way." Throwing her hands in the air, Lou marched down the hall to her office, slammed the door behind her and leaned against the door. Tears welled in her eyes and threatened to spill over. How could Brad do this to her? This story could have all the elements readers wanted. Drama, heartache, and the hope of a happy ending. A lot like her own life with the drama and heartache, though she was still looking for the happy ending.

Lou flinched. Her recent break-up with Chris Walker, another reporter at the paper still weighed on her heart. Chris had seemed different from the other men she dated, though when he said he liked her simple look, the remark had confused her.

They had been dating for three months and she thought it was going well until she caught him playing post office with the mail room girl. Her best friend Julie, who worked in the graphics department, tried to warn her Chris had a roving eye, but Lou wouldn't listen.

Then she saw it for herself.

When she confronted him, Chris tried to laugh it off saying it was just a joke, but Lou could tell by the way he looked at the girl, she was the one being made a fool of. To make matters worse, she learned he had put in for the same position.

Lou slumped into the chair behind her desk and scanned her surroundings. She was lucky to have her own office, but this one could belong to anyone who worked at the paper.

Not a single picture hung on the muddy shade of tan walls. Her desk, a cheap imitation woodgrain, was the type every office store carried. Besides her computer and desk phone, her nameplate, reading lamp, and desktop calendar. Nothing that was personal adorned it.

Even the chair sitting in the corner frowned at her with its shabby tweed cover. The room stood for her life, bare and lonely. Lou looked down at her clothes and sighed. If she got up and stood against the wall, she would disappear like a chameleon hiding from its prey.

Julie had been trying for months to get her to put some color into her wardrobe, but Lou liked comfort. Simple makeup, a little lip gloss, mascara and wrangling her curly hair away from her face into a rubber band was her beauty routine. Her basic work outfit was white blouses and khaki slacks which she wore for every occasion. She pulled at a loose thread on the hem on her shirt and realized for the first time how bland she must appear to the rest of the world. No wonder Chris went looking elsewhere.

Lou tried to push the dreary thoughts aside and pulled out her story file. Amazement still coursed through her that no one else at the paper, including Chris, had caught wind of this human-interest piece before she did. It started when she read a "letter to the editor" inquiring if anyone had information about the crosses on Bakeoven Road, forty miles west of The Dalles. The woman said she had been driving the twenty-six miles from Highway 97 toward Maupin when she spotted them, counting six. Her curiosity had gotten the better of her, so she stopped to get a closer look and was shocked at what she saw written there. After reading one, she drove back and read the others.

Each cross had a person's name and a date, along with a single sentence. But these crosses differed from the usual roadside memorials. Instead of marking the day the person died, they celebrated the day they *survived!* After reading the woman's letter, Lou wanted more information. She searched the Internet for any mention of crosses on Bakeoven Road but was disappointed how little information existed. This only fueled her curiosity—she needed to see them for herself.

Lou doodled on her desk mat, remembering the trip to Maupin and the ensuing drive down Bakeoven Road and back. The sight of the crosses along the roadside and reading the names, dates, and inscriptions had brought her to tears. By the time she returned to her office, her perfect story had been born.

Brad had liked the concept and agreed this would make a great human-interest piece, giving her the go-ahead. She spent the next few days searching old phone books and the Internet hoping to find the six people. To her surprise, they were alive, and living in or near The Dalles and planned to start her interviews soon but now wasn't sure.

The scene in Brad's office had been a crushing blow to her ego and she wondered if he thought she wasn't up to the challenge by assigning this guy to help her. Doubt crept across her mind. She had to pull herself together. This was her chance to prove to Brad and Chris, she was the right person for the job—only problem now: Jason Peterson.

Lou closed the file in front of her, slid her chair back from the desk, and rolled her neck from side to side. The mention of Chris was affecting her more than she realized, and their breakup had shaken her self-confidence. Lou didn't trust anyone, and this Jason person wasn't welcome. This was her story and her town. She sounded like the sheriff from an Old West film with her "don't come to my town" defiance. She could challenge him to a shoot-out at high noon in the middle of the parking lot, then laughed at the thought. She closed her eyes, leaned her head against the headrest and inhaled a deep breath until she could no longer hold it and exhaled. She wasn't ready for the change that was coming.

Jason Peterson sat in the dark living room of the apartment he had rented after the sale of his house two years earlier. The apartment lacked updating in years. Floral wallpaper covered the walls in large pink and mauve cabbage roses. Dark wood molding surrounded the window frames, where heavy velvet curtains shut the morning light out. A rotary phone sat on the antique walnut end table next to his chair, clanging with the tone of a school bell through the room. With each ring, the sound vibrated though his body, causing him to cringe and squeeze the arms of the broken-down recliner he had been sleeping in. Jason's breathing raced and the urge to jump up and run from the room washed over him. Where would he run? Another empty room?

Jason hated the panic attacks that paralyzed his body whenever he closed his eyes. His therapist told him this was a normal reaction after what he had been through, and to give it time.

The phone rang again.

Jason yanked the receiver, knocking the phone to the floor. "Hello!"

"Whoa... No need to yell."

"David?"

"Yes, Jason."

"Sorry, Boss."

"Never mind. Why didn't you answer your cell phone, and why aren't you in the office? I've been waiting four days for you to show yourself."

Jason winced at David's words. He had turned off his cell phone and forgot he gave David his home number for emergencies. He had missed another deadline. "Hey, sorry, man. Time got away from me."

"Don't give me that, but I didn't call to lecture you."

"Listen, David." Jason tried to rub the sleep from his eyes.

"No. You listen, Jason. Be here in one hour, not a minute later, or you can clear out your desk." David hung up the phone.

Jason shook his head to the sound of silence echoing on the line. A stabbing pain surged between his temples, as a vile taste rose in his throat. Rushing to the bathroom, he upchucked the last of his dinner from the night before. Laying on the floor waiting for the waves of nausea to subside, he wondered what Annie would have thought of his behavior.

Shame washed over him as he reached for the handle to flush the stench away. He pulled himself up off the floor and stared in the mirror. Cheese from last night's pizza hung on the whiskers of his grungy five-day beard. His dark-brown hair stuck out in all directions, with gray strands at the temple making him look older than his twenty-eight years.

When did he stop caring? He used to be clean-shaven, pay for a good haircut, and wear nice clothes. Now he considered himself lucky if he had clean underwear. With no time to waste, he stripped out of his stained shirt and baggy sweatpants, dropping them onto the pile of dirty clothes in the corner before stepping into the shower.

David was right

He had been making excuses not to go to work and wished the water would wash the pain away. Jason shut off the water and grabbed a towel. With a quick glance at the clock on the wall he realized he'd have to hurry to make it on time. His job was the last thing he still had. He didn't want to lose it too.

David Walters, editor of the New York Post, finished what he had been working on before looking up to face his employee.

"Hello, Jason." David stood and offered his hand. "Nice to see you're still with us." Jason had squeaked in just under his hour ultimatum.

Jason sighed in relief and accepted David's strong familiar grip. He had given Jason his first break right after college. Over the last six years, David helped him hone his craft. But since the accident two years ago, Jason's head hadn't been in the game. The thought it disappointed his mentor made his stomach turn.

"I'm sorry for yelling on the phone this morning."

David cracked a smile as he sat. "Forget it. I'm glad you're here."

Jason relaxed into the chair in front of the desk. "Thanks. And about the deadline. It won't happen again, I promise."

David shuffled the papers on his desk, ignoring the comment.

"I have an interesting story I want to tackle with another paper, so I'm sending you to The Dalles, Oregon."

"What's in Oregon?"

"The best story of your career—and a chance to get your life back together. I'm doing this because I care about you Jason, but here's the catch. You leave in the morning and your flight's at 8:00 a.m. That should put you in Portland around nine, with the time change. It takes ninety minutes to drive to The Dalles, plenty of time to get to your appointment by 1:00 p.m. Your tickets are at the front desk and the contact information is in this folder."

David pushed the folder towards Jason.

Jason flipped it open and scanned the information.

"What makes this newsworthy?" A sudden chill snaked along his spine, urging him to object. He couldn't do this. He needed to say no, but he kept his mouth shut. David cared, otherwise their meeting would have been his termination.

"There's more to the story. And I want you to find it."

Jason sat back in the chair. "Why me? Don't you have a flunky reporter who can write this story?"

David turned his chair away from him and Jason knew he had to change his attitude and quick.

"You're right, this might be something," Jason tried to sound convincing. "I can hash this out in a few days."

David turned back around to face Jason. "True but take your time. Let's see how it goes. Here's a company card to use for expenses. My secretary has booked you a room at the local Motel 6."

"You're kidding me—aren't you?" He waited for the punch line. "Motel 6?"

David stifled a laugh. "Yes, Motel 6. And when you get to Portland, a rental car will be waiting."

"Where is this place?" Jason was beginning to think this was to be his punishment for bad behavior. Exiled to the West Coast.

"Jason—enough with the questions." David's voice was sharp with irritation. "You can get that information from the rental car agency, just do what I pay you for and get the job done."

Without another word, Jason left, stopping only long enough to retrieve the envelope waiting for him at the front desk before hailing a cab. When he returned to his apartment to pack, he stood in the shadows of the living room, surveying the emptiness before him.

He realized his life was just as empty and went to his bedroom, grabbed his duffle bag, and stuffed in his laptop and recorder along with his whatever clean clothes he could find. Suddenly overpowered with exhaustion, he flopped on the bed and figured he might as well try to sleep.

Six a.m. would come soon enough.

Chapter Two

The airlines had packed the Tuesday morning flight to Portland with a multitude of travelers, including families with screaming children, who were giving him a headache. Problems with the rental car agency only heightened Jason's foul mood by the time he got out of the terminal and onto the freeway.

To make matters worse, the air-conditioner in the Ford Escort struggled to keep up with the heat, while he tried to cope with the fact, the rental car agent gave him, a guy that stood six-feet tall, a compact car. Disgusted, he pushed on until he reached the exit for The Dalles City Center. Even with the help of the GPS on his phone, he still made a few wrong turns before he arrived at his destination.

Jason parked in the gravel lot next to the whitewashed, block-wall building of The Centennial newspaper and noted the temperature sign on the corner registered ninety-nine degrees and the time showed one-minute past one. Beads of perspiration trickled down his temples as he exited the car and walked through the front doors into the lobby. Cool air greeted him, and he stood for a moment letting his body temperature drop, while he scanned the office and its surroundings.

The décor looked to be something from the 1950s. Dark wood paneling covered the walls and sun-faded mini blinds hung in the windows, casting striped shadows across the worn linoleum floors. This office was nothing like the chrome-and-glass-covered high-rise buildings in New York City. Instead of fine art, pictures of cowboys and, yes, Indians hung on the walls. In the middle of the lobby, sat a brown leather couch, checked with age. Next to it was a rustic wood coffee table covered in newspapers, most likely today's edition.

Jason noticed a young woman sitting behind a desk on the other side of the room with her back to him. Her shoulders swayed to what must be music from the earbuds in her ears and played with her bleached blonde hair while snapping her gum. Jason figured she must be the receptionist and not over nineteen or twenty. Her clothing portrayed a Western style, if you called it that, with her ruffled red-checkered blouse and blue denim skirt.

As he approached the counter, she seemed oblivious to the fact he stood behind her. Irritated at her unprofessionalism, he reached over the counter and spun the chair around to face him.

"Hey!" She yanked out the earbuds. "Sorry, sir. Can I help you?"

"Yes, I hope you can help me, Miss … ?"

"Karol with a K."

"Well, Karol with a K, I'm here to meet Brad with a B."

"And whom do I say is asking?"

"Tell him Jason Peterson is here."

Karol snapped her gum at him. "Are you someone special?"

The question caught him off guard. "So, Brad's office?" He had to remind himself he wasn't back home.

The girl stood and spun on the heels of her shocking red cowboy boots and motioned for him to follow. "What a jerk," she mumbled under her breath as she headed toward Brad's office.

Jason followed, ignoring her remark. Why was he being rude to her? She wasn't the one responsible for him being here.

Karol stopped, pointed at the door, then turned and walked away without saying a word.

Jason's pulse raced, and his palms grew moist as he knocked on the door, then opened it without waiting and walked in.

"Brad Perkins?" Jason asked the man sitting in front of him.

11

"Yes? And you are?" Brad set the paper he'd been reading aside.

Jason moved closer to the desk. "I'm Jason Peterson—from the New York Post. You were expecting me."

Brad stood and extended his hand. "Nice to meet you, Jason. I've read your profile—impressive."

Jason accepted Brad's firm handshake and winced.

"Thanks, or I should say, don't believe everything you've read."

Brad grinned. "Please sit. Can I get you something to drink? Water? Coffee? Tea?"

"No, thank you." Licking his lips, Jason realized his mouth was dry. "On second thought, water sounds good. Is it always this hot out here?"

Brad turned in his chair, reached into the little cooler sitting on the floor next to his desk and retrieved a bottle of water. "Here you go. It can get unbearable even with air-conditioning once summer sets in."

Jason twisted off the cap and guzzled half the bottle, trying to quench his sudden thirst. "Thanks—so, what's the angle on this story? David said something about people surviving accidents on some road. Not sure what makes that newsworthy." He tried to sound casual as he put the cap on.

"It's an interesting story. An urban legend around here. You'll be working with my top reporter, Lou McClelland, who will give you the details."

Jason adjusted himself in the chair. "Hey, wait a minute. I work alone."

"Not on this one. This is The Centennial's story, but we're sharing bylines with your paper. Didn't David tell you that?"

Jason shook his head.

"Anyway, that's the least of your problems."

Jason frowned, wondering how it could get any worse. "What problems?"

12

Brad leaned back in his chair and chuckled to himself.

"I must warn you; Lou isn't thrilled you're here."

"And why is that?" He wasn't thrilled either.

"Let's just say, Lou's a little possessive about the story."

"Is Lou here today?" Jason wanted this meeting over as soon as possible. Exhausted from the trip and the heat, he wanted to check into his hotel room, take a quick shower, and grab a short nap before tackling the assignment.

Brad pursed his lips, as if trying to keep from smiling, then stood. "Yes, Lou's been waiting for your arrival." Ushering Jason out the door, Brad pointed down the hall. "Lou's office is the last one on the left. Good luck." He gave Jason a pat on the shoulder before closing his door.

Jason stared down the hall, wondering what Brad was up to, then shrugged. Not wanting to waste any more time, he headed down the hall to find Lou. He figured meeting man-to-man, would help clear the air.

Lou had spent the morning going over her notes, making sure everything was in order when this Jason person, as she kept referring to him in her mind, arrived. It was nearing noon, and she couldn't remember if she had eaten breakfast, but the growling of her stomach assured her otherwise.

She decided she had enough time to get something from the vending machines in the snack room. The choices lacked in the healthy food department, but who was she to complain when her refrigerator at home hadn't seen fresh groceries in a month. She hated going shopping and usually stopped for fast food most of the time.

Lou settled on yogurt pretzels and a diet coke, figuring it sounded healthy and retrieved her goodies. Back in her office Lou finished her snack, then rearranged the folders and notes on her

13

desk again. Next, she moved her desktop calendar to the other side and slid her name plate closer to the edge. Bored, she checked her watch. It was after one. Maybe she had lucked out and Jason wasn't coming.

Rising from her chair, Lou peeked out the small window in her door for any sign of the elusive reporter. She was about to turn away when she saw Brad's door open and a man exit. This must be Jason. He paused as if in thought before heading her way with a determined scowl on his face. She would bet money he just learned he would be sharing the story.

Lou hustled back to her desk, gathered her notes, and slipped them into her desk drawer. *No reason to give the enemy the secrets yet,* she chuckled at herself and barely sat, when she heard a rapping on the door, and it opened. In front of her stood a tall, good-looking man. His piercing brown eyes danced with flecks of gold and she had to stop herself from staring. She was reacting more like a love-starved teenager than a professional woman. His wavy hair was the shade of dark chocolate and looked good enough to eat.

She wondered if she still had that half-eaten box of chocolates in her bottom drawer of her desk. Then she remembered Chris gave them to her, and she vowed to throw them away. As she studied him, Jason continued looking at her as if he might be in the wrong office.

"Something I can help you with?" she asked. She was trying to keep her voice light but professional, and her mind off food and other things that made her want to blush.

"Ah, yeah, I mean, I'm Jason Peterson and—"

"Yes, I know who you are. Care to come in and sit?"

Jason nodded, grabbed the tweed chair, and slid it closer to the desk before closing the door. "Thanks. I'm here to see Lou and would appreciate if you told him I'm waiting." Jason leaned back in the chair and folded his arms.

14

Lou bit the inside of her mouth. It would be easy for him to assume "Lou" was a man. It was her own fault since she hated her full name—Louise and shortened it to Lou. It sounded more professional when she came to the paper and had kept it that way.

Lou looked down taking a moment to compose her words before she spoke. "Well, Jason, I won't get in trouble telling you my name, though you might not like it."

Jason sat in awkward silence, scanning the office until he caught sight of the nameplate on her desk. "You're Lou?"

"Yes, that's me. Is that a problem?"

"But I..." Jason shook his head and grinned. He looked as if he were weighing his options before he spoke. "My apologies for assuming you were a man."

Lou wanted to be mad but let it slide. Jason seemed normal enough—so far. It wouldn't be hard working with him, besides, she could pick his brain, as Brad suggested. Jason *was* from New York City, a place she dreamed of going someday. She leaned back in her chair and imagined herself walking through the doors of the top newspaper in town. A place where everyone knew her name. It sounded like that old sitcom *Cheers*. She needed to get a life.

She heard him clear his throat. "Hey, Lou?"

Lou snapped her mind back to the present and sat upright in her chair.

"Sorry. Just thinking about the story." This man flustered her. After breaking up with Chris, she had sworn off men. Workplace romances just didn't work. "When can you get started?" she asked, trying to regain control of her runaway emotions. "Are you familiar with the story?"

"No. I have a few notes from my boss. He said it had to do with people surviving an accident or something. I'm not sure what makes that a story. Brad said it's some kind of urban legend. Although around here, I'd call it rural."

15

Lou opened her desk drawer, pulled out two file folders, and handed one of them to Jason. "You're telling me you know nothing about the story you came all the way from New York City to do?"

She didn't care if she sounded hostile.

Jason shook his head. "No, I don't. Why don't you enlighten me?"

Lou shuffled the papers on her desk. Jason's questions irritated her. "Everything you need is in that file. I've spent hours doing the research and setting up these interviews. Until you familiarize yourself with the story and the three survivors, I've assigned you, there isn't much for us to discuss. Look Jason, I don't mean to sound rude, but I've been working on this story for over two months and was ready to continue. That was until yesterday when Brad informed me you were coming."

"So, you knew who I was?"

"Yes."

Jason seemed to relax, but the muscles in his neck twitched.

"Why the hard-nose act? I only found out about the story yesterday myself."

Lou shrugged her shoulders. "No act. This is my story, and I don't want to share it, but management has ordained otherwise so I guess we tolerate each other. Read the file, make notes if you must, and be back here tomorrow morning by nine a.m."

Standing, Lou held out her hand. "Nice to meet you, Mr. Peterson."

Surprised by Lou's abruptness, Jason rose and clasped her outstretched hand in his. Electricity surged between them, causing her to release her grip and step back.

"Okay—tomorrow—nine a.m.," he rubbed his fingers together as he opened her office door. "Anything else, Boss?"

Jason must have noticed the tingle too, but she noted the sarcasm in his voice.

16

"No, that's all for now. Please be on time. It took a lot of persuading to get these people to talk."

Lou picked up her bag and moved by him out into the hall, heading for the front door. As she passed by Brad's office, she caught his eye and gave him a dirty look, to which he responded with a laugh and a wave. Well ahead of Jason, she breezed past the front desk where Karol had her nose in one of her fashion magazines and made her way to the parking lot. Sitting next to her well-worn Jeep Cherokee, a small car sat which must be Jason's rental and she wondered how he fit into it. With a grin, she slid behind the wheel of her own vehicle as Jason came around the corner of the building. Their eyes locked for a moment. A tickle of sweat dripped down her back, making her squirm against the seat. Lou hoped it was from the heat and not from his gaze. She gave him a quick wave before she exited the parking lot.

Jason waved back as Lou drove away, leaving a trail of dust behind her. Lou's choice of vehicles intrigued him, though it suited her. Tough, but with soft edges. No wonder Brad had a smirk on his face when Jason left his office. The joke was on Jason.

Lou's tough act had surprised him, but he understood the importance of setting one's territory. Jason waited for the dust to settle, before yanking open the door to his piece-of-crap rental car and slip into the driver's seat. Checking his instructions, he punched in the address for the motel into his cell phone's GPS. Ten minutes later he had checked in and headed to the second floor to find his room.

It was average, nothing compared to the suites he usually stayed in. A queen-sized bed was sitting, centered against the wall and across from the bed, on the dresser, sat a small flat-screen television. Next to that, a desk with a single chair. The bathroom had only a shower, but it stocked with clean towels, shaving cream, razors, soap, and deodorant. All the things he just realized he had forgotten to pack.

Jason set his bag on the chair, spotted the air conditioner, and switched it on. It wasn't long before the circulating pump caught up and the cool air swept across his face. Relieved, he stripped down to his boxers and T-shirt, flopped on the bed, and fell fast asleep, not moving until morning.

Lou had caught Jason's awkward wave in her rearview mirror and smiled. She enjoyed watching the big man squirm. She knew it wasn't a nice thing to do, but she couldn't help herself. Besides, he was too attractive for his own good. Lou didn't trust him. If she was being truthful, she didn't trust men, period. Her father disappeared when she was seven, and she never heard from him again.

After years of having to endure her mother complain how rotten men were, and catching Chris cheating on her, Lou was thinking her mother might have been right. She hadn't dated in months, instead she had poured her time into her work.

Lou pulled into the driveway of the house she had shared with her mother until a year ago. The problems began with Mom forgetting how to load the dishwasher or fix her hair. As Mom's behavior worsened, the doctors diagnosed her with rapid onset dementia devastating Lou. Over the next couple of months, Lou tried caring for her mother, but when she grew violent towards Lou, she feared for both their safety. After consulting with the doctor, Lou agreed Mom needed to be in a care facility, where the staff where trained to manage people with dementia. Even though they rarely got along, Mom was the only family Lou had. Six months later Mom died, and an emptiness had covered Lou like a never-ending fog.

Standing on the porch, Lou realized she was still trying to come to terms with her loss. She gazed out over the front yard that needed tending, ashamed she had let it get this way. Mom had always kept the flower beds full of flowers of every color, but now they lay covered in weeds—unkept—like herself.

Life with her mother had been hard, but it was familiar. It never dawned on her to moved out on her own. She had just stayed while she and her mother had a love-hate relationship with each other to the end. While growing up, there were things Lou wanted to say or ask her mother, but never garnered the courage.

As for her father, she had no clue where he might be or if he was still alive, or if she cared. He had walked out on them, on her, and left her with an unstable mother who took pleasure in sucking the life from her. Her father should have protected her, instead he deserted her. She doubted if she would ever forgive him for abandoning her.

Lou shook her head as if doing so would dislodge the unhappy memories, slid the key into the lock, and opened the front door. More emptiness met her as she set her bag on the table in the kitchen. When she pulled the fridge door open, not much met her gaze. Half a dozen outdated eggs and a partial block of moldy cheese sat on the top shelf in the dim light. Two English muffins lay next to left-over Chinese, along with a dried-up beef rib. She would have to throw everything away, but she wasn't in the mood to clean her refrigerator tonight.

Disgusted, she slammed it shut and opened the cupboard door. Lou grabbed a box of crackers and poured herself a glass of water and settled on the couch. She wanted to refresh her mind for her interview the next day. Every time she read her notes about the survivors, her spine tingled, raising the hairs on the back of her neck. Each person said a young woman, they called their angel, had helped them. It didn't seem possible for the same person to be at every accident—unless.

Lou had her doubts, but something kept telling her to keep an open mind. She rested her head against the couch remembering when she was younger. She loved to sit on her father's lap, nestled against his chest, while he told her Bible stories. After he left, she kept asking God to bring him back. He never did. So, Lou gave up asking.

The one bright spot in her life was her friend Julie. Lou wasn't one to make friends easily, but she and Julie hit it off from the beginning, when Julie came to work at the paper two years ago. She was there for Lou when she had to put her mother in the home and later, helped Lou through the funeral and a shoulder to cry on when Chris broke her heart. But Julie had her own life. She had recently married and moved to Portland. Though they talked every day, she missed her best friend.

Lou tried to shove away the memories invading her thoughts and focus on her notes. Content she had missed nothing, she set the file aside and shuffled toward her bedroom. Tomorrow would be a new day and a new set of problems.

How to deal with Jason and her sudden attraction to him.

Chapter Three

Jason woke to a beeping noise echoing through the room and turned his head toward the nightstand. Seven a.m. flashed in green across the screen of the clock radio as he reached over to shut off the buzzer. He didn't remember setting the alarm but was grateful the last person had and that the nightmares had left him in peace for once. He sat for a moment trying to stretch the kinks out of his back. Jumping up he stubbed his toe on the corner of the nightstand launched him into a cursing streak as he hobbled to the bathroom.

Once he finished dressing, he settled at the little desk to scan the file Lou had given him. Why David would send him to do a story about this country road or the fact it had a bunch of crosses on it baffled him. He still didn't understand what made this newsworthy.

A sudden vision of a cross sent a flash through his mind of his wife, Annie, and their daughter, Sophie, at their own funerals—so vivid his hands shook. This whole story idea was absurd, and he would put an end to it right now. Picking up his cell phone he punched in David's number, but voice mail greeted him. Angry, he threw his phone on the bed. As he paced back and forth, trying to calm the pounding in his head. He cursed himself for being weak, then picked up the file and resumed reading.

Jason's first interview would be with a man named Harold Joner. After checking the information sheet, he noted Harold's birthdate. He was nearing ninety-nine years old and Jason wondered if Harold still had his memory intact or would the

21

interview to be a total waste of time? Jason figured this whole story was a waste of time, but David had sent here him to do a job.

He remembered Lou said they each had three interviews. Confused, Jason flipped through the file but didn't find any further information. He slid the file into his bag. What kind of game was Lou was playing? He made a mental note to question her when he got to the office, then picked up his gear and headed out the door.

Passing through the lobby, he snagged a cup of coffee in hopes it would help wake him up before his meeting. Once outside, the morning sun began to heat the surrounding air. Sweat dripped from his temples by the time he reached his rental car and he prayed his deodorant would hold out.

She was reading through files on her desk when he entered her office.

"Morning, Jason. Can I get you coffee?"

Well, at least she used his first name today. He watched how she bit her lower lip as if she was nervous. It made him smile.

"No thanks. Got a cup at the motel, though I'm sure yours is better." He pulled the chair by the door over to the desk and sat next to Lou. Her lavender perfume triggered a memory of Annie.

Lou must have seen the sudden pained look that crossed his face. "You okay?" she asked.

Jason choked down the lump in his throat. "Yeah—sure." He lowered his head for a moment then flipped open his file. "I checked over the file you gave me. Come on, Lou—you believe this crap? And what's with this Harold Joner guy? You sure this guy's still alive or can remember anything?"

Lou picked up her copy of Harold's file. "Yes, he is. And I'm keeping an open mind. I realize this may not be up your alley as far as investigative stories go, so you're free to pack your bag and leave. As I told you yesterday, I'm ready to do the story, and I won't have any trouble doing it alone."

Jason sat erect in the chair and jerked his head back. It didn't take much to get her riled. "Sorry if I upset you. We both have a job to do. Can we start over?"

Lou bit her lip again. "Fine. You're right. Let's just focus on the story."

"Is there anything else you want to discuss?" Jason stood by the door with a frown on his face.

"No, that's all I have for today. Go do your interview then meet me back here tomorrow morning, same time, and we can compare notes." She played with the pen in her hand. "What's wrong now?"

Jason flipped the file open again. "You said we have three interviews each but there's no information in this file on the other two."

Lou tilted her head to the side. "I'll give you the next file after you're done with your first interview. No point muddling your mind."

Her bossy tone was getting on his nerves, but he let it rest for now.

"Okay, I'll see you tomorrow."

Jason shoved the file into his bag, pushed the chair back to its original place, and walked out the door. By the time he reached his car, he was shaking again. He didn't know what was happening to him and slammed his fist against the car door. He should give up and let Lou keep her story. The thought shocked him. What was he thinking? He wasn't a quitter, and he would not quit now. He would show her what he did best.

Investigate.

Lou pondered Jason's behavior. Brad hadn't told her much, but after she had gone to bed last night sleep evaded her, so she got out her laptop and searched the Internet. Now she understood why this story must be difficult. Lou was sorry for his loss, but life goes on and she had a job to do. She knew she was overdoing it with her bossy attitude, but she couldn't stop herself. She was tired of being second best in her life or with her job. Nor would she let Jason's presence derail her plans proving to Brad she had what it took to be an investigative reporter.

The one thing that worried her was that Brad had given them only a month to get the story wrapped up and ready for publication. Lou flipped the page of her desktop calendar, counted the weeks. That would put them at the end of September if everything progressed as planned.

Lou picked up her file and settled back in her chair. Bill Owens was her first interview and lived in the town of Rowena, fifteen miles west of The Dalles then she realized she would have to leave now the time to make it to her appointment on time.

Chapter Four

Harold Joner sat in his wheelchair watching the sparrows hop from branch to branch outside the window of his room.

The Heavenly Estates Retirement Home was turning out to be a lovely place to live since his arrival five months earlier. His wife, Eleanor, had died three years ago, then his only son, Roger, died from a heart attack the following year. Harold had no one else since Roger never married and when it became difficult for him to live at the ranch alone; he made the choice to come here. He even brought some of his favorite possessions to make it more like home.

The room wasn't large compared to his old bedroom, but it was comfortable. He had a private bathroom and large windows overlooking the rose garden. The office staff and nurses were nice and took loving care of him. And he had even made new friends.

Harold spent the best part of his day gazing at the garden. The roses, in soft pinks, corals, and scarlet reds, lined the walkway to a concrete fountain standing next to a white gazebo. On the other side of the gazebo a yellow rosebush stood alone. It looked like it was guarding something and the first time he saw it, the rose stirred a memory of long ago.

Harold's gaze wandered to the empty rocking chair next to the window, and a lump formed in his throat. Eleanor had rocked their son in that chair when he was a baby. Now it sat in the room with her favorite quilt across the arm, as if waiting for her. It didn't seem right that he should outlive them both. He wanted to join Eleanor and Roger, but God must be keeping him around for something greater. He just didn't know what yet. Memories had been flooding back ever since that reporter from the paper called. He hadn't thought about the cross for years.

Jason smiled at the old man in the wheelchair watching him as he approached. For someone close to one hundred years old, Harold sported a full head of shocking white hair, and his green eyes sparkled as Jason came closer. Harold's shoulders hunched forward and his hands, twisted from arthritis, lay folded in his lap.

"Mr. Joner?" Jason held out his hand. "My name is Jason Peterson. I'm here doing a story for The Centennial and New York Post newspapers. May I sit?"

"Yes." Harold shook Jason's hand with a firm grip, then released it and motioned toward the chair by the wall. "You can call me Harold."

Jason pulled the chair over to the little table next to Harold's wheelchair and sat.

Harold let out a deep sigh. "I hear you're wondering about my cross out on Bakeoven Road."

His voice caught Jason off guard. Though aged, it was clear, and it appeared his memory was intact. "Yes, I am. If you don't mind telling me about it."

"Not at all son." Harold straightened himself in his wheelchair. "Some things shouldn't be forgotten."

Jason pulled out his notepad and recorder. "Is it okay if I record this?" He set it on the table. "It helps me keep the facts straight."

"No problem. Use whatever you need." Harold waited until Jason gave him a nod to start his story.

"As I recall, I'd been working the south field, plowing and planting from dawn to dusk. It was taking longer than it should have. My tractor was old and held together with bailing wire and a prayer. We had one thousand acres, my wife, Eleanor, and me and

I was doing everything possible to make a go of it. We were dry wheat farmers. Do you know what the means?"

Jason shook his head. He was a city boy. "Sorry, I don't."

"Dryland farming means you rely on good old Mother Nature's rain and snow to water the fields. The year before it had been a dry spring and almost put us under with a poor crop." Harold paused for a moment as if searching for the next memory.

"After reading the *Farmer's Almanac,* I was sure this year would be wetter. I finished the last turn, slowed to a stop, and watched the sky. Clouds were forming, getting darker and darker, with what I hoped would be a strong downpour."

"Did it start to rain?" Jason flipped the page of his notebook and wondering where this was going.

Harold glanced down at the wedding band on his finger. "No, it didn't, and it made me mad." He turned the ring on his finger.

"Mad at who?"

"At the land, at my wife, and at God. Eleanor and I had a fight the night before. I thought I was doing my best, but if I was honest with myself, it wasn't enough for me either. If this crop failed, we would have to move. The lease stipulated you had to make a living on your property within five years to keep it, and this was our last year. I never told Eleanor we didn't own it when we got married. She believed the property belonged to me, and now I was on the brink of losing the farm and my wife if things didn't change. I was a prideful man. Wouldn't ask for help, and, worse, I never offered it. It's a bad place to be in your heart and mind. When my neighbor Jim Wheeler got hurt, I wouldn't take the time to help him with his crops. Should have helped ..." His voice got softer.

Jason glanced up from his notepad to see Harold's eyes closed.

"So, Harold, can you tell me what happened next?"

Harold's eyes fluttered open.

"Oh, yes. I was done seeding and sat there thinking how miserable my life was. The sky kept getting darker, but still no rain. Cursing at the clouds, I fired up that old tractor and stomped on the gas pedal sending it racing as fast as it would go across the field toward the road. I didn't see the boulder until it was too late. The left tire hit the side of it and flipped the tractor over into the ditch, crushing my left arm between the hood and the ground knocking me out."

Jason flinched as if in pain himself. "How long were you unconscious?"

Harold shifted in his chair. "It must have been at least ten or fifteen minutes before I woke. I tried to pull my arm free, but the pain shot though it so bad I screamed. Darkness was falling, and fear settled over me and I wondered if this was how I would meet my Maker and, if so, would God accept me after I'd been blaming Him for all my problems. Well, I pulled at my arm again, but it wouldn't budge. I knew if I didn't get it free, I would die out there alone."

Harold rubbed his arm as if reliving the pain and the memories.

"I didn't want to die. I wanted to hold my wife and tell her how sorry I was, and I wanted to apologize to my neighbor for not helping him in his time of need. While I lay there, I realized it would be too late for any of those things." Tears rolled down Harold's face.

Jason feared he wouldn't be able to hold back his own. The talk about Harold's wife dug deep into his own soul, and his heart ached for Annie. Jason handed him a box of tissues from the table. "Here, Harold."

Harold pulled out a tissue and wiped his nose.

"Can you tell me what happened next?" Jason asked.

Harold sat up in his chair with a determined look on his face.

"I don't recollect how long I lay pinned me under the tractor when a hand touched my shoulder and I lifted my head. A young woman stood there smiling at me and I asked her if she was The Angel of Death coming to take me."

"Did she answer you? What did she say?" Jason leaned forward in his chair. "Can you describe her?"

Harold smiled.

"Her voice was soft. Only a whisper. She said she was there to help me. As for describing her, I would say she was eighteen or twenty. Dressed in a long sleeve white blouse and a black skirt that hung below her knees. She had long, dark-brown hair and a strange shape, on the side of her face. Resembled a wing, as I remember. I closed my eyes for what I thought was only a moment, but when I opened them again, my arm was free, and I was sitting next to the tractor."

"What about your arm?"

"It was bandaged with strips from my shirt, keeping me from bleeding to death. I looked around, but I saw only empty fields. Even though I was alone, I wasn't afraid. I'm not much of a praying man, but I asked God for another chance after He had sent an angel to save me. I tried to get up, but the pain was so bad, I guess I passed out again."

Jason flipped another page and glanced at his recorder. "What happened then? Who found you?"

"From what I learned later, Eleanor got worried when I didn't come home and called my neighbor Jim Wheeler. He was the man I didn't help." He still appeared ashamed for his behavior. "Eleanor somehow she convinced Jim to look for me. He found me lying against the hood. I asked him how he found me, and he said a woman's voice kept calling to him. He said he followed her voice until he saw the tractor and found me next to it. Jim lifted me over his shoulder and carried me back to his truck, then drove as fast back to my house. The doctor was on another call, so Eleanor and Jim set my arm and bandaged me."

"Did he mention seeing the young woman?" Jason wondered if Harold had been hallucinating.

"I asked him later, but he said no. Eleanor and I spent time talking while my arm healed. I told her about the angel and how I asked God to forgive me. We cried and agreed this was a second chance." He adjusted himself in the chair again. "I pledged to change my ways and be the best husband and friend I could, by helping others for the rest of my life. Well, things turned around for us. The crops were bountiful, earning enough to make the farm ours forever. The following year we had a son, Roger. Jim and I became best friends, and I sat with him the day he died, a year before Eleanor. As for the cross, it appeared along the road where the tractor tipped over about a week after the accident. No one ever talked about it. But I knew who put it there," he said with a grin.

"One last question, Harold, do you remember what it said?"

"Oh, yes, it said, Harold Joner, saved to be a husband, father, and friend, August 2, 1948." Harold closed his eyes as if exhausted from telling his story.

Jason turned off the recorder, stuffed it and his notebook into his bag. He patted Harold's shoulder, "Sleep well, my friend. You deserve it."

Harold responded with a soft snort.

Harold's story of his love for Eleanor hit Jason hard. Why wasn't he given more time with Annie and their baby? Why didn't they get a second chance? Life wasn't fair. On his way past the front desk, he let the nurse know Harold may need help, then walked out into the summer heat.

⌒

Harold waited until he was sure Jason left his room before he reached for the phone and placed a call to his lawyer. After finishing his conversation, he knew he had done the right thing.

The story had brought back so many memories and peace flowed over him as he drifted off to sleep, for real this time, and sensed Eleanor's presence behind him.

Chapter Five

With the help of her MapQuest directions, Lou found Bill's apartment complex in Rowena and parked. It was a two-story building that sat on the edge of town overlooking the Columbia River. From her vantage point, she watched the wind surfers dancing across the water like butterflies, in hopes it would help calm her nerves. Someday she would try that, then chuckled to herself. She wasn't the sporty kind.

Lou grabbed her bag; made her way to the door she had listed on her notes and rang the bell. When the door opened the man's black shirt and the cross around his neck surprised her. She couldn't help but notice the jagged scar that ran down the side of his face.

"Ah... yes... I am looking for Bill Owens. I'm Lou McClelland, a reporter for The Centennial." She began to wonder if she had knocked on the wrong apartment.

"You've found him. I'm Pastor Owens." He stepped back to let her enter. "Please come in."

"Thank you, Pastor Owens." Lou took a quick scan around the modest apartment. It was small and tidy, with simple furniture, but had a homey look something her own home didn't have.

"Please, call me Bill. No need for formalities here." He motioned her toward the kitchen and a small alcove off the living room, just big enough to hold a small table and two chairs.

Lou pulled out a chair and sat, then reached inside her travel bag to retrieve her small recorder, setting it on the table.

"Do you mind if I tape our conversation?" She couldn't believe how nervous she was doing this interview. This was part of her job, but self-doubt was chipping away at her confidence. What if she failed? She was sure Chris wouldn't mind if she did. She wondered if Jason felt this way.

Bill shook his head then seated himself across from her. "No. I mean, sure. What is it you want to know?"

Lou adjusted her chair, straightened the recorder, then pushed the play button. "As I mentioned on the phone, the paper is doing a story about the crosses on Bakeoven Road. I believe one of them has your name on it."

Bill leaned back in his chair. "I hadn't thought about that cross for years until you called."

"I realize it's been awhile, but what can you tell me about your accident?" Lou picked up her pen, ready to take notes to help keep her hands busy and try to calm her nerves.

"As I remember, I just turned twenty-one and quit my job at a landscape company. I'm not a slacker, I wanted to work with computers—they were the up-and-coming thing but without college, I didn't have a chance. When I told my dad, I wanted to take a break and figure out what I wanted to do in life, he had a fit. Back then we didn't get along much. I rode off on my motorcycle for a weeklong trip through Oregon hoping to clear my head."

"Is that when the accident happened?" Lou was trying not to seem pushy.

Bill nodded. "About four days into the trip, I camped in Maupin, along the Deschutes River and hooked up with two other bikers. They told me about a shortcut back up to Highway 97, called Bakeoven Road. They said the twenty-six miles of cool switchbacks and straight stretches were a biker's dream road. From what they were saying few people traveled it, just the local farmers and ranchers who lived nearby or the lucky few who discovered the road. That night we drank a lot of beer, and I woke up with a major hangover. I should have slept a few more hours or stayed another day, but the road called me."

"Do you remember what happened next?" Lou flipped the page on her pad. She could do this; she just had to relax and believe in herself and, Lou admired Bill's courage to stand up for himself and leave home. Why hadn't she ever done that?

"Leaving the campground, I rode the curves out of the canyon and was up on the flats riding full-out when I rounded a corner and got the bike too close to the edge of the road. The front tire slid into the soft gravel and the next thing I know, I'm off the road into the sagebrush and rocks." Bill stood, stretching his back, then reached up and touched the scar on his face.

Lou couldn't help but ask. "Did you get that from the accident?"

"Yes." Still stroking the scar, he turned toward the window. "When I crashed, my helmet saved my life, or so I thought."

"Why do you say that?" Lou's curiosity was building.

Bill turned to face her. "After going off the edge of the road, the bike hit a boulder and stopped dead. It sent me flying over the handlebars and I landed in a clump of sagebrush with a piece of a branch stuck through my cheek."

Lou cringed and ran her tongue on the inside of her cheek to quell a wave of nausea. A tender tummy, she recalled her father calling it. The flashes of memories about a man she hardly remembered unnerved her. And why now, after all these years?

Bill returned to his chair. "I thought I would die, and I started to cry. Don't look so surprised, even a man can admit he cries. Anyway, I lay there in shock about to give up when I felt a warm hand caress my cheek. Before I knew what was happening, the stick was pulled from my face. The pain shot through my head as if something had hit me with a hammer, and I passed out."

34

"What happened next?" Lou realized she was sitting on the edge of her chair.

"When I woke, I was sitting against a tree and my helmet was sitting next to me. I felt my cheek, and there was a bandage on it and my left leg was hurting. When I looked down at it, a splint made with branches and strips of fabric was holding it together. A young woman sat next to me, holding my hand. Her touch swept any fear from my mind, and I understood I would be okay."

Lou felt the excitement rising in her chest. "Did she talk to you or tell her name? Did you see anything unusual about her looks or clothing?" Lou flipped the page of her notebook, writing, just in case the recorder didn't work.

Bill put his hands up to stop her. "Slow down a minute with the questions. Her voice was soft, and she told me this wasn't my time to die, that God had a plan for my life. I didn't grasp what she meant. The pain was so bad I kept fading in and out, but I remember she wore a black skirt that ended at her ankles and long sleeve white blouse. It sounds crazy, but everything was out of sync that day."

Lou pushed herself back in the chair and nodded. "I'm sure it was, Bill, and it must be hard talking about this. Is there anything else you remember?"

Bill sat staring out the window, as if searching his memories, then sat upright in his chair. "Oh, I remember now, she had this strange mark shaped like a wing, running from the edge of her chin to the top of her forehead. I must have passed out again, because the next thing I remember, the same group of bikers I had camped with, found me about an hour later. They used their cell phone to call for help. While we waited for the ambulance to arrive, I kept asking if anyone had seen a young woman. They said no and figured I was hallucinating from my injuries, though they couldn't explain who bandaged me. I don't know."

Reaching up, he touched the cross hanging from his neck.

The sight of Bill's cross caused a memory to flash through Lou's mind. She was five years old and remembered her mother dancing around the room to a Christmas song on the radio, while she sat on her father's knee. He had handed her a box tied with a red ribbon and remembered how excited she was opening it to find a gold cross. She closed her eyes for a moment, remembering how gentle his big hands were putting it around her neck. In a reflex action, she reached up to her neck. The necklace wasn't there, and her eyes snapped open.

"What did the doctors say about your injuries, if you don't mind my asking?"

Bill rubbed his cheek again. "They said I was lucky to be alive. The stick just missed going through my eye, straight into my brain. Still gives me the creeps thinking about it. My left leg had broken in three places and required surgery. When I realized I wouldn't be able to take care of myself, my dad came to get me from the hospital. In the beginning, it was hard for both of us, but by the time my leg healed we were best friends again."

Lou admired him for working things out with his father and wondered if she could do that with hers, if she ever saw him again. She doubted it, and a wave of resentfulness rushed over her for what she had missed.

"When did you learn about the cross?" She asked, trying to shake the emptiness.

"Not until three months later, after I healed. We took my dad's truck out to the crash site to get my bike. When we got there, I wasn't sure if it was the right spot. Then I saw a white cross on the side of the road. My first reaction was that someone died in the same spot until I read the words."

Lou stretched her shoulders. "What did it say?"

36

Bill played with the cross around his neck. "Bill Owen, saved to serve, along with the date, May 14, 1971. I didn't understand what it meant, but it dropped me to my knees. I swore not to waste the second chance it gave me. While going through physical therapy for my leg, I met a young boy recovering from a car accident. He lived in a foster home and I wanted to help him. So, I started working at the Boys Club, where he would come to play. That's when I discovered what I wanted to do and applied and was accepted to the seminary to be a youth pastor. This has been my life for forty years."

Lou set her pen down for a moment, trying to digest what he told her. Do we get second chances? Lou had quit believing long ago and had to force her mind back on track. "One last question, then I will get out of your hair. How old do you think she was?"

Bill shrugged. "I'm not sure, about nineteen or twenty. Why do you ask?"

Lou flipped back through her notes. "The others who share crosses on Bakeoven Road describe the same young woman at each of their accidents, dating from 1948 to the last one on June 18, 2017. Do you have any idea how that's possible?"

Bill shook his head. "I don't. I only know she saved my life."

Lou closed her notebook, shut off her recorder, then slid them into her bag.

Thanking Bill for his time, she headed back to The Dalles and her office. She spent the next two hours working on her notes until she was satisfied with what she had written so far. Leaning back in her chair, she stretched her arms over her head, and reflected on her career. She had started at the paper right out of high school and liked what she did, most of the time but yearned for better stories. Stories that would get people's attention, mainly Brad's.

After she discovered the story about the crosses, she prayed this would be her big breakout piece. Now with Chris up for the same position and Jason in the picture, she wasn't sure anymore. They were both seasoned writers, and she was still learning. Lou wasn't as tough as she put out there, and a nagging doubt crossed her mind again. What if Brad thought Chris's story, was better than hers or that Jason had written their entire story and refused to give her credit? The what ifs were making her tired.

Lou pushed up from her chair and headed home. Once she got there, she stood in the empty doorway engulfed in the silence and remembered she hadn't gone grocery shopping. She started to dial Julie's number but stopped when she remembered Julie lived in Portland now. Disheartened, she went to find a place to eat.

Chapter Six

The interview with Harold had taken longer than Jason expected and by the time he returned to his room and worked a couple hours, his stomach growled, and he noticed it was after 5:00 p.m.

Picking up his jacket, he exited the building, and strolled along the street, passing the few restaurants available. Nothing appealed to him until he got a whiff of roasted garlic.

An early dinner crowd packed The Branding Iron as he pushed his way through the swinging saloon doors. The place, like The Centennial's lobby, had an Old West theme, with wagon wheels and other Western décor hanging from the walls and ceiling. If he had the time while in town, he might read up on the local history.

The place was overflowing, and it didn't look like he would find a place to sit when he spied a couple getting up from a booth. He hurried over and slid onto the well-worn seat as they exited. He was scanning the menu while he waited for the waitress to come and clear the table and was still mulling over the selections when he heard someone call his name.

"Hey, Jason, mind if I join you?"

Jason looked up and saw Lou standing next to the booth. Her hair hung below her shoulders, surrounding her face in soft curls.

"Go ahead," he stammered, motioning to the seat across from him.

Lou slid into the booth and tucked a stray curl behind her ear.

"The place is so crowded tonight. I was about to leave, then I saw you sitting here alone."

Jason cleared his throat and wiped his sweaty palms on his pant legs. "No problem, I just arrived and was lucky to find a booth myself."

She looked different. The harsh lines he'd seen on her face earlier had faded away under the shadows of the hanging wagon wheels. "The smell of roasted garlic called my name. What about you?"

Lou scanned the menu. "Well, I got home and remembered I haven't gone grocery shopping and wasn't in the mood for moldy cheese and crackers. The roasted garlic here is the best in town."

Jason flipped over his menu. "My—never mind..." He stopped in mid-sentence, his voice catching. "The smell drew me."

"Me too, I come here often. They have the best ribs in town if you don't mind the mess."

Jason gave a nervous laugh. "Ribs, you say. I love ribs, with lots of garlic, and fries too."

"Yes, me too. The orders are large here and I shouldn't ask, but would you mind splitting one with me?"

"No problem. But on one condition." His eyes met hers for a moment.

"And what's that?"

"Only if I buy dinner."

"Okay, but next time I buy."

"Fair enough." Jason could tell she was as nervous as he was, and the fact she mentioned there would be a next time enticed him.

The waitress arrived, cleaned the table, and took take their order. After she left, Jason realized he forgot to ask Lou if she wanted something to drink. "Did you want a drink, a beer or something besides water?"

Lou shook her head. "Water is fine. I don't drink."

Jason was thankful he hadn't slipped and ordered a beer. He'd made a promise to himself when he left New York City, that he wouldn't take another drink. The pull had been strong, but he had fought the urge.

As they waited for their food, an awkward silence fell over them, but once the plates arrived, they wasted no time devouring the stack of ribs.

"Sorry, I just can't help myself." Lou set the stripped bone down on her plate, licking the sauce off her fingers.

Jason lay his rib bone down and wiped his mouth. "You're right. These are great. There's nothing this good at home."

Lou laughed. "You mean the big city of New York doesn't have ribs?"

"Well, okay, they have ribs. Just not this good." He gave her a stern look. "If you tell anyone I said that I will deny every word," then he laughed.

Lou smiled. "My lips are sealed." She ran her finger across them in a zipping motion. "But only after I finish my dinner."

Jason tried to remember the last time he had been this comfortable with a woman since Annie's death. Even though Lou acted tough on the outside, he suspected she was hiding a softness and wondered if he would discover it while he was here.

"So, how was your interview this afternoon? You were right about Harold; he sure likes to talk."

Lou wiped her mouth and set her napkin down. "It was very informative. Did Harold mention a young woman helping him?"

"Yes. He said she was young, eighteen to twenty. There was a wing shaped mark on the side of her face. Why?"

"Bill Owens, that's the man I interviewed. He mentioned the same birthmark. The thing I don't understand is that Harold's accident was in 1948 and Bill's was in 1971 and they saw the same woman, even dressed the same."

Jason nodded. "Yeah, that's strange. Oh, that reminds me do you have my next interviewee. I was hoping to read the file over tonight."

"Sorry, I didn't bring the folders with me. I hadn't planned on seeing you until tomorrow morning."

Jason shrugged. "No problem. It's been a long day."

After they finished, Jason paid the waitress and walked Lou to her car. "Thanks for the company."

Lou tossed her purse on the seat and turned toward him. "Hey, no problem, and thanks for dinner. It's nice to talk to someone besides myself. It can be a one-sided conversation, for sure."

Jason had an impulse to kiss her but stopped himself and stepped back. "Yeah, I know what you mean. Thanks again, and I'll see you in the morning."

Lou slipped onto the seat then looked up at him. "Where are my manners? Can I give you a ride to your motel?"

Jason shook his head, shutting the door between them. "No, but thanks for asking. I think I'll try to walk off the ribs." He patted his stomach.

"Sure, no problem. See you in the morning." Lou started the jeep, put it in gear, and pulled away from the curb, leaving him standing near the street corner.

Jason waved as she drove down the street. Something about Lou brought out emotions he hadn't experienced in years, but it only confused him. He wanted to get on with his life, but felt if he did, he would dishonor what he and Annie had shared. Emotions swirled through his mind as he walked back to his motel.

Chapter Seven

Sleep proved difficult for Lou that night. She lay staring at the ceiling for hours until she fell asleep, bombarded with wild dreams about Jason. This left her more flustered than ever. She never had dreams about Chris the whole time they had been dating.

By six-thirty she was wide awake, and by eight, she was heading to the office. To avoid having to talk to Karol, Lou used the back entrance then stopped by the break room to snag a much-needed cup of coffee to help her focus. Jason would be here soon, and it embarrassed her to even face him after what she'd been dreaming.

Julie had been pushing her to date again but the pool of single men in The Dalles was a little empty so ending up an old maid was more likely her fate. She was about to take a sip of her coffee when Jason swept through the door and dropped into the chair in front of her desk startling her.

"What the—" she yelled as coffee flew over the front of her white blouse and in her lap. Jumping up, she slipped, sending the chair sliding backwards. She landed on the floor, wedging her between the desk and the wall.

Jason sprang from his seat and leaned over the desk. He was struggling to keep from laughing. If looks could kill, Jason would be dead by now as Lou sat in a heap on the floor, her hair askew, with coffee still dripping off her desk onto her clothes. He reached out his hand. More embarrassed than mad, she accepted it. As he pulled her to her feet, she glanced at her clothes, and started to giggle until she was laughing so hard, she almost fell over again.

"Jason—look—what you did!" Lou gasped between breaths, holding on to the edge of her desk.

"I'm sorry, Lou. I didn't mean to startle you." Jason yanked off his knit-shirt and sopped up the rest of the coffee on her desk, before offering the shirt to her to blot her clothes

"Are you okay?"

Jason stood in front of her—shirtless. If someone walked into her office, they would never believe her explanation. Lou reached for the shirt and dabbed the front of her blouse and pants, before handing it back to him.

"Thank you. Now please put your shirt back on before someone comes in here."

Jason stared at her then down at the soggy shirt he held.

"You can't expect me to put this back on—it's wet and stained with coffee."

Lou rolled her eyes, staring at the muscles on his tanned chest. His arms were well-developed, and she had to fight the urge to climb over her desk straight into them. "For heaven's sake, Jason, it won't kill you. I still have my clothes on, and they're wet. Please get dressed."

Jason slipped the shirt over his head, pulling it down over his chest. "Happy now?"

"Yes, thank you." She waved a hand at him. "You can go."

"What about our meeting today and the next interviews?"

Lou picked up the papers that barely missed getting ruined by the coffee and stacked them on the corner of her desk. "I was about to tell you, before my coffee ended up on my blouse, that they postpone our interviews until tomorrow afternoon. So, you're off the hook today and I suggest you go back to your motel room for some clean clothes." Lou checked the time. "Then meet me back here around one, and I'll give you your next assignment."

"Just like that?" Jason gave a low growl, expelling curse words.

"Yes, just like that. Now, if you will excuse me, I'm going home to get out of these wet clothes, and I suggest you do the same. And you might want to ask housekeeping to soak that shirt for you before the coffee sets, or the stains won't come out."

Lou picked up her bag and strolled past him toward the door without another word, then slipped out the back door before she burst out laughing again. The whole scene was unbelievable. It wasn't his fault. She was the one who had been daydreaming, but the look on Jason's face had been priceless after she told him to put on his coffee-soaked shirt.

The curse words had surprised her, but under the circumstances, it amazed her she hadn't slipped a foul word herself. The morning breeze was drying her clothes fast, making her shirt and pants stiff from the coffee. She needed to get home and change before things got further out of control.

Jason had cursed under his breath as she walked by to see if she would respond, but she slid past him to the door without a word. It wasn't the Christian way to act but he couldn't help himself. Who did she think she was dismissing him like a schoolkid? What was it about this woman that got his blood boiling in under thirty seconds? Lou was a nobody, just a small-town reporter with a bad attitude. He waited until he was sure Lou was gone before he left her office.

As he passed the front desk, Karol took one look at his stained shirt and snickered. Not wanting to explain, he pushed through the glass door out into the morning heat. He had only been here two days and hated this town.

Back at his motel, Jason stomped down the hall to his room and stripped off his dirty shirt before the door closed behind him. He was about wad it up and throw it away until he remembered he only brought three shirts with him. Once again, he slumped on the bed and hung his head in his hands. This self-pity thing was getting on his nerves, and he needed to put a stop to it. Fine, if that's how she wanted to be, he could play hardball too, but first he needed new clothes.

Jason pulled on his last clean shirt and grabbed his keys then stopped in his tracks. He yanked his wallet out of his back pocket and counted forty dollars. Disgusted, he was about to throw it against the wall when he spied the company credit card David had given him for expenses and grinned. His lack of clothing made this a company expense.

Lou pulled into her driveway and parked. A smile crossed her face as she sat thinking about the morning and the crazy scene in her office. Jason had looked sexier than ever without his shirt on, and the vision made her blush as she hurried into the house for a much-needed shower to cool her rising emotions.

Wrapped in a towel, she dug through her closet. She was giddy as a schoolgirl hunting for the perfect outfit for the school dance. Until she realized she had nothing exciting to wear. The only clothes hanging in front of her were more khaki slacks and white shirts. Julie was right, she needed to add some life into her wardrobe and promised herself she would go shopping, someday.

Lou grabbed another shirt and a pair of slacks, but when she checked herself in the mirror, the same beige person gazed back at her. Studying her image, shook her head in disgust, then gathered her hair and fastened it high on her head, leaving a few curls falling around her face. She thought about adding color to her pale face but wasn't sure the last time she had bought any cosmetics.

Rummaging through the bathroom cabinets she found her minimal choices. Not wanting to overdo it, she settled on blush, mascara, and lip gloss, then had to fight the urge to wash it off her face.

She knew she needed to take more time for herself. Eat better, even exercise. The idea made her chuckle. Exercise was not one of her strong suits, but it wouldn't hurt to investigate it.

Lou thought about grabbing lunch but remembered she still hadn't gone shopping and had wasted three hours getting cleaned. Instead, she headed back to the office. When she got to the parking lot, she didn't see Jason's car, and neither was Chris's.

She had been avoiding Chris since the break-up as much as possible and was polite whenever she saw him, but nothing more. Now thinking about it, he never acted too upset and Lou realized she had to let it go. She continued to sit in her car, trying to calm her jittery nerves but she knew if she stayed there much longer Jason would arrive.

The whole idea of arriving first was, so she had time to rein in her runaway emotions before she saw him again. What was wrong with her? She knew from her last experience; workplace romances didn't work. Okay, so he didn't work for her paper, but he lived in New York City and would go home after they finished the story. She didn't need to get involved with another reporter and gave herself a mental slap.

Lou grabbed her bag, walked to the back door, and tried the knob. The door wouldn't open. She must have locked it this morning after she came in. She searched through her bag for her key, but it was nowhere. Then she remembered she set the key on her desk right before Jason came rushing in, and the whole coffee scene happened. Frustrated, Lou kicked the door. Her plan was to slip in through the back door unnoticed. Now she would have to go through the front past Karol. Lou hadn't clicked with Karol the way she had when she met Julie and Lou wouldn't consider them friends. Lou talked to Karol since she came to work at the paper six months ago but kept it casual. Karol was only eighteen with too much flash for Lou's taste. Not trashy, simply different with her red cowboy boots, and denim skirts. If Lou admitted it, she was envious of Karol's ability to be herself, no matter what anyone else thought.

The sun was getting hotter, and Lou knew she couldn't stay out in the heat any longer. With only one choice left, she whisked through the lobby door, flashed Karol a smile—who sat with her mouth open—and strode to her office as fast as she could. Once inside, she shut the door and collapsed into her chair. This whole idea was stupid, she told herself.

Jason drove around for an hour looking for a men's clothing store, only to discovered he would have to buy his new clothes at the local Fred Meyer all-in-one store. It bewildered him you could shop from the food section to home improvement and everything in-between and would have liked to explore, but his need for clothes came first.

Though the men's department was limited, Jason was able to find comfortable jeans, six T-shirts, and two nicer pull-over shirts. He figured it wouldn't hurt to clean up his act. After adding in the essential socks and boxers, he was ready to go. Once checked out, he headed back to his motel and changed. He had spent more time than he planned shopping, and it was getting close to his one p.m. meeting with Lou and the thought of seeing her excited him.

Lost in her own misery, Lou was unaware the door had opened, or that Jason walked in—until she swung her chair around to find him staring at her. The surprised look in his eyes and his sly smile made her uncomfortable. She wanted to run straight to the bathroom to wash her face and undo her hair.

"Hello, Jason, I didn't hear you come in—again." She had to fight the urge to release her hair from the pins holding it. "I might have to put a bell on you."

48

Jason dropped his bag on the floor. Lou watched the stunned look flow over his face. Her cheeks matched the glistening shade on her lips. Lips that wanted to kiss him.

"Might not be a bad idea." He laughed.

She tried to remember what he referred to—praying she hadn't spoken those words aloud.

"It would save you dry-cleaning bills." He said.

Lou fidgeted with the files on her desk. "Why don't you sit, and we can discuss the interviews for tomorrow."

Jason slid the extra chair to the side of her desk and sat. His nearness caused her to tense, so he moved the chair back a little.

"Okay, Boss, I'm ready. Who's next on the list?"

Her attraction towards Jason grew stronger each time she was near him, and it shocked her. What did she know about him other than he was a reporter from New York City and his family had died? Well, she knew he liked ribs; he liked to joke with her, and he made her heart do flips. Chris had never made her heart do flips. But was that enough to risk getting involved with Jason beyond work? She was more confused than ever as she picked up the first file, flipped it open before sliding it toward him.

"Your next interview will be with Brandon Johnson, age nineteen, who works at the pizza parlor in a small town called Maupin, thirty-six miles from here. The information is in the file."

Lou sounded blunt and regretted it.

Jason took the file and skimmed the information.

"Does everyone talk about this woman helping them?"

"Yes." She kept her voice subdued. "They gave the same description. Harold saw her first, over seventy years ago, but each person describes her the same way—young and with the mark on her face. There can only be one explanation, Jason. She's an angel—or—a ghost."

"Come on, Lou. You don't believe in ghosts, do you? There must be an explanation for what they saw. That's why it's called investigative reporting."

Lou wasn't so sure but decided not to argue the point right now.

"You're right, Jason. I need to look at this story without attaching emotions to it. Stick to the facts. Though it's hard not to get emotional hearing their stories. If the others are like Harold's and Bill's versions—we'll just have to wait until we're done, then decide. Sound fair to you?"

"Sounds fair."

Jason got up and slipped the file into his pack. "So, who is the third person on my list?"

Lou relaxed, leaning back in her chair. "We can discuss that after we get done tomorrow. If you don't mind, I want us to focus on one person at a time. Your appointment is at noon. It will take you forty minutes to get to Maupin. I'll be going to Dufur, but my appointment isn't until four. It's closer, only about twenty minutes away."

Jason winced.

Lou watched the pained look cover his face. "Now what's the problem?"

"There's a lot of driving involved with this story." He shuffled his feet toward the door. "It's so different out here. Wherever you want to go requires driving—for hours. In New York City, you take a cab to your destination. You don't worry about anything besides tipping the driver."

Lou laughed. "Yes, there is Jason. Tomorrow's trip is short compared to where you are going the next day."

Jason shot her a concerned look. "And where is that?"

"Madras. About two hours from here."

"Two hours! You've got to be kidding."

Lou flashed him a wide smile. "No, I'm not. But we can talk

50

about that later." She liked the banter between them. "Don't be such an old man. The driving will not kill you, and you might even enjoy it."

Jason made a pouty face. "I don't know, Lou." He dropped his head.

Lou realized he was playing her and laughed along with him. "You had me for a minute." She tried to regain her composure.

"You looked so serious." Jason laughed again then stopped.

Lou saw the same look on his face from the restaurant. She wondered what caused him to look so depressed. She put the files back in her drawer. One moment they were having an enjoyable time, and the next it was as if he flipped a switch, shutting her out. She had enough on her own mind, without worrying about him. There were things that needed fixing at her house and she still hadn't cleaned out her mother's room. She didn't know if she could. Though they never had a close relationship, Lou had to admit—she missed her mom and that living alone was harder than she ever imagined. Sometimes the silence could be unbearable.

Lou stood and handed him another one of her cards, brushing her fingers with his.

"Okay, well, I guess that's it for today. If you have questions, you have my number." Lou's legs wobbled, threatening to give out any moment. She rested her hand on her chair for support. "Let's meet here tomorrow around six. That should give you time to get back, eat and freshen up, then I'll give you your last file."

"Ah... sure, six is fine, and if I have questions, I'll call you." The door closed behind him.

Lou sank into her chair as tears bubbled over her eyelids, spilling down her face. She didn't know why she was crying and reached for a tissue to dry her eyes; she discovered her mascara was streaking down her face. No wonder she didn't enjoy wearing makeup and pulled her compact from her bag to survey the damage. The sight caused her to cry even harder until she had a runny nose along with the black streaks under her eyes. It took the rest of the tissues in the box to clean her face before unclipping her hair and letting it fall. She just wanted to go home.

Lou grabbed her files and the back-door key for the parking lot, thankful for the back exit. She wasn't in the mood to walk past Karol looking this way. Before she opened the outside door, she said a silent prayer, hoping for once God would answer and Jason had left. But standing in the empty lot, Lou slumped with disappointment. For some silly reason she thought Jason might wait for her. She knew this roller-coaster of emotions needed to stop.

Feeling depressed, Lou retrieved her cell phone and dialed Julie's number, but it went to voicemail. Lou knew she was being overdramatic, and her friend didn't need to listen to her whine while she was enjoying the happiest time of her life. Lou hung up without leaving a message. Besides, what was she going to say? That she was attracted to a guy she just met? Lou needed to face the truth about her attraction to Jason or nip it in the bud now— she couldn't have it both ways.

Irritated with herself, she drove home.

Chapter Eight

Jason made it back to his motel room, pulled the drapes, and sat in the dark. Despair and loneliness swept over him. Hunger pangs poked at his stomach, but fatigue overrode his wish to eat and he lay down on the bed. He tried to keep his eyes open, but thoughts of Annie and Sophia drifted through his mind until he fell into an exhausted sleep.

Three Years Earlier

"Jason... Jason... it's time," Annie whispered in his ear, trying not panic. She had been having contractions for the last three hours, but ignored them, thinking it was just indigestion. Now the pains were coming rapidly. "Jason!" Annie pushed harder against his shoulder.

Jason rustled from his deep sleep to see her staring at him. "What's wrong, Annie?"

"The baby! It's coming!" She cried as another contraction rushed through her body.

"Are you sure, honey?" The look on her face prompted him to jump out of bed. He hit his knee on the nightstand as he hobbled to the dresser to grab his clothes.

"I'm sure! Hurry, or this baby will be born right here!"

Jason called his sister Joan, before they left, and within two hours, Sophia Maria Peterson came screaming into the world, eight pounds, six ounces and in perfect health. She had curly, dark hair like her father, her mother's button nose, and Annie's green eyes too. He was strutting around when Joan and Fred arrived to

53

see their first niece. Two days later, Jason and Annie took their new baby home.

The months flew by, and the day Sophia tuned eleven months old Jason had to leave on assignment overseas.

"I don't want you to go, Jason." Annie set Sophia in her playpen surrounded by her favorite toys. "You promised. No more overseas jobs."

Jason came to his wife's side and put his arms around her. "I'm sorry, honey. David needs me to do this one last story and I promise I'll be home for Sophia's birthday. I love you Annie, more than you'll ever realize."

Sophia giggled and reached for him. "And you too, little lady." Jason bent down, scooped her up into his arms.

Jason reached for Annie in his sleep, calling her name, before he woke with a start and realized it was morning. This was the first dream of her he'd had since arriving in The Dalles, and it shook him to the core. His body ached, and his mouth was dry. When he sat up and swung his legs off the bed and realized he still wore the clothes he had on yesterday. His head pounded as if he'd been drinking, and for a moment, he worried he'd gone off the wagon.

He scanned the room but didn't see any beer bottles and sighed with relief. After a quick shower and dressed in his new purchases, he headed to the lobby. He stopped to grab a cup of black coffee and a donut from the tray before getting on the road.

The directions Lou gave him made the drive easy. As he followed the road down the hill into Maupin, he wondered if he would have trouble finding the pizza parlor. He needn't have worried. It was the only one in town.

Jason pushed open the door to a tinkling sound from a bell hanging on the top.

"Sorry, we're not open yet." A teenage boy was wiping the

counter with a rag.

"I'm looking for Brandon Johnson." Jason watched the kid for a moment. Tall, close to six-two. Thin, on the lanky side.

"That's me."

"Hi, I'm Jason Peterson. The newspaper called you."

"You're early."

"Yeah, no traffic."

Brandon came around the counter and offered his hand. "Nice to meet you. My mom said you wanted to know stuff about my accident."

"Yes. Can we sit?"

Brandon motioned him to the nearest booth. "Want coffee or something else to drink?"

Jason shook his head. "No, thanks." He reached into his jacket and pulled out his notepad and recorder.

"What's that for?" Brandon gestured at the recorder.

"Hope you don't mind. It helps me keep the facts straight."

Brandon shrugged.

"As the reporter told your mom, The Centennial, along with the New York Post, is doing a story about the crosses on Bakeoven Road. Can you tell me what earned you a cross?"

Brandon stretched out his long legs as he leaned back in the booth. "That was a crazy couple of days. I'd been helping my dad and the volunteer fire department put out a range fire the day before and into the night and I didn't get very much sleep before I left for work. I was driving here to Maupin from Shaniko, and, man, was I tired." He glanced at Jason watching as he took notes.

"Go on." Jason noticed the animation on Brandon's face as he talked.

"Oh, yeah. The cops figure I dozed off for a second and my foot pushed down on the gas pedal. They think I was doing close to sixty miles an hour when my car flew off the edge of the road. I woke to being bounced over the sagebrush for a wild ride until I hit the power pole and the car stopped." Brandon paused; his eyes wide.

"That pole snapped right in half, landing on the hood, and staring me in the face. Everything happened so fast I didn't have time to react, but something had pushed me against the seat, holding me there."

Brandon sat forward, putting his hands on the table.

"It was weird, like time stood still. There was silence all around me. The pole smashed the dash down to the seat pinning my right leg. I tried to pull it free, but the pain hurt so bad I flopped back against the seat. That's when I saw her standing outside the car."

Jason flipped the page as the recorder whirled in unison, getting every word. "Who did you see?"

"A woman about twenty years old. She told me to stay still, and that help was coming. It scared me and I wanted to call my folks. I reached into my pants pocket for my cell phone, but it wasn't there and remembered I left it sitting on the charger at home. When I tried to move again, she reached through the window and took my hand and I stopped struggling. Must have passed out for a while until I heard people calling my name. I tell you, I wanted to cry like a baby for my momma!"

Brandon stiffened. "Hey, don't put that in the story," he pleaded.

Jason smiled. "No problem, man, I won't say a word. To tell you the truth, I've had a few of those moments myself."

Brandon seemed to relax. "Thanks, dude. You're a cool guy."

"Do you remember what the woman looked like?" Jason leaned against the booth cushion, trying to push out the knot forming in his neck.

"She wore a long, black skirt that came to about here," he motioned with his hand to his calf, "and a white blouse. Oh, and she had this wild-looking mark on her face. Kind of like a wing or something. Seemed odd, though."

"Why do you think?"

"She reminded me of someone from the old days. You know, a pioneer woman sort of."

"How long do you think you waited until someone rescued you?"

"I'm not sure. When the pole broke, it knocked out the power. A farmer came looking for the break. He found me sitting there in the car and called. Later my dad told me how he and mom freaked out when they got the call."

Jason could sympathize with the fear the boy's parents must have felt getting that call. "Was the woman still there? Did the farmer see her or mention her to you?"

Brandon shook his head. "Now that I think about it, I didn't see her after I opened my eyes again. We had to wait for over an hour for the power company before they got me out. I kept asking if they saw her, but everyone said no. While I sat there waiting, the rescue squad talked about how it was a miracle I survived. You should have seen where the telephone pole landed. The airbag didn't go off, and I didn't have my seatbelt buckled."

Brandon put up his hand as if to stop Jason's next comment.

"I know, it was stupid. They couldn't figure out how I didn't go through the windshield. I tried to tell them about the hands that held me, but no one would believe me. They said I was hallucinating or something."

"What do you believe happened?" Jason turned his page and stretched his legs under the table.

Brandon got up from his seat. "I'm not sure, but something or someone kept me from going through the windshield. After the emergency crew got me out of the car, I rode in the helicopter to the hospital. Too bad I got so banged up because flying was cool."

Jason nodded. "Yeah, been in a few copters. So, can you tell me about your injuries?"

Brandon rubbed the lower part of his right leg. "Crushed the bones in my leg, which took three operations to fix. The doctor had to use lots of pins and metal to put it back together. Cracked my back too and had to wear an itchy back brace for six weeks. The recovery was tough, but I made it. Did what they told me. I didn't want to be a cripple at sixteen. Sometimes the chilly weather makes it hurt, but the doctor says it will get stronger with time."

"What are your thoughts about the cross with your name on it?"

"My family and friends wondered if it would show up, you know, since they were becoming a legend along the road." Brandon cocked his head to the side. "After ten days in the hospital, I got to go home. On the drive back, I saw the cross near the place I crashed and asked my dad to stop."

"Do you mind telling me what it says?"

"Brandon Johnson, saved to excel in life, June 12, 2015. Tell you, man, it creeped me out seeing my name on it. I'd seen the others along the road but had thought little about them until I had my own."

"And what did you discover?" Jason appreciated the wisdom Brandon had gained beyond his years. He tried to remember himself at that age and admired Brandon's drive. The worst injury he ever had was a broken toe, and the thought of spending time in a back brace and a leg cast made his skin crawl.

"Learned if an angel saves you, you better take it as a sign to do something with your life!"

"You believe she was an angel?"

Brandon turned and gazed out the window at the valley. "What else could she have been? It took me an extra year being out of school so much, but I graduated this year. In the fall, I start at the community college. Got me a scholarship in automotive repair.

Someday I'll have a shop of my own." A proud look covered his face.

Jason stood and walked over to Brandon. "I want to shake your hand again, young man. I'm sure you will go far in your life. Take care of yourself. Second chances don't come every day."

"Thanks, I will." Brandon walked into the kitchen.

Jason gathered his things, strolled out into the humid air, and got into his car. The weather report called for another scorcher, as he started the engine and cranked up the air conditioning.

He was sweating as the familiar feelings of emptiness rushed over him. Why had these people survived when Annie and Sophia didn't?

Questions continued to haunt him as he guided his car onto the main road when a sudden urge to drive Bakeoven Road came over him. The road out of the canyon almost made him dizzy until he reached the top of the hill. The road continued into the long stretches and sweeping curves. He was enjoying the scenery until he came upon the first cross. The sight of it made the hair on the back of his neck stand at attention. Even though the crosses showed a testament of survival, it made him pay closer attention to the road. He wondered if this was Harold's cross and slowed down, so he could read the name. It said Brandon Johnson.

He traveled on until he came upon the next cross. This one said, Bill Owens. That was the man Lou interviewed yesterday.

About halfway down the twenty-six-mile stretch of pavement, he approached a dip in the road where a huge bush grew, overtaking the draw. It looked to be a wild rosebush from the few dried flowers remaining. As he drove by, a strange sensation tugged at him and stayed with him as he drove past the third cross.

This one was Harold's. As he traveled on, he passed three more, slowing enough to read their names. Jenny Taylor, Caroline Mason, and Linda Roberts. The sight of the six crosses overwhelmed him, and he pulled over to the side of the road, staring out over the vast expanse of desert. Something inside him was changing. The emptiness he felt before he came to The Dalles and met Lou was filling with new hope and he wanted to talk to her.

Chapter Nine

The morning started with one headache after another for Lou. First, Brad called her at home, wanting an update on the story and reminding her of the deadline. Lou reminded him Jason had arrived only three days ago and things were progressing as planned. Flustered by his call, she hung up on him, snatched her bag off the counter, and headed out to her jeep, only to discover it wouldn't start.

"Oh, great!" Lou pounded her fists on the steering wheel in frustration. "What else can go wrong today?" When she yanked her bag onto her lap, the strap caught the passenger door handle, spilling the contents over the floor. Lou wanted to scream. She leaned over, retrieved her cell phone, and called for a tow truck to haul it to the mechanic's. After she picked up her things, she sat waiting for the truck to arrive and worried if it didn't show up soon, she would have to call and cancel her interview.

Lou was reaching for her cell phone when the tow truck pulled into her driveway and parked next her jeep. After she explained what happened, the driver popped the hood and checked the battery.

"Looks like your cables came loose, Miss. And they're corroded." He walked to his truck to get his tools. Returning he used a metal brush to clean off the cables, then tighten the bolts, before he hooked up his jumper cables.

The jeep started.

Lou would be the first to admit it was a bucket of rust, but she loved her jeep.

"Thank you so much," she told the driver. He left it charging before he removed his cables and tossed them back in his truck then wiped his hands with a rag.

"Hey, no problem. But replace the battery cables as soon as you can."

Lou nodded. "You're a lifesaver. How much do I owe you?" She hoped this wouldn't cost a fortune. She was lean until payday.

"Not a thing, Miss. You only needed a jump."

Lou stood in shock for a minute, then hugged the man.

"Oh, thank you, thank you." She released him and stepped back.

The driver smiled and returned to his truck. He still had a big grin on his face as he drove away.

Lou jumped back in the jeep, making a mental note to get those cables replaced soon. She would have driven down to the local auto store but didn't want to be late for her interview. Thanks, to the nice tow truck driver, she should be able to make her appointment on time.

The trip to Dufur allowed her time to gather her thoughts and Lou wondered if Jenny would mention a young woman helping her too. She also wondered how Jason's interview went. Seeing him later, even if it was just to discuss the story, excited her until a wave of dread hit her like freezing water, shocking her back to reality.

When they finished the story, he would return to New York City. There was nothing to keep him here. Then she had a crazy idea. What if she dragged the story out a few days longer and they could get to know each other better? Something about him made her feel alive again. Lou shook her head. What was she thinking? She had a story to write and didn't have time for these wild thoughts.

By following her MapQuest directions once again, she found Jenny Taylor's home on the north end of town and rang the doorbell.

The door opened. "Hello. Can I help you?" The woman asked. "Yes, hi, I'm Lou McClelland from The Centennial newspaper. Are you Jenny?"

"Oh, yes. Where are my manners? Please come in," Jenny moved back so Lou had room to enter.

"I appreciate you taking time to talk to me today." Lou stepped inside the house. The living room welcomed her. Styled in the Victorian era, the room had a warm rust-colored couch, matching floral side chairs, and cream-colored lamps covered in old-fashioned lace shades. Nothing compared to Lou's living room. Her mother never changed a thing, and neither had Lou, even after her mother died.

"No problem. Would you follow me into the kitchen? We can talk in there." Jenny led the way to a table set with two glasses and a pitcher of lemonade.

Lou couldn't help but look around the sunny room, with its cream-colored lace curtains, bright floral prints on the chairs, and fresh flowers on the counter. Another pleasant change from her beige kitchen counters. They still had the mushroom canisters her mother probably bought after she married her father. Even her kitchen table wore the faded plastic floral tablecloth she remembered her mother bringing home when she was ten. The visions forced Lou to admit she needed to change her life, and soon.

Jenny motioned for Lou to sit at the table. Chocolate chip cookies sat piled on a plate in the center of a lace doily. She poured them each a glass of lemonade. The fragrant aroma from the cookies made Lou's mouth water with anticipation. She took the glass and downed half the cool liquid before setting it on the table in front of her.

"Oh, my... this lemonade refreshing. I didn't realize how thirsty I was."

Jenny smiled and sat across from her. "So, what can I do for you?" She offered Lou the plate of cookies.

Lou took a cookie and set it on a napkin, fighting the urge to stuff it in her mouth. She couldn't remember the last time she tasted fresh-baked cookies. She set the cookie aside and reached for her notebook and recorder.

"Do you mind if I record this?" She adjusted the recorder and pulled out her favorite pen. "It helps me with the details."

"I guess it would be okay." Jenny sounded hesitant.

Lou smiled and pushed the record button. "As I mentioned on the phone, the paper is doing a special article on the crosses along Bakeoven Road." She couldn't resist any longer and broke off a small piece of cookie and slid it into her mouth, savoring the warm chocolate. She noted Jenny's apprehension, so she continued.

"The police report states on July 20, 2002, you were traveling with your daughter, Molly. Is that correct?"

Jenny took a deep breath, before exhaling. "Yes. We were going to Maupin from Shaniko to pick up diapers. Brian, my husband, came home from Salem the day before and forgot get them. How do you forget diapers?"

Lou could hear the rise Jenny's voice rise.

"I love my husband, but those were trying times for us. Brian's family had bought the only hotel in the tiny town of Shaniko, out in the middle of nowhere. We, along with Brian's older brother, Kevin, and his family, agreed to move from Salem to help run it with his mom and dad. Brian asked me to marry him right before we were to leave, though his father wanted us to wait a year or two. At least, until after the hotel was running on solid ground."

"Did Brian agree with his father?" Lou wasn't sure if she had struck a nerve.

Jenny shook her head and straightened in her chair.

"No. Brian was twenty-one, and I had turned eighteen. He said he didn't want to wait; he wanted to get married right away so I agreed. Soon after we arrived in Shaniko, I found out I was pregnant. Brian never said, but I'm sure his parents thought I was expecting before we got married." Jenny picked up her glass and took a sip before she continued.

"At first we had fun. The whole town, twenty-five people, rallied around the hotel, helping where they could. They were like a huge extended family. Brian and I were living in a one-bedroom house next to the hotel. Now with a baby coming, I felt terrified. The closest hospital was in The Dalles, sixty miles away. Brian's parents are wonderful, but I had no family close. They lived in Salem. I tried to put on a brave front, but as the time got closer, I just couldn't do it. So, I left Shaniko to stay with my parents until the baby arrived."

"Did Brian go with you?" Lou took a sip of her lemonade.

Jenny turned toward the kitchen window. "Yes, he did, although it caused a rift in his family."

"Why?" Lou snapped off another piece of cookie.

"They thought he should stay and help with the hotel. It was hard on us, but we made it through the birth of our daughter, Molly, in December 2000, then moved back. The hotel was doing well, and I worked on weekends cleaning rooms, which left the weekdays to be with Molly. Brian was the first to get restless. There wasn't enough to keep him busy, so he returned to his old job in Salem. He couldn't afford a place for us yet, so he stayed with a friend, leaving me in Shaniko."

"How did that set with his parents?" Lou wondered if something else was bothering Jenny. "It must have put you in an uncomfortable spot."

Jenny twisted the napkin in her hand. "The separation was hard on me. It left me so lonely and I was becoming angry. I know he was doing the best he could for us, but I felt left out. Molly had just

65

turned two, and I was trying to potty train her. That weekend the weather had changed, causing everyone to snap at each other from the heat."

"Is that when you drove to Maupin?" Lou turned the page of her notepad "Can you tell me what happened that day?"

"It's so hard reliving that day. Anyway, I strapped Molly in her car seat for the ride to Maupin. I was down to six diapers by the time he got here on Friday and my nerves were raw. I was still furious with Brian."

Lou gave her a puzzled look. "Why, what happened?"

"I should have been more understanding since he had driven four hours to get home. Instead, I yelled at him and I told him he was irresponsible and, as always, I must take care of things. I knew I wasn't being fair, but at that moment I was tired, hot, and mad. People don't realize what it takes to live out here in remote Central Oregon. You don't pop off to the store whenever you want to." Jenny paused. "Do you want a couple more ice cubes?" She stood and walked to the freezer. "They seem to have melted."

"Yes, thank you." Lou held up her glass.

"Molly and I left Shaniko around 9:00 a.m., and it was getting hot out. About eight miles out of town, a tire blew on my Ford Explorer. It happened so fast there wasn't time to react. The car careened off the road, and we rolled three or four times." Her words came quickly. "The backdoor latch broke, causing it to fly open, and the belt holding Molly's car seat snapped, ejecting her out the door."

Lou gasped. "What happened to Molly? Was she hurt? What about you?"

Jenny caught her breath. "The car stopped on its hood, leaving me hanging upside down by the seatbelt. The air was hot and stagnate and not one sound came from the backseat. It took me a few minutes to pull myself together. When I looked behind me, I saw Molly's car seat wasn't there and I started screaming."

Jenny got up from the table and walked to the sink. She stood with her back to Lou. When she turned around, Jenny saw Lou staring and covered it with her good hand.

"I'm sorry, I didn't mean to stare. Did that happen in the accident?"

Jenny returned to her chair, keeping her hands in her lap. "Yes, it crushed my hand between the dash and the roof." Her voice was so quiet Lou could barely make out what she was saying.

Lou sat forward. "Go on," she urged.

"The pain was horrible. The more I tried to pull it free, the worse it got. It hurt so bad I wanted to quit until a woman's voice told me Molly needed me. I tried again and my hand slid free. At the same time the seatbelt let go, and I tumbled onto the windshield and lay there, not sure what to do until I noticed my door had sprung open in the crash, so I crawled out and sat next to the car. It was so quiet not even a bird sang. I wanted to go to sleep and would have, if I hadn't felt a hand touch my shoulder. When I looked up a young woman stood next to me, smiling. I glanced down at my hand expecting to see it torn to pieces, but it had wrapped it in a cloth bandage."

"Can you describe her? The woman?" Lou tried to quell the excitement in her voice.

Jenny sighed. "I'm not sure, but she might have been about my age. Nineteen or twenty and dressed in black skirt and white blouse. She had her hair pulled back, tied with a blue ribbon, and she had a glow about her that's hard to explain. Almost heavenly if you know what I mean."

Lou didn't want to press, but she needed to know. "This must be hard for you Jenny, but do you remember if she had a mark on the side of her face?"

Jenny leaned back in her chair. "Yes, she did. Shaped like a wing, as I remember. Why? Is that important?"

"It could be," Lou jotted in her notepad. "What happened next?"

"I'm not sure how, but she got me to my feet and told me my daughter needed me. That's when I started to panic, looking around for Molly. The woman held me for a moment, pointed toward a juniper tree. As I stumbled toward it, a whimpering sound was coming from beneath the tree. Molly was sitting upright, still strapped in her car seat. From the marks in the dirt, someone had turned the seat upright and cleaned the dirt from her mouth and nose. Molly took one look at me and started wailing. That woman saved our lives that day, I just know it!" Jenny burst out.

Lou waited for her to gain control.

"I'm sorry. Even though it's been fifteen years since the accident, it's still fresh in my mind."

Lou nodded. "That's okay. I'm sure if it happened to me, I'd still be reliving it too. Take your time and continue when you are ready."

Jenny nodded. "After I got to her, I was afraid to take her out of the car seat, that I might hurt her, so, I dragged her with my good hand toward the road."

Lou reached for another cookie. "Was the woman still nearby?"

"No, I didn't see her anywhere, but each time I wanted to stop, her voice whispered in my head urging me to keep going. She said help would come, and I believed her."

"How long did you wait until someone found you?" Lou prodded, trying to keep her talking while resisting the urge to eat a third cookie.

"I'm not sure. We landed off the road a good distance. The sun burned right above us, getting hotter by the minute. Molly was so quiet, I kept stopping to check on her. After I got back to the road, we sat in the middle, waiting for someone, anyone to find us. I wasn't afraid. I felt we were being watched over and thirty minutes later, the local road crew came upon us and radioed for help."

Lou glanced at her watch. Even though she needed to wrap up, she wanted to give Jenny time to tell her whole story. "Is there anything else you can remember about that day or the woman who helped you?" Jenny believed what happened, but Lou had to ask.

"Do you think you imagined the woman?"

Jenny gave her a strange look. "No. I know what I saw and heard that day."

"Does Molly remember anything about the accident?"

"Not at first. Later she became quiet and clingy. Brian and I, well I hate to say it, were thinking of separating. I couldn't take the isolation anymore. After we got home from the hospital, we realized this was a second chance. Two months later, we understood how blessed we were to have each other and Molly."

Lou cocked her head, intrigued. "Why, what happened?"

Jenny leaned in toward Lou as if to make sure Lou heard her.

"Molly had trouble sleeping, so we asked her if she wanted us to read her a story. She said she wanted to talk to the angel. When Brian and I asked her what angel, she told us about the woman who wiped the dirt from her face before I found her. Stunned, I asked Molly if she could describe her. In her little voice, she said the lady had a funny mark on her face. I broke down crying. Brian was confused so I explained how this woman helped me that day. I've told no one else about her until now."

Lou stretched her back, giving Jenny time to compose herself.

"When did you find out about the cross?"

"We moved back to Salem soon after the accident. I didn't know about the cross until we returned to Shaniko for a family reunion two years later. It's a somber experience to see your name on a roadside cross. I went to school to become a teacher, and Brian started his own company. After I graduated, we moved here to

Dufur. It's still a small town, but closer to The Dalles. I love the school here. We visit his family, and Brian's business is doing well."

Lou reached for her glass and finished her lemonade.

"One last thing, do you remember what the cross said?"

Jenny gave her a nervous laugh. "It was a prophecy."

"Why is that?" Lou asked.

"Because it said, Jenny Taylor, saved to teach, July 20, 2002."

Lou closed her notebook and gathered her things. After thanking Jenny for her hospitality, she made her way back to her car with a baggie of cookies. Once inside, she sat mulling over what she learned. The pieces were falling into place. If the next interview went ahead as planned, she would have plenty of information to write her half of the story. Lou popped a cookie in her mouth and put the jeep in reverse.

On the drive home, she wondered if that had happened to her and her mother, would her mom have saved her? She didn't think so. Disappointed by the thought, she reached for another cookie. By the time Lou returned home, she was giddy with anticipation for her meeting with Jason at six and would need to step it up if she wanted to get back to the office on time.

Lou retreated to her bedroom and stared at herself in the mirror. Same shirt, same pants. She had to admit, Julie and even Chris had been right, she was boring. Not trying to let that get her down, she rummaged through her closet looking for anything she could wear that wasn't beige. She was about to give up on the whole idea until she spied a lavender floral-print summer dress hanging in the back. She didn't have the faintest idea the last time she had worn it or if it would fit but deiced to be adventurous and shed her shirt and slacks.

Nervous, Lou slipped the dress over her head, praying it would fall into place. To her amazement, it slid on without getting stuck on her hips. Not bad, she thought, until she realized she didn't have shoes to go with it. Loafers or tennis shoes made up her shoe collection—nothing that would look good with a dress. She was about to take it off, then remembered her mother always wore sandals and dressy shoes.

Lou crept down the hall to her mother's bedroom. She hadn't been inside since the funeral six months ago and wasn't sure if she should borrow a pair, then realized it didn't matter. Standing at the door, emotions flowed over her. During her teen years Mom had little interest in showing Lou the finer points of being a woman. She was either in a deep depression or bouncing off the walls, so Lou learned about makeup from magazines or by watching her mother from the doorway. She knew no matter how hard she tried, she would never be as beautiful as her mother and had to accept the truth about herself. She was plain. Melancholy and the urge to cry swept over her but she stopped herself. She would never shed another tear for her mother.

With a new resolve Lou pushed the door open and walked to the closet that held her mother's shoes. At least, she and Lou wore the same size. After surveying her choices, she settled for a pair of low-heeled strappy sandals in white. Sliding them on she did a little turn in front of the full-length mirror and liked what she saw. Not too fancy, but at least she wasn't wearing beige and smiled at herself. She suddenly felt a chill and hurried out of the room as if she might get caught if she stayed any longer. Lou knew it was silly to feel this way, but she couldn't help it. With one last look in the mirror, she decided to leave her hair down, added lip gloss, and called it good.

⌣

Jason returned to his room and noticed the maid had been in to clean and the best part, she had turned on the air conditioner. She even filled his ice bucket. He made a mental note to leave her a nice tip at the end of his stay then headed for a shower. Once he dressed, satisfied with his new clothes, he slapped on aftershave and was ready to go.

When he pulled into the parking lot and didn't see Lou's jeep. His watch flashed ten minutes to six, he was early, so he waited in the car. Even with the air conditioning on, the heat made him sweat. Nervous, he checked his reflection in the rearview mirror, making sure he had nothing hanging out of places it shouldn't. He was still studying himself when he saw Lou's jeep come around the corner and park next to him. He straightened the mirror, praying she hadn't seen him primping and laughed as he got out of the car.

Jason walked over and opened her door. He was speechless when Lou slide from her seat and stood in front of him. She was pretty as a pixie from a heavenly garden in her floral dress. Her hair flowed around her face in waves, and her eyes danced in the sun's light, while her lips glistened, inviting him to kiss them. His heart was bouncing like a ping-pong ball in his chest.

Lou watched his face and smiled. "Hello, Jason."

"Lou," he stammered, "you… you sure look nice this evening."

"Thank you. You look nice too. Is that a new shirt?"

Jason looked down at his navy polo shirt. "Yeah, got it a Fred Meyer's. What do you think?"

Lou tilted her head. "That color looks good on you."

Jason grinned. It had been a long time since he received a compliment on his clothing. He usually stuck to jeans and T-shirts.

"Thanks. The sales lady said the same thing. I guess she knew what she was talking about."

They both stared at each other.

"Lou—"

"Jason—"

"No, you go first. I mean, shall we get out of this heat?"

"Yes, that would be a good idea." She unlocked the back door and hurried past him into the coolness of the hallway.

Jason followed and shut the door behind them. He was so close to her he could smell the fragrant scent of her shampoo. It was light, with a touch of lavender, and reminded him of Annie. That had been her favorite fragrance. He groaned and murmured Lou's name.

Lou remained silent in the hall as she searched his face.

Jason saw the longing in her eyes. No longer able to fight his feelings, he pulled her into his arms, crushing his mouth against hers.

Lou responded, until she pulled back, surprised, and overwhelmed by their connection.

"Oh—I mean—that, what a kiss." Jason tried to catch his breath.

Lou licked her lips. "What a kiss yourself but we can't do that again, we should keep this professional. Don't you think?"

Jason gave her a sheepish grin then pulled her into his arms once again. "Sure." He kissed her forehead, then her nose, before returning to her lips. "If you think so."

Lou relaxed in his embrace, then just as fast, released herself from his arms. "Jason—we must stop—we can't do this in the hall. What if someone comes by and see us?"

Jason looked around, remembering where they were. "Well, I guess they would get an eyeful but you're right." Turning, he held out his hand to guide her down the hall towards her office.

Lou accepted his outstretched hand and followed him to her office door with a grin on her face. The office staff were gone, and the paper crew worked in a different part of the building. She and Jason were alone like two teenagers sneaking around. Lou unlocked her door then moved across the room to put distance between them and turned on her desk lamp. Jason closed the door and locked it. She turned as he approached, putting her hands up to stop him from coming any nearer. She wanted Jason. More than she had ever wanted a man. But what did they know about each other? And the story. She had to remember the story.

"I'm sorry, Jason, but we can't do this." Fighting the urge to jump into his arms again, she turned and retreated to safety behind her desk. Jason wore a confused look. She had felt a connection when they kissed but now, in the light of her office, guilt caught up with her as if they'd done something wrong.

"You're right, Lou. I apologize. I don't know what came over me, but it won't happen again." He pulled the chair in front of her desk, instead of next to her as before, and sat.

A sudden chill covered the room, and Lou shivered.

"No need to apologize. I was a willing participant, but it's better if we keep this professional. I'm not ready for a serious relationship and I'm not sure if you are, either. So, friends?" She hoped he would say no—that he wanted more.

Jason squirmed in his chair. "Sure, Lou. You're right, just friends—for now."

Lou chewed on her lip and looked down at her desk. She wanted to kick herself for being such a fool. She could tell he liked her. But was she ready to take a chance and trust him with her heart? Lou had done that with Chris, and he had crushed it to pieces. She swallowed the lump in her throat, picked up the files for the last of their interviews, and handed Jason his. Their eyes met with such longing, they both turned away.

For the next hour, they talked about the similarities of the cases.

Lou shuffled the papers on her desk. "I guess there's nothing more to discuss. Unless you have questions about your interview in Madras tomorrow."

"No questions." Jason closed his folder.

"How about we meet for dinner and figure out how we write this whole story?" She watched him lick his lips and felt her heart skip a beat.

"Sure, dinner sounds good. What do you suggest?"

"Do you like Chinese? I know a wonderful place on Main Street. We could meet at six, if that's okay with you. That should give us enough time to get back and freshen up before dinner.

Lou knew she was talking too much, but she didn't want the conversation to end yet. She knew as soon as it did, he would leave. She scribbled the address on a sticky note and handed it to him.

Jason sat forward, reached for the note, tucked it in his shirt pocket and shrugged.

"Okay, then." He stood. "See you at six."

Before she had a chance to respond, he was out the door leaving her stunned, as she gazed around the empty room. Lou wanted to run after him but felt anchored to her chair and sat in the silence, scolding herself for letting the best thing to come into her life get away. She put the file in her bag, shut off the light and drove home, her heart aching for Jason.

The drive back to the motel left Jason in a foul mood. One, he was hungry, and, two; he realized as soon as he walked out the door he longed for more. As he passed a McDonald's, his stomach gave out a growl. Fast food wasn't his favorite, but for tonight it would do.

Chapter Ten

Lou rose early after another restless night and was on the road by 9:00 a.m. Her final interview was in the small town of Shaniko, more than an hour away. The same town Jenny had talked about. Lou had done research after she returned home and discovered the town considered itself Oregon's oldest living ghost town. The population was about thirty-eight people.

The article told how Shaniko had been the end of the line for the railroad in 1901, shipping wool and grain from Oregon to the seacoast for sale. Fascinated with its history, she made a note to consider the town for a feature story later. Right now, she had the best story of her life and trusted fate stepped in the day she discovered that letter to the editor.

Lou tried to take her mind off Jason, as she drove, with little success. Was he thinking of her too? Her heart fluttered, but she kept trying to convince herself she wasn't ready to get involved with anyone, including Jason. Besides, she was sure he still had issues about his wife and daughter, otherwise he wouldn't be here to work on this farfetched story. Sure, the story would help to advance her career, but what good was it for Jason? With the interesting stories he'd covered, this must seem boring.

While driving through the rolling hills and deep valleys, Lou relaxed against the seat. She wondered how the early settlers ever traveled up and down these hills in wagons. The wheat fields had turned a golden yellow like the song. Amber waves rushed across the hills, pushing against the deep-blue sky. She was enjoying the drive until she crossed the bridge out of Maupin and started up the hill. Her full attention now focused on the road. Lou hoped she wouldn't get carsick. Motion sickness plagued her for as far back as she could remember. She had never been on a carnival ride in her life and barely handled speed bumps. Once she drove out of the curves onto the straight part of the road, she let out a deep sigh of relief until she passed the first cross and the hairs on the back of her neck stood up on end.

Each time she passed another cross something pulled at her. The sensation grew stronger when she drove by a large wild rosebush, bigger than any rosebush she had ever seen. Though the blossoms were long gone, the vines blanketed the side of the ravine with leaves a deep forest green. Lou wondered how it ever got there. She wanted to stop but kept going. The drive to Shaniko had taken longer than she planned.

Lou pulled into the tiny town and drove around the short streets until she reached her destination. A small manufactured home, about a thousand square feet, sat back from the main road and overlooked the vast empty rangeland. Only an occasional juniper tree dotted the landscape, but the view of the mountain ranges was breathtaking. Lou never realized what she had been missing until she stood taking in the beauty surrounding her. She decided she needed to travel more.

After retrieving her bag, Lou began working her way to the front porch. Kids' toys lay strewn across the porch and around the yard. She wondered if this was what it was like to have children. Then cringed at the thought. She never thought of herself as a mother, besides with her upbringing she would probably be a bad one and tossed the thought aside.

Lou rang the bell and waited. She was about to knock when the door opened. A woman about her age sported a sling on her arm and a bandage on her forehead. Two massive black eyes still bore shadows of purple and yellow.

"Hello? Are you Linda Roberts?"

The woman pushed the screen door with her good hand. "Yes, I am. You must be the reporter from The Dalles."

"My name is Lou McClelland." She reached for the door and held it open. "Do you need help?"

"No, but thanks for asking. You could close the door for me, I need to sit."

Lou shut the door as Linda settled into a recliner that sat in the center of the living room. "I'm sorry to bother you. I realize it hasn't been that long since your accident." Lou saw the pain etched on Linda's face as she adjusted her body in the chair and felt bad for disturbing her, but she needed this last interview.

"Give me a minute to catch my breath. The doctors say I need to move more, but they aren't inside this body." Linda shifted in her chair. "That's better. It's easier on my hips to sit. What did you say your name was?"

"Lou McClelland."

"I'm sorry for the mess. The kids try to help, but they're just kids. My mom comes by and takes them for a while, so I can sleep."

Lou looked around at the clutter. Dishes lined the counter and clothes piled on the couch waiting for someone to fold them. More toys lay scattered on the floor, and she fought the instinct to pick things up. Not wanting to stay longer than necessary, Lou grabbed a dining room chair, brought it into the living room, and set it next to Linda's recliner.

"Thank you for seeing me. I appreciate your help with the story I'm writing. Do you have help here?"

Linda groaned as she adjusted herself again, trying to get comfortable. "Like I said, the kids try to help. We have been staying at my mom's house since I got out of the hospital, but the children were tired of sleeping on the floor and wanted their own beds. I wanted to come home too and we just moved back three days ago."

Lou nodded and reached into her bag and panicked. She had left her recorder sitting on her desk at the office and would need to rely on old school note taking. With her pen in hand, she was ready to write. "If you're up to talking, what can you tell me about the accident?"

Linda played with the hem of her blouse, pulling on a loose thread with her uninjured hand.

"I didn't remember much in the beginning, but now it's coming back in bits and pieces. We'd gone for the end-of-the-year school concert in Maupin. School was out, but they had postponed the concert because the music director fell and broke her arm," Linda paused. "I'm sorry, I seem to ramble. We were on our way back to Shaniko. Tina, my oldest girl—she's fourteen—she plays the flute in the school band. She was sitting in the front with me. Mindy— she's seven—and Kenny, the baby, he's two." Her voice cracked. "They sat in the back. And I buckled in them in case you want to ask."

"No, though the report said you weren't wearing your seatbelt." Lou tried not to sound judgmental. "Why not?"

Linda pulled the thread out before answering. "It was a stupid mistake."

"What do you mean?"

"About six miles from town, Kenny started getting fussy and kept trying to undo his belt, so I stopped the car to check on him. After I got back in the van, I forgot to buckle my belt before taking off again. It was muggy out, so I had the window down."

"What happened next?" Lou knew the basics from the police report, but not the details.

"Well, I rounded the corner, and some animal stood in the road. I know you're supposed to just run them over, but I couldn't do it, so I swerved. The van slid into the soft shoulder of the road and I lost control of the steering wheel. It sent us off the side into the juniper and sagebrush. The van rolled, ejecting me out the window."

Lou cringed. "What about the kids?"

"The van came to a stop upright, with the kids still strapped in their seats."

"And you?"

"I landed about ten feet away. The sound of my children crying filled the night air. From the pain I felt, I knew it was bad and couldn't move my right arm. I wanted to get up to find my children, but a woman's voice told me not to move. She held me in her arms. She told me the children were safe and she would stay until help arrived."

"Do you know where she came from?" Lou's heart raced as she listened.

"No. Bakeoven Road isn't traveled much at night. Fortunate for us, Debbie Hopkins, another mother from Shaniko, was right behind us in her car. They live up the street. She saw the van roll, stopped, and called for help. She was a godsend too."

"Why do you say that?"

"She got to my children and stayed with them until the medics could check them out. After that, she took them to my mothers, who was home with a sinus infection. She lives here in town too."

"Did you see her face? The woman who helped you?"

"My eyes wouldn't focus, but as the sirens and flashing lights screamed toward us, I looked up and saw a strange mark on the side of her face. I wanted to touch her, but my hands wouldn't move, and everything went black. Four days later I woke up in the hospital. I don't even remember the helicopter ride to the trauma unit in Bend."

"Do you know if anyone else saw the woman who held you?"

Linda signed. "I asked about her, but no one had seen her. They said I must have been dreaming."

Lou shifted in her chair. "Do you think you were dreaming?"

"It's possible. But a dream or not, I don't believe I would have made it without her help. The doctors said if I had moved, the nerves in my back would have severed, paralyzing me, or worse, I would have gone into shock and died. It stills gives me shivers remembering that night."

Lou leaned forward and patted Linda's hand. "I'm sorry for your pain."

Linda gave her a weak smile. "Thank you, but don't worry. When you think your life is at its darkest, a light shine through changing it forever."

"Mind if I ask why you say that?" Lou admired Linda. Here she sat bruised and broken, but she talked of hope.

"During my therapy sessions, I met a man recovering from a back injury. We had time to get to know each other during our sessions. The attraction was mutual. We realize it's sudden but believe that fate brought us together and we're getting married next year, on the anniversary of the accident."

"That is wonderful. What do your children think?"

"They're more excited than we are. My ex-husband left us 2 years ago, and now Charles—that's his name—is ready to take on the bunch of us. It's more than I ever dreamed."

Lou sat back in the chair, reflecting what Linda had told her. Could someone find a love that fast? Her mind wandered to Jason until Linda moaned, snapping Lou back to the present.

"One last thing before I go so you can rest. When did you notice the cross on Bakeoven Road? Have you seen what it says?"

"Not yet—it's too hard to travel yet. The day I got out of the hospital, my mother told me about it, though I wasn't sure what it meant at first."

"Why is that?" Lou was curious.

"It said, Linda Roberts, saved for true love, June 18, 2017. I guess I was saved to find Charles, who has promised to love me and my children forever."

Lou closed her notepad and stuffed it back in her bag.

"Thank you for talking to me, Linda. I wish the best to you and Charles, and to a speedy recovery."

Linda started to rise.

Lou put up her hand. "No, please, you stay put. I can show myself out." She returned the chair to the kitchen, said goodbye and left Linda sitting in her chair with her eyes closed.

While she made her way to her car, Lou no longer doubted that the same young woman had ministered to the victims. One question that kept crossing her mind. Why did this woman appeared on just this country road when people needed help? It still mystified her.

As she backed out of the driveway and headed out of town, she wondered if Jason had finished with his interview in Madras. She thought about Linda finding love and if it was possible. Once again, she had second thoughts about just being friends with Jason and decided she would talk to him tonight about the possibility of a relationship.

Jason's mind was on Lou and their kiss; he didn't even mind the two-hour drive to Madras. He could still taste her soft mouth on his, and it made his heart dance a jig. This was crazy—they'd just met—but he couldn't help how he felt. He checked the address one more time before he pulled into the driveway of a modest-size house that reminded him of the one where he and Annie had lived. He would still be there if things had turned out.

The sudden memory caused his pulse to throb in his temple as he parked the car, alerting him of a panic attack coming. He tried to remember what his therapist had taught him about taking deep, long breaths until he regained control. Jason concentrated on his breathing until he felt his heart slow down then opened his door, retrieving his bag. He walked up the two steps to the front door and pushed the buzzer. The door squeaked open and a small, silver-haired woman, with dark-rimmed glasses that made her look like a wise, old owl, answered, surprising him.

"Can I help you?" The woman behind the screen asked.

"Hello. Are you Caroline Mason? My name is Jason Peterson. Lou McClelland said she spoke with you on the phone about an article." He hoped the woman remembered the conversation.

"Oh, yes, please come in." She pushed the screen open and stepped back.

Jason grabbed the door and walked through before it slammed behind him, causing him to jump. "Sorry about that. It slipped out of my hand."

"Don't worry. That old door does it to me too. If you would take a seat on the couch, I'll take the chair. It's better for my knees."

She motioned him toward the worn floral couch.

Jason waited until she sat before he took his place on the couch.

"I'm not sure what Lou told you on the phone, but the paper is doing a story about the crosses on Bake Oven Road and—"

Caroline gasped. "You mean there are other crosses?"

"Yes, six of them, counting yours. You weren't aware of the others?" He opened his notepad and set his recorder on the coffee table. "I hope you won't mind if I record this?"

She shook her head. "That's fine. I guess I never noticed if there were others. I haven't driven that stretch of road since the day I returned and looked at mine. It's a sobering effect when you see your name on a roadside cross."

"I imagine it can be. Would you tell me how you came to have one?" Jason pushed the record button.

Caroline sat back in her chair, silent for a moment, then cleared her throat. "You need the story before the cross to understand it." She twisted the handkerchief she held in her hands. "For the better part of my childhood I lived at the orphanage in The Dalles. I still remember how I cried and begged my father not to leave me. He told me to stay quiet as he walked away, and I cried until I fell asleep against the door. It must have been after midnight when a voice woke me. I thought my father had returned. There was a woman kneeling next to me and I tried to push myself further into the corner."

Sophia's face flashed before Jason's eyes, and the image cut deep into his mind at the thought of someone discarding a child as if she was garbage. "Who found you?"

"A nun who ran the place. I remember looking up at her and pleading, 'I want to go home. Can you take me home?' I was only six years old and my clothes were dirty. My hair, which used to be brown, was in a ponytail and I held on tight to a tattered stuffed dog."

Caroline dabbed at her eyes beneath her glasses. "The nun was at a loss for words then saw the note pinned to my coat. She took the note and read the scrawled words. 'Her name is Caroline, and she just turned six. Can't care for her or myself. Her mother is dead, and I have no one else. Please take care of her and tell her I love her and I'm sorry.' He signed it Carl Mason. Sister Mary Elizabeth— that was her name—picked me up and held me close. Afraid and tired, I gave no resistance and clung to the nun's neck holding my stuffed dog. She carried me through the door, closing it to the outside world."

Jason forced the lump down in his throat. "This must have been difficult for you. Would you prefer not talk about it?" He was sorry he had come.

"No, I want to tell you. If you can put up with an emotional old woman."

84

"Are you sure?" He leaned forward on the sofa.

"Yes, let me continue. She took me to the nursery to join the other children. Six boys and five girls, ages from six months to fifteen. For the first few days, I kept watching, waiting for my father to come back, but he never did. The days and years flew. Since my father was alive as far as we knew, no one could adopt me. I kept hoping he would come back someday and get me, but it never happened." She dabbed her eyes again. "The nuns tended to our needs: clothing, food, and schooling. Early on, I learned to follow the rules and stay out of trouble. On the outside, I did whatever they asked of me, but inside I seethed with a growing hate and hardened my heart toward my father for leaving me, and toward God for not answering my prayers to bring him back. When I graduated from high school at eighteen, I entered college through a scholarship from the local church. That's when I decided I wanted to work for children's services to help children like me never feel alone. After getting my degree, I moved here to Madras and settled into my job as a caseworker. I never married. Instead, I've spent my life devoted to the children placed in my care." She waved her hand. "I don't need much. What I have makes me grateful. For a long time, I didn't think I would be happy again."

"Why is that? Don't you believe you deserve happiness?" Jason wondered the same thing for himself. Didn't he deserve to be happy too?

"For a long while I didn't. I had so much hate built up against my father and God until I received a letter in 2001."

Jason perked up at the mention of a letter. "A letter? Was it from your father?"

"Yes. The return address was from the hospital here in Madras, ten blocks from where I live. I must tell you, emotions rocked me to the core. I didn't know whether to open it or throw it away?"

"What did you do?" He couldn't imagine what she had been

85

thinking.

"Ended up stuffing it in my jacket pocket and continued with my day too shocked to deal with it."

Jason understood about one's mind running amuck. His had been doing that ever since Annie and Sophia died.

Caroline unfolded her handkerchief and folded it again in a nervous motion. "Then, if you can believe this, I forgot about the letter. It wasn't until the next week when I was in The Dalles checking on a new case and I stopped for lunch. I reached into my coat pocket for a hanky, my hand touched the envelope and I remembered what it was, and my hand began to shake." She sighed before she continued. "I pulled it from my pocket and set it on the table in front of me. My heart pounded as I smoothed out the wrinkles. Couldn't believe I had forgotten about it. Something I'd been waiting for my entire life. Turning it over, I opened the envelope, and pulled out the letter."

"What did it say?" He urged her.

Caroline looked around the room. "I wondered how he got my address or what he wanted. I stared at it for a long time without reading it, then crumpled the letter and stuffed it back in my pocket." She began to cry.

Not sure what to do, Jason reached for a package of tissues he kept in his pocket and handed it to her. Her story was hitting him harder than he realized.

"Thank you." Caroline sniffle and wiped her nose. "My feelings were torn between wanting to run to him, or to forget the letter ever came. I needed to talk to someone and went to see Mother Superior and ask for her guidance. Mother Superior told me it was God's will that I got the letter. She said I needed to see my father and try to accept what he had to say with an open heart and left the convent drained. I wasn't sure what I wanted to do about him."

Jason flipped the page. "Did you go to see him?"

Caroline shook her head. "I didn't get a chance. On the drive back from The Dalles, so many questions swirled through my head as I drove through Maupin. I didn't realize I had turned onto Bakeoven Road until I came up out of the canyon through the curves going too fast and lost control of my car, dropped over the embankment and rolled twice coming to a stop, teetering on the edge of a cliff."

Jason flinched at the vision.

"All I remembered is seeing a bright light before everything turned black." She stood and walked around the room. "When I woke up, my head hurt, and my forehead was bleeding. My legs wouldn't move, and panic flooded through me. I thought I would die and was ready to give up hope until I saw a young woman standing outside the car. She said help would come but I began to panic until she reached in through the broken window and touched my shoulder. Peace flowed over me, and I was no longer afraid."

Jason leaned forward, stretching his own back. "Can you describe her?"

"She was in her early twenties or younger. Her long, dark hair hung to her shoulders, and I saw a mark on her face. It resembled the shape of a wing. She wore a long, black skirt just below her knees and white blouse. I think I passed out again because the next thing I remember I was outside the car. A fabric bandage covered my forehead, and my legs were wrapped in splints made of broken branches tied with the same white fabric."

"Did you see her after you woke?" Jason rested against the cushion.

"When help arrived I was so confused and kept asking if anyone saw her, but they said no. As they carried me away from the wreck, a crunching sound stopped us. We watched in horror when the car rolled over the cliff, crashing two hundred feet below in the gully. I heard them say it was a miracle the car had stopped where it did, and I was able to get out."

Jason took a deep breath, holding it until his lungs burned before he released it. He wondered if Annie and Sophia had seen the van before it hit their car or realized what was happening to them. He prayed they didn't know and wished someone had been there to help them. Each time another person told him how they survived, he wanted to scream. He knew he had to get over their deaths. But a deep sense of gloom swept over him, causing his chest to constrict so tight he thought he would pass out.

"Sorry. What happened next?" He forced himself to regain control.

"Are you okay, son?"

Jason wanted to get out of there. He needed air—he needed his life back. "Yes. Thank you for asking. It's just a headache, but please, continue."

Caroline rose from her chair and hurried into the kitchen. She returned with a glass of water and a bottle of aspirin. "Here take these. No need to suffer." She handed them to Jason before she took her seat once more.

Jason swallowed three tablets with the water then set both on the coffee table.

"Thank you. I appreciate your kindness."

She reached over and patted his hand. "They rushed me to the Madras hospital, where I remained in intensive care for four days. After my mind cleared, I remembered the letter and asked if my father was a patient here since the letter had a return address from the hospital. The nurses said they would check into it. Hours later, they returned with a box holding my father's belongings. He had died of a massive stroke the same day I arrived at the hospital. I held it and cried."

"Do you mind telling me what was in it?" Jason tried to sound interested as the pain still throbbed in his temples.

"More letters—years of them. Written, but never sent."

"Did you ever read them?" He hoped the aspirin would kick in soon.

Caroline sighed. "Yes, though it took me a while. The first one was dated a month after he left me on the orphanage steps in 1951. He wrote how he tried to care for me after my mother died but had fallen into a deep depression. One night after I fell asleep, he said he came into my room with a loaded gun. He had been drinking and planned to shoot me, then kill himself."

Jason's stomach turned, and he had to force himself to continue with the interview. "What happened?"

"He said the gun was ready to fire until someone or something touched his shoulder. He said he looked but saw no one in the room. It was just the two of us. Whatever it was, stopped him, and he ran out into the street, and threw the gun down the sewer grate. He bundled me up and took me to the nuns. Then disappeared from my life."

Jason felt drained. "How about the other letters?"

Caroline looked shaken. "Each letter kept saying how sorry he was and hoped someday I would forgive him. After my broken legs healed, I had to go to The Dalles to pick up his ashes. They don't have a crematorium here in Madras. I avoided driving Bakeoven Road on the trip in, but something compelled me to take it on the way back. As I drove around the curve where I had crashed, my breathing quickened. A white cross stood on the side of the road and I stopped. To my shock it said, Caroline Mason, saved to forgive, June 12, 2001. I sank to the ground in front of it and cried as the anger I had been holding against my father washed from my heart."

She sat up straight. "That's when it became clear what I had to do. I hurried back to the car, grabbed the container holding his ashes and returning to the cross, I found a stick and dug a hole in front of it, setting the container inside and covered it with dirt and rocks. With a pen from my coat pocket I scratched, CM RIP, on the bottom of the cross and said a prayer. I realized my father had saved my life, so I could help others and worked another ten years and retired in 2011."

Jason closed his notepad, and after turning off the recorder, he put them back into his bag. He sat back against the worn couch for a moment, trying to gather his thoughts before standing.

"Thank you for your time today, I'm sure it's difficult reliving the wreck."

"Thank you for coming and reminding me of what I have." Caroline followed him to the door and touched his arm. "I hope you find peace in your life, young man."

Jason could only manage a nod, turned, and walked to his car. He wanted to yell or blame someone for his pain. So many feelings ran though his head. Hope and forgiveness, moving on, starting over, letting go. He never thought this story would bring to the surface the feelings he'd tried so hard to bury the last two years. His mind drifted to his meeting with Lou later tonight. Something was happening to him. Yes, they had only met, but she had opened a door in his heart, one he believed closed forever. A smile crossed his face. He wanted to kiss her again.

Chapter Eleven

Mulling over the pros and cons of the story, Lou turned on to Bakeoven Road and headed back toward Maupin. After her conversations with Bill, Jenny, and Linda, Lou was believing something, or someone, on this stretch of road helped people in need. As she passed the first cross, it reminded her to keep her mind on her driving. When she got close to the wild rosebush she had seen earlier, something shiny caught her eye, and she felt the urge to stop.

"That's odd," Lou mumbled to herself as she pulled over and parked her jeep at the edge of the road. She didn't hesitate to work her way down the steep embankment, using the sagebrush to keep from sliding down the hill, along with the rocks she displaced until she reached the bottom. The rosebush was even larger than it appeared from the road. Looking up, Lou could barely see her jeep.

"Wow. It's a long way down here. Someone could get lost and never be found." Her voice faded into the empty landscape, sending a chill up her back, along with the thought this wasn't a good idea. But her curiosity took over, pushing her to search for whatever had caught her attention.

The wild rose vines were still full of leaves and heavy with thorns and Lou recalled reading somewhere that wild roses lasted only a month or two after blooming so with the dried petals shriveled on the ground, she figured it must have bloomed around the first of June. She was sorry she missed it and hunted for something to lift the prickly vines.

Lou found a broken juniper branch she could use and trying to

91

be careful not to get scratched, she started her search. Thirty minutes later, sweat trickled down her brow. The air was hot and silent. She could hear not even the sound of chirping birds as she continued to poke through the branches and was about to give up until she saw the edge of a rusted, old bumper.

Lou lifted a large cluster of vines, exposing a truck fender. Shocked, she stumbled backwards, catching her pant leg on a thorn, and tearing a hole in the fabric. Fear gripped her, and she wanted to run straight up the hill to the safety of her jeep, but she stood her ground and freed herself from the thorny vines. She continued to work until she got to the side of an old truck. Lou moved closer, using her stick, and making sure she watched for rattlesnakes.

Determined more than ever to expose the truck, Lou moved the vines away until she could get to the driver's side door that hung open. The seat was bare. Most likely stripped by sage rats to build their nests, leaving behind a patchwork of fabric and springs. Inside she could see the glove box sprung open. Whatever papers might have been inside, had long ago blown away, leaving no clue who owned the truck or how long it had been here. Disappointed, dirty, and exhausted, with blisters on her hands, Lou was about to give up and leave when she saw something wedged under the seat.

Lou checked for critters, before she reached down and pulled out a metal box. Lou felt her pulse quicken as she pried open the lid. Inside lay a small, leather-bound journal. She lifted it out of the tin and brushed off years of dirt before she opened the front cover. On the first page, the name Kelly Turner, RN, April 11, 1930. Excitement vibrated through her and she closed it gently, afraid she might damage the delicate pages. She wanted to get back to her office to read it but wanted to document the truck with a picture. But when she reached into her pants pocket for her phone, she realized in her hurry to climb down, she'd left her cell phone in the jeep. Lou stood for a moment thinking over what she should do next. She wasn't sure how much of the truck she had uncovered, or if anyone could see it from the road, but didn't want to take any chances. Using her stick and avoiding the thorns as best she could, she recovered the truck.

Satisfied, Lou tucked the metal box into her blouse, then scrambled up the steep cliff to her jeep. Where had the truck come from and how long had it been there? Was this Kelly person the one who had been driving it? If so, what happened to her?

Lou's hands trembled as she pulled the metal box out of her blouse and stashed it inside her bag for safekeeping. Her hands still shook as she tried to get the key into the ignition. After several failed attempts, she succeeded and headed towards Maupin. Seven miles before the curves, a loud popping noise startled her, and the jeep pull to the right. "Crap!" she yelled, realizing she must have blown a tire. The last thing she remembered was the sound of breaking glass before silence engulfed her.

Jason turned off Highway 97 and drove along Bakeoven Road one last time. He thought about Caroline, Brandon, and Harold, and how similar their stories were about the person who helped each of them but had his doubts this person was an angel. Because if angels existed, why didn't they save Annie and Sophia? He had so many questions about life and loss, but he was not finding the answers he wanted. He wanted to go home. But to what? An empty apartment? An empty life? If he didn't come through with the story, he might not have a job either. And what about Lou? What if he opened his heart, and she rejected him?

The idea horrified him, but decided he had to take a chance and talk to her tonight at dinner and pray she felt the same. His mind was still on Lou when he passed the first couple crosses. When he approached the dip in the road where the wild rosebush grew, the hairs on his neck stood on end again. It had happened the first time he passed it on his drive to Madras and had creeped him out. As he rounded the next corner, he saw flashing lights ahead and saw an overturned vehicle off the road. It looked like a jeep—Lou's Jeep Cherokee!

Jason skidded to a stop, jumped from his car, and rushed toward the mangled vehicle.

"Lou! Lou!"

"Hey! Hold up, Mister", the sheriff called, stopping him before he could reach the jeep. "You can't go over there".

"I need to get to her!"

"Who?"

"Lou—Lou McClelland. That's her jeep, isn't it?"

The sheriff flipped open his notepad and checked the name on his report. "Yes, it's hers, but she's gone".

Jason thought someone had stabbed him through the heart and sunk to his knees. "No! She can't be!" He screamed, shaking his fists to the sky. "Not again. Not again".

The sheriff put his hand on Jason's shoulder. "Sorry, son, I meant to say they airlifted her to the hospital in Bend".

Jason's head snapped up, searching the sheriff's face.

"You mean she isn't dead?"

The sheriff helped Jason to his feet. "No, she's banged up bad. She was awake when they got her out, and she kept mumbling something about an angel and her bag. We sent the bag with her. She should be in the ER by now".

Jason grabbed the sheriff's hand and shook it. "Oh, thank you. Thank you. When you said—I thought—. But where's Bend? He looked around as if he stood on another planet.

"Try to calm yourself. Bend is about eighty miles south on Highway 97". The sheriff pointed. "You go back to the main road, turn right, and follow it until you pass through Madras,

Terrebonne, and Redmond; then another twenty miles to Bend. Watch for the hospital signs. You should arrive in about ninety minutes". He peered at Jason. "You okay to drive?"

Jason took a deep breath. "Yes, I have to get to her".

The officer gave him a sympathetic look. "She your wife?"

Jason shook his head. "No, but someday".

"Well, son, no reason to waste your time standing here. Just make sure you drive the speed limit. I don't want to be scraping you off the pavement next". He returned to the business at hand.

Jason got to his car and slid behind the wheel. She's alive! She's alive! He kept repeating the words in his mind as he turned the car around and headed to town.

The miles flew by as he passed through one town after another. He had to make it this time. He was thinking he would never get there when he saw the city limit sign for Bend. As he followed the hospital signs, he found the emergency entrance, parked, and headed for the desk. His breath sounded ragged when he approached the front desk. "Excuse me".

"Yes, can I help you?" The woman replied and set down her crossword puzzle book.

"Please, can you tell me where Lou McClelland is? Helicopter brought her here". His legs wobbled, requiring every ounce of energy to stay standing.

The receptionist checked the patient board. "Yes, she is in ICU. Are you family?"

Jason had to think fast. "I'm her fiancée. She has no living family, so please let me see her". He wasn't sure if Lou had any family. He hoped the nurse wouldn't call his bluff.

"Visitors are allowed for five minutes each hour. Check in with the nurse before entering her room". She replied.

"Thank you". Jason looked down the hall in a daze. "How do I get to ICU?"

"The ICU is on the second floor. Remember, only five minutes for visiting", then she returned to her puzzle book.

Jason staggered to the elevator and pushed the button. Watching the numbers descend from the fourth floor, he didn't want to wait and hurried to the stairwell. The nurses' station was right in front of him when he exited out of breath. After he explained who he was looking for, the nurse gave him a visitor's name tag and showed him to Lou's room.

He stood in front of the door and waited for permission before he slid the door open unprepared for what he saw. Lou looked so small and fragile lying between the sterile white sheets as the nurse hustled around her.

Jason moved to the side of her bed and stared in shock. If not for the monitors above her head, beeping in rhythm with her breathing and pulse, Jason would have thought she was dead. Tubes snaked in and out of her body, and her soft curly hair lay matted against her face. A bandage covered her forehead, and bruises had formed on her right cheek. Jason ached to hold her and protect her, but he could only wait and pray. The nurse stood next to Lou writing something on a chart. She acknowledged him before she turned and left the room. Five minutes later, the nurse returned and signaled it was time for him to go.

Turning to leave, his foot caught the chair that held Lou's bag. They hadn't put it away yet, and the contents scattered across the floor. The bag had pens and notepads, a small hairbrush, rubber bands, and even an extra pair of socks. Stooping to pick up the spilled items, Jason couldn't help but smile when he saw the tube of cherry lip gloss, she had worn the night he kissed her. He stowed the items back into her bag, surprised at how heavy it felt.

Jason was about to rise when he saw a metal box under the chair. Curious, he opened it to find a worn book resembling a journal. He closed the lid and slipped it into his jacket pocket for a closer look, but by the time he found the ICU waiting room and dropped into the nearest chair, he was too exhausted. Leaning his head against the wall, he dozed to visions of another hospital flashing across his mind. His sister, Joan, and her husband, Fred, stood in a bright white empty hall. They were crying, holding their arms out to him. As he approached them, a guttural scream erupted from his own body, jerking him awake.

Confused, Jason looked around the empty room until he remembered where he was. Checking the clock on the wall, he saw he'd been asleep for almost an hour. Jumping up, he hurried back to Lou's room, but she was still asleep. He stood next to her until his five minutes were up, then retreated to the waiting room to continue his vigil. The minutes ticked by, turning into hours.

Each time he sat watching Lou's shallow breathing, he prayed, begging God to let her wake up, but nothing happened, and he would return to his chair in the waiting room.

Twelve hours passed in a blur since Lou arrived at the hospital, and Jason worried she might never wake up again. He questioned why God had to be so cruel. Why now?

He hated hospitals. Pacing around the waiting room, he wondered if he should call someone?

Brad? Should he call Brad?

What about David?

Or Joan?

Chapter Twelve

Joan Holden stood at the kitchen sink washing the dirt off her fresh-dug carrots, surprised her husband, Fred, had grown them. He was turning out to be a backyard gardener. It amazed her the new things he wanted to try. She remembered the day she had met him six years ago at an art lecture at the Grey Art Gallery in New York City. She had been watching him study a painting by Rembrandt and liked his smile.

Though a large man, about six-feet tall, and showing gray at the temples, Joan felt at ease when she walked over and stood next to him. Caught up in the painting's beauty, her purse slipped out of her hand and spilled at his feet. She watched in horror as the contents spread across the floor. When she bent down, so did the man next to her, and they bumped heads, which sent her into a fit of giggling.

After retrieving her items, Joan thanked him again and blushed when she looked in his eyes. Her heart melted. He introduced himself as Fred Holden, and when he invited her for a cup of coffee, they talked for hours. Fred had retired from the police department and was following his wish to take art classes. He said he never married because he hadn't wanted to put a wife through the worry of his job.

Joan told him she had just retired from the title company where she had worked for twenty-five years and was pursuing her love of the arts too. From that first meeting, they were inseparable. They spent time together, going on coffee dates, visiting art exhibits, and taking long walks. When he asked her to marry him, she said yes without reservation.

She and Jason had lost their parents during Joan's senior year in high school, the same year Jason had turned nine. She took over the role of the parent, pushing her own life aside. For the next ten years she worked hard, making sure Jason had what he needed. She made sure he graduated from high school and stood in the audience when he graduated from college. Another ten years had passed her by. Joan wasn't bitter; she loved her brother, but now it was her turn, though she still fussed over Jason when he would let her.

Joan hadn't heard from him since he left for the West Coast and was worried. She was drying her hands when her cell phone rang, and she recognized his number.

"Well, hello, Jason. It's about time you checked in with me".

"Joanie" His voice was so low she wasn't sure if it was him.

"Jason? Is that you? What's wrong? Are you hurt?" Frantic, she hurried through the kitchen door into the backyard to find Fred.

"Fred! Fred! Come quick, something's wrong with Jason".

Fred came running from the garage. "What is going on, Joan? Why are you yelling?"

She handed him the phone. "Jason—something's wrong—please talk to him".

Fred looked confused as he took the phone. "Jason? This is Fred. Are you okay?" After hanging up, Fred stood with a bewildered look on his face. Still staring at the phone, he turned to face Joan.

"Well? What did he say?"

"That reporter, Lou McClelland, the one he's working with on the story, she had an accident and—"

"Oh, no!" Joan put her hand to her throat. "Is she?"

Fred put his arm around his wife. "She's alive. Jason says she has a broken arm and cracked ribs, along with a concussion. She's in a coma. He said it's too early to tell how serious that might be until she wakes up. He's staying at the hospital with her".

Joan buried her head in Fred's chest and sobbed. Fred tried to assure her that Jason said he could manage this. They had no choice but to trust him.

"There, there, Joan". He kissed the top of her head. "Jason will be fine".

Joan looked up at him. "Are you sure?"

"He said he would call again as soon as he had more information. He asked me to call David and let him know what happened. Do you have David's number, by chance?"

Joan nodded then retrieved her address book. "Here is his cell phone number". Joan sat on the kitchen stool while Fred talked to David.

"David said he would give Jason a call later". Fred slid onto the stool next to Joan. "For now, all we can do is wait and pray".

Tears slipped down her cheek. She wondered why Jason was at the hospital. Didn't this Lou person have a family of her own? After Annie's accident, he could barely take care of himself, and buried his pain in a bottle. It took a lot of coaxing, but she talked him into seeing a doctor and saw a change right away. He was returning to his old self. Now, with this new crisis, she worried he wouldn't be able to handle things if the woman died. It sounded as if he cared for her more than just as a colleague.

Forty-eight hours had passed since Lou arrived at the hospital and noises began to seep through the fog in her mind. People were talking, and she recognized Jason's voice. Her head pounded, it clouded her memory, the rest of her body ached and even her eyes refused to open, as if something lay on top of them. Exhausted, she drifted off to sleep again as images and sounds came rushing at her.

Lou remembered the hopelessness she felt when the jeep ran off the road, trapping her in the mangled metal and feared she would die until a young woman's voice spoke, telling her to stay calm. The woman was young. About twenty years old, dressed in a simple white blouse and black skirt. She had her deep brown hair tied back with a ribbon, exposing a wing-shaped birthmark that covered most of the right side of her face. Lou tried to reach for the woman, but her right arm wouldn't move. The young woman touched her shoulder and Lou felt a calm flow over her and closed her eyes. When Lou opened her eyes again, she was sitting beside the jeep and her right arm was in a sling of white muslin. Another piece swaddled her forehead. She turned her head, looking for the woman, but she saw no one and everything faded to black once more to the sounds of voices yelling and sirens filled the air.

Another three hours passed before Lou began to fully wake from her deep sleep. She was tired of lying there and forced her eyes to open this time. A woman in a white coat stood with her back to Lou, saying things Lou couldn't follow. Frustrated, Lou focused on where and what surrounded her. When she turned her head, she saw her right arm covered in a cast, suspended in traction bar and her other hand had an IV line attached. When she tried to take a deep breath, she got a stabbing pain in her side, which caused her to wince. Her pulse began to race, sending the monitors into spasms, screaming through the silence, then footsteps rushed into her room.

Jason had just sat in the chair near Lou's bed when the alarm blared from the monitor, startling him. He jumped up to see Lou's eyes move around the room. He wasn't sure if she recognized him or understood where she was but felt grateful; she was awake.

"What happened?" Lou looked from the nurse to Jason.

"Now, don't you be moving, Miss Lou". The nurse was

101

adjusting her pillow.

Jason touched Lou's hand and was going to tell her about the accident when the doctor entered the room to check on her. After a quick examination, the doctor declared she would survive, with months of recovery ahead, then he left the room.

Lou reached for Jason's hand and tried to sit up, only to have pain shoot through her side. "Oh, that hurts". she hissed.

"How about you use this?" The nurse said, handing Lou the bed's controls. "This will save you from hurting yourself". She showed Lou how to raise the top of the bed until she sat upright.

Lou gave her a half-smile, relaxing as best she could against the pillow. "Okay, that is better".

A smile spread over Jason's face.

"What happened? How long have I been here?"

"Slow down, Lou. You've been in a bad wreck and..". His voice wavered. "And I thought I lost you".

Lou held his hand tighter. "It's okay, Jason. I'm too ornery. Haven't you noticed? Tell me what happened. I remember that I stopped for something". Anxious, Lou's eyes darted around the room again. "Where's my bag?"

Jason reached into his coat pocket and pulled out the metal box.

"Is this what you're looking for?" He set it on the bed next to her. "I knocked over your bag and it fell out, so I put it in my pocket for safekeeping".

Lou released his hand and reached for the metal box but stopped. "Did you open it? Did you read the journal?"

"Yes, I opened it and no I didn't read it. Why? What is it?"

Lou groaned from the pain. "I'll explain that later. Can I have something to drink?" Licking her dry lips, she nodded toward her bedside table out of reach. "I'm so thirsty".

Jason pulled the table closer, handing her the cup with the straw. Lou fumbled, trying to get it into her mouth.

"Here, let me help you". He held the straw to her lips, as she inhaled the liquid, quenching her thirst. She had a frown on her face. "It will be okay. I'm here. You don't have to worry".

Lou pulled her hand back. "I'm not worried".

"Well, what's the problem?" He sounded confused at her response.

"I saw her".

"Saw who?"

"The angel".

Jason gave her a skeptical look. She had hit her head. "Can you describe her?"

"I woke when someone touched my shoulder. She looked so young, and her clothing—the white blouse and plain black skirt. The birthmark on her face was just like the others described. I closed my eyes and when I opened them again, I was outside the jeep and she wasn't there". Lou leaned back against the pillow, motioning with her good hand for him to open it. "I'm not sure who this belongs to, but unless we read it, we'll never know. Will you read it to me?" My head aches.

Jason opened the lid and removed the journal then sat down in the chair next to the bed. "Are you sure you feel up to doing this, Lou?"

Lou nodded at him. "Please, Jason".

He opened the cover, turned to the first page, and began to read to her.

April 11, 1930

Today I turned twenty. The sisters gave me this wonderful leather-bound journal to write in, and it fills my spirit with love for them. I am still trying to adjust to the fact I have finished my two years of schooling to become a nurse and will receive my certificate on Friday. I am excited to start my new job as the Wasco Circuit Nurse and will see to the health of the ranchers and farmers. A new experience lies before me, and now I will give back to those who helped me. Sister Abigail wants me to stay at the orphanage, but I have taken up too much of their time since arriving here as a baby. How the years have flown. Though difficult I believe I am who I am because of their love. Life here has made me strong and I am ready for the task at hand. My job as a circuit nurse will be a long and, a lonely life, but I know God has chosen me for this work. The sisters and I spent the morning preparing the truck they have given me to drive. Though it was a challenge, I conquered the shifting of the gears. Mother Superior gave me a doctor's bag that she once used, to carry my medical supplies. Life is changing so fast it's making my head spin. In two days, I will travel from Bend, going north on the old stage road now called Highway 97. They have given me a map marking where I turn off the main road onto Bakeoven Road, where it will take me to the town of Maupin. I'm told it should take about five or six hours to reach my destination. My only fear is running out of fuel, but Mother Superior said the farmers are hospitable and I just need is to ask. The hour is late, and I must try to sleep.

April 13, 1930

I have only a few moments to write before it's time to leave. Excitement and apprehension swirl through my head, and I wonder if I am ready for the next chapter in my life. Part of me wants to stay within the safety of the orphanage, but it's time for me to move forward. The head of nursing has arranged for me to receive my lodging in Maupin. From there I will travel along the twenty-six miles of Bakeoven Road, tending to the farmers and ranchers, including the town of Shaniko. As I look from my window for the last time, the morning sun is bright against the soft clouds on the horizon, casting rays of amber and pink high into the sky. The sorrow of leaving tugs at me. The time to leave has come and I am grateful for a warm spring has arrived early in the high desert. It will be good for traveling.

Jason paused and glanced over at Lou. "What's wrong, Lou, are you in pain? Do you want the nurse?"

Lou shook her head. "She was a circuit nurse. I've read about them. They traveled the farm roads helping the locals". Lou stopped talking for a moment. "Jason—she was a nurse—don't you see?"

"So, what's that—oh—now I understand. She was a nurse, but why—unless. You don't think she's some ghost, roaming the road for years, do you?"

Lou nodded. "Who else could it be? She helped Harold, Brandon, Caroline, Bill, Jenny, and Linda—and me. I have to know what happened to her".

Jason turned the page.

April 14, 1930

It has been a long day. The trip to Maupin is taking longer than expected because of a flat tire on Bakeoven Road. I am less prepared for this journey than I thought and was lucky a rancher happened by. I watched in amazement at what it took to change the tire. The rancher, Devon Ward, had been on his way to town to summon help for his sick family. God worked in His own way bringing us together. I informed him I am the new county nurse and agreed to follow him to his ranch and have arrived just in time. Devon's wife, Clara, and their two children, Shelly, four, and Joe, two, have been vomiting along with bouts of diarrhea for the last week. I never smelled such foul quarters as I do here. I said a prayer and rolled up my sleeves. Clara and the children seem dehydrated and I must get them to eat. But what? After searching the pantry, I made a potato broth, and set about handfeeding them. I hope my training has prepared me for this task.

Lou let out a deep sigh. "How awful not knowing if she can help them".

Jason gave her a weak smile then began to read again.

April 15, 1930

Awoke to another morning of stench to clean. The baby can barely hold his head up and I am worried about him. Devon is getting over whatever brought this on, and we are praying for the rest of them. Shelly is such a sweet child, and Clara a devoted mother. It causes me pain as she watches her children suffer. In a fleeting moment, I question if my mother worried about me before I arrived at the orphanage, or had she died when I was born? There is no time for that, with so much work to do. I scrubbed the house clean and boiled the bedding and clothes. Still, I cannot figure out what is making them sick, and whatever I give them comes back up. Tomorrow, I will try something else.

April 20, 1930

I have been so busy for the last five days; I have little time to write. Never in my life have I seen so much sickness, and I am watching them slip away in front of me. I have used everything in my medicine bag, and they are still sick. I pray and cry when I am alone. Must try to sleep. My body aches and I'm afraid of what tomorrow might bring.

April 24, 1930

Four more days have passed, and today I saw an improvement in the baby and Clara. Clara said she felt well enough to care for Joe. I have been feeding them only baked biscuits and hot tea, and it's working. Shelly is still vomiting, but the diarrhea has stopped. Devon has stayed well, so one less to worry about. I asked him if he wanted to go for the doctor. He said they didn't have one in town right now. When I asked what people did, de said they must go to The Dalles, sixty miles away. Clara and I sat and talked for a while, and she shared how she needed to get back to canning for the winter. I questioned if they had been eating anything out of the ordinary before they got sick. Clara shook her head then gasped. She got up and rushed to the pantry, returning with a jar of marmalade, and set it on the table. When she opened the lid, the foul smell repelled us, and I asked how long they had been eating it before they got sick. Clara remembered it had been at least a week and began to cry. She did not realize it had spoiled and kept feeding it to her family. Devon told her it tasted off, but she ignored him. She cried as we gathered the jars, and Devon buried the contents far away from the house. The weight of the world has lifted from my shoulders, and I believe they will get better. This has been a testament to my faith. Tonight, I will sleep in peace.

Jason paused and looked over at Lou. Her eyes had closed, and she was breathing quietly. He placed the journal back inside the metal tin before he stowed it in his jacket pocket. He figured the rest of the story could wait until tomorrow. It had waited this long—one more day wouldn't change it. Exhausted and in need of a couple hours sleep himself, Jason stopped by the nurses' station to give them his number in case anything should happen while he was gone, then walked out into the warm evening air.

He took in a deep breath then climbed into his car, shut the door, and cried. Jason had never let himself grieve after Annie and Sophia died. Now, with almost losing Lou, his pent-up emotions erupted to the surface, he wept, and the pain flooded out with them. Exhausted, he sat waiting for his heartbeat to slow and realized he was ready to live again. But, first, he drove to the nearest hotel, booked a room, and crashed.

Jason was in a deep sleep when his phone began ringing next to his head. His first reaction was something must have happened to Lou, but when he checked the number, he realized it was his sister calling. Then he remembered he forgot to call her when Lou woke.

"Hey, Joanie, what's going on?" He rubbed his eyes and tried to sound awake.

"Jason — I", she cried into the phone. "It's Fred".

Jason sat up in bed, now wide awake, his sister wept on the other end of the line. "Whoa, Joan, take a breath and tell me what's wrong".

"Fred—had a heart attack, and, and he's still unconscious. I'm scared, Jason. Please come home. I need you!"

"Okay, listen to me Joan, I'll be on the first plane out of here. What hospital is he at?"

"Saint Mary's. I'm so sorry, Jason, I shouldn't ask, but I need you. I don't know what to do".

"You don't have to be sorry. I'll be there as soon as I can. It will be okay". He wasn't sure who he was trying to convince, Joan or himself. "Fred's too tough to let this get him".

Jason said goodbye then dialed the local airport. He discovered he could fly from Redmond but would have to drive twenty miles north to get there. They informed him the next commuter flight to Portland would leave in an hour. From there he could get a connecting flight to New York City and booked the flights using the company credit card. He was sure David would agree this was an emergency.

Jason sat stunned; his mind was in a jumble. He wanted to stay with Lou, but his sister needed him. He felt pulled apart at the seams, but he had no choice. Joan had begged him to come. She had always been there for him. She had been the one to pull him through the darkness when Annie and Sophia died. Now was his turn to help her. But what about Lou? Who would help her, and would she understand why he had to leave?

When he returned to Lou's room, the nurse informed him she was still sleeping. She looked so peaceful he didn't have the heart to wake her. Leaning down he kissed her forehead and touched her cheek with the back of his hand. "I love you", he whispered in her ear. Lou stirred for a moment, as if his words had penetrated her deep sleep, but didn't wake. Jason choked back the lump in his throat and left the room, stopping at the nurse's station. "Do you have a pen and paper I could use?"

The nurse handed him her pen and a sheet of paper. "Can I help you?"

Jason scribbled a note explaining what happened and why he had to leave, assuring Lou he would be back as soon as possible. He wrote his cell number and told her to call as soon as she could, then ended the note with Love, Jason. He gave the nurse her pen back and folded the note.

"Will you please see that Lou gets this as soon as she wakes?" The guilt he felt inside for leaving her consumed him. "It's important".

The nurse took the paper and slid it into the pocket of her lab coat. "Okay, sure. I'll be sure to give it to her. Anything else you need?"

Jason shook his head, turned, and walked out the door, headed for the airport and another hospital.

Lou tossed and turned throughout the night, with visions of breaking glass and sounds of twisting metal filling her mind. By the time she woke in the morning, she was in a foul mood. Her body ached, and if she took a deep breath or tried to move, a sharp pain stabbed through her sides. The pain medication helped, but she didn't like how it made her sleepy, so she refused to take it. Her cast was starting to itch, and she had no way of stopping it. She glanced around the room and noticed Jason wasn't in the chair next to her and reached for her call button.

"Good morning, Lou. What I can do for you?" The nurse pushed the call light button. "Are you in pain?"

"Well, a little bit. But that's not why I buzzed you. I was wondering if you know where my friend is".

The nurse shook her head. "I am not sure. Would you like me see if he is still here?"

"Could you?" Panic rose in her chest as her mind ran rampant. What if he couldn't take the stress of seeing me hurt, and just left? Would he do that—just walk away, after waiting days for me to wake up and the journal? Where was the journal? A crushing pain squeezed against her chest, causing the machines to beep and alarms blaring. Lou didn't know what was happening to her.

The nurse came rushing back in and after checking her; the nurse decided Lou was having a panic attack and gave her a pain shot.

Lou felt her body begin to relax, and she drifted off to sleep, mumbling, "Where's Jason? I need to see Jason".

Chapter Thirteen

George McClelland sat in his room at the boarding house, enjoying a cup of coffee while reading the morning paper. An article about another crash on Bakeoven Road caught his eye. Tucked under the obituaries on the back page, he almost missed it. His heart raced when he read the crash victim's name: Lou McClelland. Jumping up, he dropped the paper and his cell phone onto the floor knocking the back off, as it slid across the room. Not wanting to waste time to put it back together, he hurried downstairs to use the house phone in the office.

George tapped, as not to startle the woman behind the desk before he entered. "Hey, Mary, sorry to bother you. Do you mind if I use the phone?"

Mary Carpenter looked up from her paperwork. "Sure, George. What's the hurry?"

"I dropped my phone on the floor; it's in pieces. My daughter's been in an accident. She's at the hospital in Bend". He was out of breath.

"Oh my. Is she going to be okay? Where did it happen?"

"On Bakeoven Road. How many wrecks on that stretch of road?" His hands shook as he flipped through the phonebook looking for the number.

"I'm not sure but I've heard six crosses have appeared". Mary rose from her desk and took the book from him. "Let me help you, George. Can you drive, or do you want me to come with you?"

George wasn't sure. His last treatment at the clinic three days ago had left him tired. "Thanks, Mary, I'm fine. First, I need to call and get an update if they'll give me one. She probably listed me as deceased on her forms, but I need to try". He would welcome her company but knew he had to do this alone.

Mary patted his arm and handed him the phone after dialing the number. She offered him her chair, but he waved her off, so she returned to sit and wait while he made his call.

George leaned against the desk as the phone rang and rang. He was about to hang up when the operator came on the line.

"St. Charles Medical Center. How may I direct your call?"

"Um — yes, I would like information about a patient. Her name is Lou McClelland".

"Are you a family member?"

George paused for a moment. "Yes, I'm her father. Can you tell me her condition? Is she going to be okay?" The sound of feet shuffling across the floor grated on his nerves as he waited for the person on the other end of the line to continue talking.

"Let me look. You say you're her father?"

"Yes. I'm George McClelland. I've been out of town, so she probably didn't have my number". George felt the hesitation.

"I guess it would be okay. The records show she has a broken right arm, three cracked ribs, and a mild concussion, which has cleared. They should release her tomorrow. Do you want me to connect you to her room?"

George panicked. "Oh, that won't be necessary. Let her rest. I'll call back tomorrow. Thank you for your time". He hung up the phone.

"Well, George?"

A wave of nausea rushed over him, and he grabbed for the nearest chair. "Sorry, Mary, give me a minute, will you?"

Mary rose to get him a glass of water. "Here, George, drink this". George took the glass and gulped down the cool liquid. "Thanks Mary, you always know what to do". He set the glass on the desk.

"Don't keep me in suspense—how is she?"

"She has a broken right arm, three cracked ribs, and a mild concussion. The doctor is releasing her tomorrow".

Mary made the sign of the cross and said a silent prayer. "What do you want to do, George? Didn't you tell me her mother died before you moved back?"

"Yes".

"That settles it. She needs your help".

"What if she won't let me?" He leaned back in the chair.

"I don't know, but she will need help until her ribs heal and they remove the cast. The doctor may not let her go home unless she has someone to help her".

Mary reached out and touched his hands. "You should call back and talk to her".

George patted her hand. "Thanks, Mary. I think I'll just show up tomorrow, that way Lou won't have a choice if she wants to get out and not go to a rehab facility".

"Whatever you think, George, just let me know what happens".

George got up, came around the desk and gave her a kiss on the cheek. "Don't worry. I'm not giving up my room. This is only temporary. As soon as I know what's going on, I will let you know". He was so nervous when he returned to his room, he wasn't sure what to do. He wanted to rest, though sleep eluded him.

George rose from his bed, opened the closet door, and pulled out a wooden trunk the size of a toolbox. He set it on the table next to the wall and slid his hands over the smooth wood finish. The motion calmed his nerves. He opened the lid, lifting out a tray that held carving tools and set them on the table, then took out the wooden figurine he had been carving. It was of a little girl holding a teddy bear. He had started it after his return to The Dalles, hoping to give it to Lou someday. George had learned to carve from his father as a young boy, but he had put it aside for years.

113

It wasn't until after his surgery he picked it up again to help calm himself during the long hours of treatments for prostate cancer.

He'd been in town for four months undergoing chemo and living at Mary's Boarding House while he was trying to gather the courage to call his daughter. The problem was, he didn't know how Lou would take the return of her long-lost father. He hadn't seen or talked to her since Vivian forced him to leave. It hit him hard when he realized sixteen years had passed.

After a restless night he was up early and ready to leave. Mary had stood at the door with tears in her eye, and he assured her he would be back. He watched her waving as he drove away to his uncertain future.

Lou sat on the edge of the bed trying to put the clothes on the hospital had given her, since they destroyed hers after the wreck, with little success. She couldn't manage the simplest of tasks. Her ribs still hurt when she took a deep breath or tried to bend, and the cast on her arm itched, keeping her in a foul mood. After several failed attempts, she gave in and asked the nurse to help her dress. It felt good to be in regular clothes again.

Five days had passed since the accident and another three days with no sign of Jason. No one knew where he was. Lou had called Brad, but only got his voice mail saying he had left on vacation and wouldn't be back for two weeks. She tried to find the number for the paper but couldn't remember if it was the Times or the Post or one of three other papers listed. Frustrated, she gave up trying and each time she called Jason's cell phone, the voice mail came on.

After the fifth time, she stopped leaving messages. Emotions ran though her in waves, and she didn't know how to deal with the feelings she felt for him. She wondered if he had felt the connection too, or had it just been the whole story thing pulling them together?

At first, she worried something happened to him, but now she was mad.

Mad he had the journal.

The doctor had been in earlier and told her she would need help at home. She lied and said she had it covered. She called Julie in Portland, thinking she might ask her to come and help her, but the call hadn't gone as she planned.

"Hey Julie", Lou tried to keep her voice calm.

"Lou! It's so great to hear from you. You'll never believe what John and I are doing today".

Lou could hear the excitement in Julie's voice. "Well, I won't know until you tell me".

Julie laughed. "Right. We are going on the Sternwheeler for a ride today. Tomorrow, we are off to the beach for a week. Oh Lou, I am so happy".

Lou wanted to scream, instead she kept her voice as light as she could. "That's wonderful. You deserve it". She could hear John's voice in the background telling Julie to hurry.

"I'm sorry Lou, John is calling me. Was there something you called about?"

Lou knew she couldn't say a thing about the accident or Julie would drop what she was doing and rush back. She was that kind of friend, but Lou would not ruin Julie's trip for any reason. "No... I just missed my friend, and I wanted to say..."

"I'll be there in a minute John. I'm sorry Lou, what did you say?"

Lou winced in pain. "I said, I missed you and hope you are having the time of your life".

"Thank you, Lou, and I miss you too, but we will see each other soon. I hate to cut this short, but John insists we get going. Lou?"

"Yes?"

"Are you okay? You sound like you have something on your mind".

"Oh, I'm fine. Can't I miss my friend? Now go catch up with that handsome husband of yours and I'll call you in a few weeks after you've settled into your new home. Don't worry about me".

"Love you Lou".

"Love you too Julie". Lou hung up and realization hit her hard. She had no one. She was alone.

Lou signed with relief for the fact she didn't have to worry about her mother, then felt ashamed of herself, but it was true. Her mother's dementia had gotten so bad before she died that Lou would have been taking care of her mom, instead of her mom taking care of her.

She got up and walked over to the mirror and frowned at the woman staring back at her. Black stitches stuck out on her forehead like an extra eyebrow, and the bruises on her face had turned a sickly shade of purple and muddy yellow. They covered her right arm in a cast to her shoulder, and she was lucky she had only cracked ribs and hadn't sustained internal injuries.

Lou returned, and she sat on the edge of the bed, looking at the cast on her arm. She wondered how she would dress herself at home. The more she thought about it, the more upset she became and reached for the pillow. She held it to her face, her screams muffle by the pillow stuffing and cried until her sides ached.

George stood outside the door watching his daughter sobbing. He was far enough out of sight Lou couldn't see him. He wanted to rush in and hold her in his arms but was afraid. She didn't know him, and he feared she would reject him once she realized who he was. He couldn't blame her, and she had every right. He just wanted a chance to make it up to her and ask for her forgiveness. At least, he had to try.

When he arrived, the nurse had informed him Lou was dressing and would have to wait before he could enter. Excitement and dread flooded over him. He was about to turn coward and walk away when another nurse came up behind him with Lou's discharge orders.

"Can I help you, sir?" she asked, pushing the door open.

Lou heard the nurse's voice and wiped her face. She saw a man standing at the door.

George stood transfixed for a moment. She looked so much like Vivian and had her mother's eyes. "Hi, Lou".

Lou looked at him, cocking her head to one side as a long-ago memory began to surface in front of her. "Dad?"

Silence.

Lou continued to stare at the man, so the nurse backed out of the room, giving them time alone. Lou plopped back down on her bed. Shock and disbelief flooded over her. Could this man be her father? Questions raced through her mind so fast they were making her dizzy. Where had he been for all these years? Why was he here now? And what did he want? Lou caught the smell of his aftershave, evoking another memory—when she sat on the bathroom counter and watched him shave. "Daddy?"

George bit his lip as he watched a full range of emotions flit across his daughter's face not sure where they would end. He hoped she would at least talk to him before she told him to get out. He could only imagine what she must think, and he couldn't blame her.

Lou groaned with pain as she tried to adjust her arm.

"Can I help you?" His voice came out as a whisper. Without waiting for an answer, George sat down on the bed next to her, taking her left hand in his and pulled her to his chest and held her close. Lou didn't resist and sobbed in his arms.

George held her while she cried. His little girl was all grown up, and he had missed it. "It's okay, Louie, let it go".

Lou accepted his comfort until he used the familiar nickname, he used to call her. He could see the anger on her face when she pulled back and stared at him

"So, Dad, what do you want?" Her voice hardened. "Why are you here?"

George could sense the chill in the air and fell silent for a moment. He knew if he hoped for any chance of fixing their relationship; he had to see this to the end. "Well—I—" he stammered, clearing his throat. "I'm here to take you home and help until you're well enough to take care of yourself. If you'll let me".

"Help me? Why do you want to help me? I haven't seen you for sixteen years!"

George flinched at her words. "I know, Louie, but I'm here now, and I want to help".

"Don't call me that".

"I'm sorry. What do you want me to call you?"

Lou scowled at him. "Call me Lou, and I'll call you George".

"Okay, if that's how you want it". Her words stung like a hornet.

Lou heaved a deep sigh. Her head ached from trying to make sense of everything that happened. First, Jason showing up and throwing everything out of whack, then those similar descriptions of the angel in the interviews and finding the diary. Add the wreck into the mix, top it off with Jason disappearing. Now her absentee father shows up to take care of her, she couldn't make this stuff up if she tried.

Looking at her arm in the cast and considering the tightness in her chest from the cracked ribs, she knew she couldn't care for herself and felt defeated. If she wanted to leave the hospital, she would have to accept his help regardless if she wanted it.

118

George cleared his throat. "Let's get you out of here". Lou pushed the nurse's call button and waited.

"Yes. Can I help you with something?" the speaker squawked.

"I want to leave. Are my papers ready?" Lou stood.

"I'll be right there", the nurse replied.

Lou tried to grab her bag and winced.

"Here, let me get that for you". George moved over to help her.

"Thanks, I can do it myself". Pain shot though her sides. "Okay, you better take it". She didn't want to admit she hurt.

George took the bag and set it on the bed next to her.

She was about to reach for it when the door opened, and the nurse came bustling through pushing a wheelchair.

"Well, missy, your limo's here to take you to the lobby", she said, sliding the chair closer to Lou.

George took this as a signal and exited the room.

Lou gave the nurse a nasty look and considered this whole part a silly rule. She could walk, but hospital policy wouldn't allow it, forcing her to settle into the wheelchair. After getting her prescription just in case she needed it at home, the nurse pushed the wheelchair to the loading zone and locked the brake on the wheels. Checking out had taken longer than expected, and it was two in the afternoon.

"Here you go, Miss Lou. Do you need anything else?" Lou shook her head and inhaled the fresh air.

"No, but thanks for your help. Hope I wasn't too much of a pain".

"You did fine. If you have any problems or experience severe pain, be sure and call your doctor". The nurse patted her on the shoulder. "I'll wait with you until your ride comes".

Lou closed her eyes and enjoyed the warmth of the sun on her face. She would have fallen asleep if her mind wasn't in such turmoil. Did George even have a car? She'd forgotten to ask.

119

Whatever it was, she didn't care. She wanted to go home, but for some crazy notion she had hoped Jason might be the one taking care of her, not her father. She wanted Jason to be different and even let herself believe—what a fool she'd been. No note, no calls, nothing. She wouldn't let that happen again. And as for her father, she would have to see if he would stay.

Men. They just kept coming and going in her life.

George struggled with his own emotions as he went to the parking lot to retrieve the car. As he exited the lot, part of him wanted to keep going, as he had done for so many years. But looking at this wounded woman-child, he knew he had to stay.

He wanted to stay.

This was his daughter. Although she may not want to admit she needed him, and he needed her. Their first interaction went better than he'd hoped. She hadn't thrown him out—she'd even cried in his arms, like she used to as a child. That got to him and he wanted to do was take care of her the way he should have years ago. He prayed this would be a second chance for both.

George pulled up to the loading zone, then hurried to open the door. The nurse helped Lou from the wheelchair into the front seat and he took her bag and medical supplies and put them into the trunk, then slid in the front next to her and noticed she had trouble getting the seatbelt buckled.

"Here, let me help you". He reached for the belt and secured it. He remembered the first time he buckled her into his big rig and smiled. Lou's eyes were closed on the drive to the house, so George took it as a sign she wasn't in the mood for conversation. He knew this must be a shock to see him and would turn back time if he could.

George pulled into the driveway and turned off the engine, not prepared for the memories that bombarded him. He knew he would have to take it slow with Lou, and sat for a moment, trying to prepare for whatever happened next. Looking over at her, he smiled. She had fallen asleep. He hated to wake her, but they needed to get into the house. He reached over and touched her shoulder.

"Hey, Lou, we're home".

Lou's eyes fluttered open. She had been dreaming of Jason.

"Jason?" she asked, trying to get her bearings.

"No, it's just me, Dad". He wondered who Jason was.

"Dad?" Suddenly she sat upright, realizing who sat next to her. "Oh, George". she corrected. "You remembered your way home".

The bitterness in her voice stabbed him in the heart. George knew he would have to accept whatever punishment his daughter dished out. "Hasn't changed much". He unbuckled his seatbelt then reached over and undid hers.

Lou just shrugged and reached for the door handle. "Ow!" she winced in pain.

"Careful, now, let me get the door". He walked to her side of the car. "No need straining your ribs just to prove a point, Lou. I'm here, so let me help you".

"Okay, George, have it your way". Lou pushed herself up from the seat. "Six weeks", she grumbled, looking down at her arm.

George chuckled to himself. She was a tough cookie, for sure. He only hoped the years with Vivian hadn't turned her against him as he retrieved their bags from the trunk and followed her up the steps. "Can I get that door for you?" Lou gave him a stern look. He backed off and waited for her to unlock the door.

Looking around the entry hall, he half expected Vivian to come from the kitchen to yell at him for being late. He sighed.

Lou looked over at him as she was lowering herself to the couch. "Something wrong, George?"

George shook his head. "No. Just memories. They sneak up on you when you least expect it".

"Yes. Yes, they do". She leaned her head back and adjusted the sling on her arm.

"Can I help you?" George scanned the room. It was if time had stood still. Lou hadn't changed a thing. Floral wallpaper still covered the walls in the living room Vivian had insisted putting up right after they moved in the house. The cream-colored drapes, though faded with age, hung on the gold rods over the windows. His brown recliner still sat in the corner next to the rose-colored couch.

"No, I'm fine. Let me rest for a moment". Her voice trailed into silence.

"Where should I put my things?" He got no response. George walked around to the front of the couch and found her asleep. A lump formed in his throat. The house felt chilly to him, so he reached for the quilt that lay in the chair next to the television and covered her. His first instinct was to pick her up and carry her to her room as he had when she was little, but he was afraid of hurting her. Instead, he tiptoed out of the room and headed down the hall.

He could sense Vivian's presence in the house as he bypassed their bedroom and the thought of staying in their old room made his skin crawl. He opted for the spare room that held a large double bed for guests, though he couldn't remember ever having anyone stay there when he lived in the house. The same floral bedspread and sheets covered the bed and next to it, the lamp stood on the nightstand, and in the corner sat the three-drawer dresser. He wondered why Lou hadn't changed things after Vivian died. Was she still mourning her mother?

The questions he had could wait. George dropped his bag on the floor, lay on the bed exhausted, and drifted off to sleep.

Lou flinched in her dreams sending a wave of pain through her rib cage, waking her. Confused until her mind began to focus, Lou realized she had been sleeping for hours. Looking around the living room, she noticed it was after six in the evening and the sun was casting long shadows across the floor. As a child, she liked to pretend dust fairies danced in the beams. When her mother was having a good day, they would pretend to see the magic fairies dancing. Then Mom would change her mind and close the drapes, shutting out the light.

Lou adjusted her sling and sighed. She thought she could jump up as if nothing had happened, hit her like a stack of bundled newspapers. Fixing something to eat crossed her mind, but she didn't have an appetite or the inclination to move. Lou tapped on the cast. The itching irritated her, and the cast was cumbersome. She didn't know how she could stand a month and a half with this thing on her arm. As for the return of her long-lost father, he could stay until she could take care of herself, then he was out the door.

Lou rested her head against the back of the couch. She vaguely recalled the ride home with George and wondered where he might be until she caught the sound of soft snoring coming from down the hall. What was she going to do with him? Depression washed over her in waves. Just a week ago, Jason had been reading to her and holding her hand. Then he just disappeared with no word. She checked her cell phone to see if she had any messages. Nothing. It was as though he never existed, but her heart didn't feel that way. Overwhelmed, she sobbed until she fell back asleep.

George stirred, worried about Lou, and got up to check on her. She was still on the couch asleep. He could remember the time she was five and got chicken pox. She had camped out on the couch for a week watching cartoons, so she would stay still and not scratch at herself. The memory of her little face, covered in spots, made him smile. George brushed a stray curl from her forehead then sat in the chair across from her. He watched her sleep until his eyes became heavy and retreated to his room. His being in the house brought up things he hadn't thought about in years, unnerving him and sleep eluded him until the early hours of the morning.

Chapter Fourteen

Three days passed and there was still no word from Lou. Jason couldn't believe he was standing in a hospital ICU, looking at another person he loved. Yes, he had said it. He loved Lou, but he hadn't heard from her since he left and figured she must be mad at him for leaving. He thought about calling but pushed it aside and direct his attention to Joan and Fred. The doctor told them if Fred regains consciousness, it would need to happen in the next few hours since he was not breathing on his own. Fred's doctor said if they removed the breathing tube, there was the possibility Fred could die. If he rallied, they would do bypass surgery.

Joan blinked in disbelief as horror crossed her face. She walked past Jason and the doctor. Jason started after her, but she held her hand up to stop him, and he understood. She had to manage this on her own.

Jason turned back to the doctor. "Do you think Fred will wake up soon?"

"It's anybody's guess. His scans look good. There was some muscle damage to the heart". The doctor skimmed the test results in Fred's chart again. "We could try weaning him off the respirator. That would be up to Joan and it could go either way".

Jason knew if it was him, he wouldn't want to live this way. After shaking the doctor's hand, he left to look for his sister and found her at the chapel, begging God to give her more time with Fred. He was about to leave when Joan turned toward him.

"How are you doing, Joanie?" He walked over and put his arm around her.

"Better". She wiped her nose with a tissue.

125

Jason wasn't sure how to approach what the doctor suggested.

"Hey Sis, I talked to the doctor after you left".

"What did he say?" Her voice cracked.

"He said Fred should wake up soon and wondered if you would consider weaning him off the respirator to see if he can breathe on his own".

"But what if he can't?"

Jason didn't want to push her, but he felt a responsibility to Fred.

"Look, Joanie, I know this idea isn't easy, but Fred wouldn't want to live kept alive by machines".

"But, Jason, he could die!"

"Yes, or he could start breathing on his own. They will hook him back up if it doesn't work, but I believe it's a chance you have to take".

Fred surprised everyone by breathing on his own, then they rushed him into surgery for a triple bypass. The surgery had been a success and the doctors were sure he would make a full recovery.

Fred opened his eyes, but it took a few minutes before he could focus and saw Joan standing in the corner whispering with Jason. His throat and his mouth felt like cotton and his mind was groggy as he tried to figure out where he was. Why he was lying in this bed hooked up to oxygen? Then he remembered being in the kitchen talking to Joan when a crushing pain hit his chest and glanced down. He could see tape running down the center of his chest and it felt tight when he tried to take a deep breath.

"Why's everyone so glum?" His voice was low and sounded raspy. He called again, but they still ignored him. Frustrated, he looked for the call button on the bed. Joan stopped talking to Jason in mid-sentence when the nurse came through the door.

"What's a guy got to do for some attention?" he said louder.

126

Joan rushed to Fred's side. "Oh, honey! You're awake. Do you know who I am?"

Fred gave her a look as if she were bonkers. "I know who you are. Alice, right?" He gave Jason a wink.

"Alice? Who's Alice?" Joan saw the childish grin on his face. "Fred Holden. If you weren't in this hospital bed". She laughed, kissing him.

Fred kissed her back and smiled. "Sorry, Joan, you guys looked so serious". He tried to move in the bed, but he was too tired. What does the doctor say?"

Joan tried to explain but couldn't get the words out. Jason moved to the side of the bed and put his arm around her.

"Do you want it sugar-coated or straight, Fred?"

"Just give it to me straight". He couldn't remember anything after the crushing pain in his chest.

"Well, old guy, you had a heart attack. When you got here, it was touch and go until they could stabilize you. You had to have a triple bypass and you will need extensive therapy to regain your strength. The doctor is optimistic you'll recover if you do what you're told".

Fred patted Joan's hand, trying to digest what had happened and was grateful to be alive. "It that it? I thought it was something serious".

Since he arrived four weeks ago, Jason had been staying at Joan's. He continued to struggle with his love for his sister, and his guilt for leaving Lou alone with no one to help her. Caught up in the drama with Joan, he spaced out, forgetting to check his phone for messages. Now, he felt like a fool for not calling the hospital to check on Lou. Jason reached into his pocket for his phone, only to discover it wasn't there. Frantic, he searched though the rest of his pockets and bag, but still couldn't find it. He must have lost it somewhere between The Dalles and New York City. Then he realized. Lou couldn't call him—he didn't have a phone. What an idiot he was and borrowed Joan's phone.

The receptionist at the hospital didn't have any information, so she referred him to the nurse who took care of Lou. When he asked how she was doing, she told him they had released Lou, and that her father took her home. Jason didn't remember Lou mentioning her father and disappointment flowed over him. No wonder Lou didn't call — she didn't need him. He still needed to get a new phone and decided it was time to check on his apartment.

It seemed like it had been years as he rode the elevator to the tenth floor. He dragged his feet as he walked down the hall and felt he carried the weight of the world on his shoulders. Stacks of old newspapers blocked the door, and he had to slide them aside with his foot, before he could unlock the door and step in. Empty beer cans still littered the floor, along with dried pizza boxes and Chinese food cartons on the coffee table and the place stank.

Jason had to face the fact he lived like a pig and the smell became stronger as he searched for the source. Entering the kitchen, he pulled cupboard door open under the sink and the foul order hit him full force. Holding his breath, he grabbed the garbage sack, and headed for the dumpster in the basement, first stopping to pick up the newspapers for the recycle bin. When he returned, he searched for a can of Lysol. After he gave the garbage can a good dose, he continued to spray the rest of the rooms, disgusted at himself for living this way.

He spent the next two hours cleaning his apartment and took four trips to the dumpster. The place was clean but smelled of disinfectant. He searched through the bathroom cabinet and found a can of lilac air freshener. Jason wasn't sure if it was better, but at least it was habitable.

As he stood back, he surveyed his accomplishment. Not bad.

With his clean up done, Jason took out his laptop, logged in and scanned his emails hoping for a message from Lou, but found nothing. There was a message from David with orders to call but Jason wasn't ready to talk to him or anyone. He cleared his mailbox before he closed his computer. Exhausted, he couldn't keep his eyes open any longer and went to his room, stripped down to his T-shirt and boxers then slipped between the clean sheets.

He was out in minutes when the dreams started.

Two Years Earlier

It was after nine in the evening in New York City, when Jason landed. Though he was tired from the long flight and in need of a shower, he just wanted to hold Annie and their baby. Tomorrow was Sophia's first birthday. Jason promised Annie he would be home in time for the party, and he had made it. He hoped they would be up when he got home. He had just retrieved his bag when his phone vibrated in his pocket. Jason saw he had missed a call from his sister while in the air.

While he waited for a cab, he set his bag down and retrieved the message. Shock resonated though his body, causing him to stumble against the wall. He could barely make out what Joan was saying. It sounded like Annie and Sophia had been in an accident and he needed to get to the hospital now. Jason grabbed his bag and cut through the line, jumping in the nearest cab, ignoring the shouts behind him, he urged the driver to hurry to the hospital.

Jason couldn't remember if he paid his fare when the cab stopped in front of the ER, but he must have since the cabbie drove away. Rushing into the waiting area, Jason knew the instant he saw the look on Joan's. The room began to spin, and Jason felt as if his body weighed a thousand pounds, pulling him toward the floor. Fred was next to him in a flash and grabbed him before he collapsed and guided him to the nearest chair. Joan hurried to Jason's side and enfolded him in her arms.

"What happened?" He could barely speak.

"Oh, Jason, I'm so sorry", Joan cried unable to stop. Fred knelt next to his wife and put his arm around her.

"Tell me what happened", Jason voice started to rise. "Tell me!"

Fred recounted what he'd learned from the police officers who came in with the ambulance. Annie and Sophia were on their way home from the bakery when a delivery van hit Annie's car on the driver's side. It pushed her car into a power pole, smashing in the back door next to where Sophia sat. The driver of the van was drunk and died at the scene. Rescue workers had to cut through the twisted metal to get them both out of the car, but the emergency crew couldn't save them.

Jason sat motionless, trying to wrap his mind around what they had old him. "I want to see them. Now!"

The ER doctor led him into the room where the nurses had cleaned them up the best they could. Jason moved between the gurneys that held his wife and daughter, touching their faces. They looked like angels and his heart wanted to believe they were only sleeping. From deep inside his belly the pain rolled up to his throat until it exploded. Jason dropped to his knees between them and sobbed until he could cry no more. When he could stand, he gave them each a kiss, then cursed God. Without another word, Jason left the room, and walked out the door into the night.

As the morning light crept through the mini blinds in his room, Jason forced his mind awake, away from the memories that haunted his dreams. Soaked in sweat and tangled in the sheets, he waited for his heartbeat to slow in his chest. Sometimes he wished the dreams would just stop. Jason wanted to be with Lou. He was an idiot for leaving her. He should have waited until she was well enough to leave and brought her with him, but Joan needed him. What was he supposed to do?

Jason flipped back the covers, untangled his legs from the sheets and sat on the edge of the bed. He needed to talk to Joan. After a quick shower, he loaded his laptop in his bag and made sure he tucked the journal in the pocket. After glancing around the apartment, he hurried out, locking the door behind him.

Joan sat in the physical therapist's room waiting for Fred to finish with his appointment. She marveled at the determination her husband showed and wondered if she would have the same strength if faced with this challenge. Since his transfer to the rehab center that morning, therapy was going well. He was regaining his strength, but the doctor reminded her Fred had a long way to go. He would have to watch his diet, exercise, and try to lower his stress.

Lost in thought, Joan didn't see Jason arrive.

"Joan. Joan is everything okay?" Jason sat into the chair next to her.

Joan saw the concerned face of her little brother. "Hey, Jason, what are you doing here today?" She studied his face. He looked like he'd aged ten years. He had dark circles under his eyes and appeared to have lost weight.

"What did the doctor say? You said on the phone they had transferred him, but I wanted to see how Fred was doing for myself".

"He's progressing better than expected after a triple bypass. His blood pressure is high, and he gets tired. Fred keeps telling them he's ready to go home". She chuckled. "You know Fred—don't tell him he can't do something, because he will try to prove you wrong. I just hope he's right this time".

Jason put his arm around his sister and held her tight.

Joan relaxed into his embrace and let him comfort her while she cried. Jason handed her his handkerchief.

"Wow, I didn't see that coming". Joan straightened in her chair.

"Joanie—I", he stammered.

"What's wrong, Jason?" She looked up at him.

"I want to go back to The Dalles, to find Lou and explain why I left and ask her for a second chance. But I don't want to leave you here alone, either", he said, his voice catching.

Joan gulped a quick breath.

"What's wrong?"

Joan felt ashamed of her weakness. "I don't have a right to ask. Would you stay, just until I'm sure Fred is better?"

Jason saw the worry on Joan's face. He wanted to leave now, but he knew she wouldn't ask unless she needed him. So, even though his heart was breaking, he would wait.

As the days passed in a blur, he kept trying to get hold of Lou. He called the office in The Dalles, and Karol said that Lou was still out and to leave a message. When he asked for Lou's number since he had lost it, she informed him Lou wasn't taking calls and hung up on him. After the third try, voice mail picked up his calls.

He called David, who mentioned he and Brad had been discussing the story. They wanted to know what was happening. Jason said he needed more time. David agreed on two more weeks. After that, he had to return to work or clear out his desk for good. He knew he had been pushing his friendship with David to the breaking point.

Chapter Fifteen

Five weeks had dragged by since Lou's first night home from the hospital. Where had the time gone? Lou got ahold of Brad, who was back from his vacation and he confirmed that Jason had returned to New York City, though he didn't know the circumstances. He told her that if she wanted him to relay a message to Jason through David, he would.

Lou started to say yes, then decided against it. If Jason wanted to talk to her, he would have called. As for the story, Brad assured her it was on hold until Lou came back to work. That eased her anxiety but without the journal, she was at a stalemate. She had no way of knowing the ending. For now, she would let it go.

Lou spent most of her days in her room sleeping. The slightest task exhausted her, and she worried that she'd never get better. The rest of the time, her mind wandered to Jason. "Why, Jason, why?" she asked herself. Her other, more pressing issue was what to do about her father. Lou had things she wanted to say, questions she wanted to ask, but each time she started to talk with him, she got angry and dropped the topic. The clattering of dishes caught her attention, signaling George must be in the kitchen. Lou decided now was the time and grabbed her robe.

George had spent the morning tinkering with his car and fixing things around the house. While cleaning out the hall closet that morning, he discovered a shoebox shoved in the back, hidden behind a suitcase. He wondered what was inside and took it to the kitchen. Lou was in her room resting, so he sat alone at the table when he cut the tape on the lid and opened it. He jerked when he saw its contents. It held letters and cards he had written to Lou. He wondered if Lou had hidden them. If so, why hadn't she written him back?

George flipped through the envelopes. Every birthday card, holiday card, and the letters he'd sent since leaving home. Until a year ago, when he gave up hope of Lou reaching out to him and stopped writing. When he pulled out one card and opened it, shock and disgust washed.

"Vivian!" He cursed under his breath. "How could you?"

It was becoming clear why Lou never wrote back and wanted nothing to do with him. Vivian must have kept these from Lou, as a way of punishing him. But why would she have hung onto them? Why Vivian did any of the things she did still stumped him. George replaced the card and the lid and was still holding the box when Lou came into the kitchen.

George looked up from the table. "Good morning, Lou". He tried to sound cheery, but his voice quivered.

"What's wrong, George? You look like you've seen a ghost".

"I guess you could more like a nightmare".

Lou sat across from her father. She appeared to be on a mission.

"Um—George, we need to talk".

He knew what she wanted to discuss.

"Why did you leave us?" she blurted. "How could you leave me with her?"

George hung his head. "I'm sorry, Lou. I didn't plan it. I had every intention of coming back".

"But you didn't! I waited for you, and each night I cried myself to sleep. Whenever I asked Mom if I made you go away, she said you left because I was a brat and you didn't like bratty kids".

"That's not true, Lou. Please believe me, it wasn't about you". He couldn't believe the depths of Vivian's hatred toward him.

Lou looked at him with doubt in her eyes. "How do I know?

134

You never called me, never wrote. When the mail came, she would say there was nothing for me. After a while, I stopped asking, stopped hoping, and stopped loving".

George tried to gather his thoughts before he spoke. "Lou, there things are I need to tell you. About your mother and why I left. Afterward, you can decide if you want me to stay or not. It will be up to you".

"What could you say to make this nightmare I've been living go away?"

George took a deep breath, not sure where to begin. "It started when your mother got pregnant when you were three. Do you remember me telling you Mommy was going to have a baby?"

Lou shook her head.

"You asked me if you could have a puppy instead".

"I remember little about that time". Lou sat up in her chair. "But—wait—what happened to the baby?"

Tears escaped George's eye. "Your brother—he came early— and there were complications. The doctors tried to save him, but he was born with the cord wrapped around his neck".

Lou's face crumbled. "What's that got to do with Mom, or how she treated me?"

"Your mother became depressed after she came home from the hospital. She blamed me for your brother dying".

Lou gave him a look of disbelief. "How could she blame you? How come I don't remember this?

George got up and paced the kitchen. "I don't know. She just couldn't come to terms with the loss, and I guess she needed to blame someone, so she chose me".

"That's ridiculous". She shifted in her chair

George returned to his seat. "It was a challenging time for your mother. After she came home, she pretended it never happened. Your mother didn't want to talk about the baby or help plan the funeral. It was as if he never existed". George choked back a sob. "I had to take care of burying him alone. She wouldn't even give him a name for the death certificate. He deserved a name on the headstone". George broke down.

Lou handed him a napkin "What did you name him?

"Raymond George McClelland, after my father, your granddad".

"Where's he buried?"

"Next to your mother".

Lou looked confused. "I thought it was your dad's grave, so that's where I buried her".

"No, it's your little brother's".

Lou sat back in her chair, shifting her arm. "That doesn't explain why you left".

George took a couple deep breaths. "Your mother's depression was hard to control. One day she would be fine, almost jovial like her old self, then the next she would sink so low she couldn't get out of bed. Once, it got so bad I had to admit her to the hospital for her own protection and yours".

"What happened then?"

"She was better for a while. The doctor gave her medication for the depression, and it helped. The problem was, she didn't like the way it made her tired, so she quit taking it. But when I tried to explain it was for her own good, she would get angry, blaming me for how bad her life turned out. Somehow, she got it in her mind that it was my fault and would punish me".

"How would she do that?" Lou leaned back in the chair.

"It doesn't matter now. Do you remember I drove my truck long-haul? Each time I got home; she would do whatever she could to make my life miserable. You were the only bright spot in my life. It was you who I came home to see". He returned to his chair.

"Remember the time I took you with me?" Lou shook her head, picking at the edge of her cast. "You had just turned six, and I thought it be good for Mom, you know, give her time to herself. I put you in the seat next to me and buckled you in and you were laughing and holding your little teddy bear. Do you still have him?"

A smile crossed Lou's face then faded. "No. Mom threw him away after you didn't come back. She said toys were for babies. When I was around nine years old, I was in my room playing with my doll. Mom was in one of her rages. She came in and snatched it away from me. She told me I was too old to play with dolls and threw it into the trash and cried myself to sleep. Later, got up and pulled the doll out of the trash, cleaned her, and hid her in my room. She's still hidden to this day. That next morning, I worried Mom would discover the doll wasn't in the garbage, but she was smiles and loving. This began the first of many outbursts, followed by her failure to remember what she had done".

George shook his head. "I'm so sorry, Lou".

"Doesn't matter; it's in the past". Lou shrugged. "You were saying?"

"After a while your mother's mood became viler toward me. She'd seem stable for a day or two then would regress so much, she once threatened to run off with you if I didn't stay away. So, I made my trips longer until I just didn't come back. But, Lou, you must know I never forgot you".

"What do you mean you never forgot me? I never heard from you again!" Lou slammed her cast on the table and cracking the edge of the part that covered her hand.

George jumped. "I sent cards on your birthdays and holidays; I wrote to you".

"You're a liar! I got nothing from you, except a life with a mother who hated me!"

137

"Please Lou, that's not true. She didn't hate you. She just hated her own life more. I wrote to you and I can prove it". He pushed the box toward her.

Lou looked down at the shoebox he slid in front of her then back at him.

"What's this?"

"Proof that I care, Lou. That I didn't forget you".

Lou reached for the shoebox but stopped short of touching it. What could this hold that would prove he loved her? How could he have left her, knowing her mother was unstable? The new revelation shed light on Mom's behavior but didn't excuse the way she'd treated her.

Lou lifted the lid and peered inside to find letters, stacks of them, addressed to her. She lifted the envelopes and spread them on the table in front of her. The postmarks dated back to the year George left and continued until six months before her mother moved to the care facility to live.

One by one, she pulled the cards and letters out of the opened envelopes. Lou's stomach turned at the sight. Lies! Lies! Lies! scribbled were over his words with a red pen. Lou read the parts of the letters she could make out. Her father told her about his travels, how he missed her and loved her, and how sorry he was for leaving her. Lou felt the hatred that had layered her heart against him start to peel away.

George rose, came around the table, and took her in his arms. Together they cried, washing away the years of hurt between them.

"Oh, Louie, how do I ever make it up to you?"

Lou grabbed another napkin and blew her nose. Her father loved her, and she had the proof in front of her. Her emotions were ragged, and she felt drained. "Well, George—I mean Dad, how about we take it a day at a time? Sound good to you?"

A smile flooded his face. "Yes, one day at a time".

Over the next week they shared memories, hopes, and dreams with each other. She had even called Julie and could keep the conversation upbeat but didn't tell her about the accident or her father's return. Lou decided she would wait until they saw each other at Christmas. During her conversations with her father, she told him about Jason and the story they were working on before the accident. She shared about the feelings she had for him until he'd disappeared with the journal and her heart.

George listened as she bared her emotions. "Did you try to call him? He must have a good reason for leaving in such a hurry".

"I called my boss, but he said Jason had gone home on personal business and he couldn't talk about it. When I tried calling his cell phone again, the operator said the number was no longer in service".

The mention of his name only refueled her anger. As soon as she was back at work, she would find out why Jason left and never tried to get in touch with her. She needed his half of the story to complete the feature and give her any chance at the new position.

During this time Lou was learning about her own feelings and her father. They made a trip to the cemetery to lay flowers at the graves. George had cried at the sight of Vivian's name on the headstone, and of their son's. Lou had stood in front of her mother's burial site, and a healing came over her, along with forgiveness toward her mother. Turning from the graves, father and daughter walked arm in arm, away from their past and into the future, whatever it held.

Chapter Sixteen

ou woke with a smile on her face. Six weeks had gone by since the accident and Jason's disappearance, and still no word from him. Something terrible must have happened. But what? She decided for today she would put it aside and concentrate on freeing her arm.

While she has been off, fellow workers she hardly knew sent her cards and emails wishing her a speedy recovery. She had been feeling alone and now realized people cared about her. She pledged to take time to get to know them better and, not stay wrapped up in her own world. Even Chris had sent her a potted plant with a generic Get-Well card. It had made her smile and Lou decided it was time to forgive him. The other pressing issue was her need to get a new car. She had totaled the jeep in the wreck. Dad said he would help her pick something out and make sure it was the right one for her. She started to protest but stopped and let him help. That's what fathers did. The one thing he couldn't help her with— the deep ache for Jason.

"You seem chipper today", George said, starting his car and backing out of the drive for the ride to the hospital clinic.

"Yep, time to get this ratty, old cast off, and get my life back", then she glanced at him. "Nothing against you. Only tired of this thing and glad they scheduled me for first thing this morning".

"Hey, don't worry. If it was me, I probably would have cut it off long ago". He chuckled. He watched a frown spread across her face.

"What's wrong, Louie girl? You look burdened. Something bothering you?"

"Oh, I was just thinking how much I've enjoyed our time together and how I'll miss it, after I go back to work. I know we haven't talked about it, but I want you to stay".

George had been wondering if she would make him leave after she got better. He wanted to stay longer until their relationship was stronger and loved spending time with Lou, but he missed Mary. They were keeping in touch by phone, and he had stopped to see her when he shopped for groceries. He worried they might lose the closeness they were building, but he didn't want to put any stress on Lou either by starting a serious relationship too soon.

"Don't you worry, I will stay as long as you need me. We'll still breakfast and dinner, and I could always bring you lunch".

Lou reached over and patted his arm. "I think I can at least make myself lunch".

While George waited in the lobby, Lou sat on the exam table, scanning an old copy of Better Homes and Gardens. Looking through the pages of decorated rooms, along with the lovely yards, Lou realized her home needed freshening up a bit. It was time to change things. Time for her to stop living in the past and move forward. She decided she would talk to him about it after they got home and was still flipping pages when the nurse came in the room.

"Good morning, Lou. How are your ribs? Any pain with them?" the nurse asked, while she took Lou's vitals and charted them.

Lou shook her head. "Only if I stretch too far, otherwise I'm great. I'll be even better after I get this monstrosity off my arm". She motioned to her cast.

"The itching is the worst. When broke my wrist four years back, and it drove me crazy. The doctor will be here in a few minutes to cut it off, and I will be right back".

"Thanks". Lou picked at the plaster. She had almost removed the bridge between her hand and thumb from nervousness and would destroy the thing if it stayed on any longer. She was still working at another loose piece when the doctor opened the door and entered.

"Good morning, Lou. Good to see you in one piece".

"Hi, Doctor Keller. It's nice to see you too".

"Ready to get that thing off your arm?" Opening the cabinet, he brought out the cast saw and set it on the tray table.

"Sure, and none too soon". She picked another chunk of plaster off next to her thumb.

"I better get to it then". He started cutting. In less than five minutes, her arm was free. He removed the gauze and wiped off the cream that covered her arm then had her try moving it.

"It looks good, but I want you to watch what you do for another two weeks. Don't put too much pressure on it or lift anything heavy", he said, making a notation on her chart

"It was a bad break, Lou, so I want you wear a splint for a while. Just to make sure".

Lou groaned.

"It won't be that bad", he chuckled. "You can take it off at night".

"Thanks, Doc. I know I'm acting like a baby, but this thing was killing me".

Doctor Keller laughed, patted her on the shoulder, and left the room.

Lou sat looking at her arm, turning it over and back again. It looked shrunken and wrinkled from being inside the cast and smelled musty. She couldn't wait to get home and take a real shower. She was still checking her arm when the nurse returned.

"Okay, ready to get out of here?" She pulled a splint from the drawer.

Lou rubbed her wrist and arm. "Do I need to wear that thing?"

"Just for a while. You don't have to wear it all the time, but you need to take it easy for a while. It was a bad break, and you want to make sure it's healed". The Velcro strap was long, so the nurse reached into her pocket for her scissors and pulled out a piece of paper with them. "Oh, no!"

"What's wrong?"

"I'm so sorry. I haven't worn this jacket since—and—I am so sorry". She handed the note to Lou.

Lou didn't know what the nurse was talking about. She took the piece of paper and scanned the hand-written message. Jason! The note was from Jason.

"When did you get this?" A lump formed in her throat.

"The night you woke up from the coma. That nice young man who had been sitting with you came by the desk. He sounded upset and said he had to leave and left the note for you. I slipped it into my pocket and was on my way to give it to you when another accident victim came in and I forgot. I'm sorry, Lou".

Lou wanted to be angry, but who was she to judge "It's okay". Lou jumped down from the exam table. "You have no idea what this note means to me".

She held the piece of paper close to her chest, grabbed her things and hurried out. Emotions rushed through her mind. Jason hadn't run off he had a reason for leaving. But why didn't he call? She read the message again. He said to call as soon as she gets this note. She had tried to call, until the operator said the number was no longer in service. Then she realized. If Jason wasn't getting her calls, he must think she didn't want him. Oh, what a mess. Lou knew what she had to do.

On the ride home, Lou looked nervous about something and kept looking at a small piece of paper in her lap. George wasn't sure what brought on the sudden change and couldn't take it anymore.

"So, Lou, besides getting your cast off, did something else happen today?"

Lou looked at the note again. "Remember the man I told you about. The one I was working with on my story?"

"You said his name was Jason. Why?"

"Remember how I said he never called or even left a note, why he had to leave?"

"Yes, I do, and as I recall, it has upset you. Has something changed that?" George recalled her tearful conversation. Lou turned to her father with the biggest smile he'd seen in a long time.

"He didn't leave because he didn't want me. He left because his sister's husband had a heart attack and she needed him".

"But you needed him too. I'm confused".

"I know, I know, but don't you see?" Lou held up the piece of paper. "He left this for me that night, but the nurse put it in her pocket and forgot about it. She found it today when she was fixing the strap on my brace".

"Okay. But I still don't understand?"

"Well, the note said to call him after I woke up, but since I didn't get the note, I never called. Well, I did, but his phone wasn't working or something and since I didn't call, he must think I don't want him in my life either".

Lou looked down at her lap.

George didn't want to sound too fatherly but couldn't help it.

"Couldn't he have called if he cared about you? Either he wants to be with you, or he doesn't".

"You need to know Jason".

"What's there to know?"

"There are things I haven't told you about him". She was playing with the paper and saw the concerned look on his face.

"Is he wanted by the police? Is he married?"

144

"No, he's not wanted by the police. He's not married. He's a widower".

"I'm sorry. Do you know what happened?"

"The night before his daughter's first birthday, his wife and child got killed in a terrible car accident".

George felt compassion for the man, knowing the pain of losing a child. "That's rough, Lou, though I'm not sure how that explains why he hasn't called you?"

Lou held up the note. "It's complicated, but don't you see? It means he was opening his heart. I just hope it's not too late".

George didn't know how to respond. It upset him this guy ran off and hurt his daughter. Hadn't he done the same thing? Turning in his seat, he saw such unhappiness in her face, and it crushed him.

"What do you want to do, Lou?" He tried not to choke up as he pulled into the driveway and parked the car.

"I want to go to him and tell him I want him in my life and, that I love him".

"That's a big step, Lou. Are you sure about this?"

"Yes. More than anything in my life".

George reached over and pulled her into his arms. After she stopped crying, they hurried into the house to figure out a plan.

First, George called the airlines and booked her a flight to New York City.

Then he called Mary to let her know he would drive Lou to Portland, so they would have to cancel their dinner date. Mary assured him she was fine and would see him after he got back.

"Hey, Dad, I didn't mean to eavesdrop, but who's Mary?" Lou asked, as they sat down to lunch. "You sounded cozy on the phone".

George set their sandwiches on the table and sat down across from her. He missed Mary and wanted to spend time with her, but

145

his place was with Lou. He wasn't sure how to broach the subject about Mary but decided to just be honest.

"She's a friend and was my landlady". He took a bite of his sandwich.

"Landlady? Where? I thought you just got into town right before you showed up at the hospital".

"Well, that's not entirely true".

Lou looked at him with questions in her eyes. "What do you mean?"

George coughed, then set his sandwich back on the plate. "I'd been staying at Mary's Boarding House for the last four months while I—"

"You what?" Lou was now standing. "You had been in town for four months, and just showed up when I needed you?"

George didn't know what to do. He should have contacted her sooner, and told her about his cancer treatments, but in her condition how could he burden her with that?

She ran from the room.

"Please, Lou don't shut me out". His voice trailed off behind her. The sound of slamming drawers echoed down the hall from her room. He didn't know how he would fix this or even if he could, but if she wouldn't let him explain.

Fifteen minutes later, her bedroom door flew open, and she came stomping into the kitchen with her suitcase in hand.

"I want you gone before I get back. How could you do this to me? I trusted you, and you've been lying to me all this time. I never want to see you again". The hate in her eyes cut him to the bone.

"Lou, please let me explain".

"Explain what?" She snorted at him. "That you're a liar? Did you mean those things you told me or were you just trying to get rid of the guilt for leaving me? Never mind. I don't need you. I was fine without you all these years". Her voice sounded cruel. "Just leave before I get back and never contact me again." Lou walked out the front door and slammed it behind her.

George collapsed in the chair, unable to move. He hoped after she calmed down, she would come back so he could explain. He walked to the front window just in time to see the tail end of a cab disappear around the corner. George turned away from the window. He went to his bedroom, pulled his suitcase from under the bed and emptied his dresser and closet. With each piece of clothing, a piece of his soul broke. By the time he finished packing, his chest hurt so bad he feared he was having a heart attack. After taking his things out to his car, he shuffled inside and called Mary.

Mary was baking dessert for the guests when the phone began to ring.

"Hello, Mary". George's voice quivered as he spoke.

"Are you okay, George?"

"I—I just wanted you to know I'll be coming back to my room, if that's okay".

"But what about Lou?"

"I don't want to talk about it. I just want to move back".

"Okay, George. Your room is waiting for you and so am I."

"Thanks, Mary—I—never mind. I'll be home soon".

Mary was standing at the front door as George drove up and parked his car. From the look on his face, she knew something was troubling him, but she couldn't imagine what brought him back here. They had talked just the other day how well things were going. She held the door open and gave him a gentle pat on his shoulder when he walked by her. Not saying a word, out of respect, she watched until he disappeared upstairs. Lord! What in the world is going on?

Mary closed the front door and returned to the kitchen to check on her pies. With George back, the house was full again, and she had to admit she liked it that way. She remembered the day George had shown up, looking for a room to rent. One of her long-time boarders had just moved out, leaving her with a vacancy. After a quick criminal background check, and the first month's rent, George had settled into the house. At first, he didn't seem interested in conversation, until one night a month later, they were having a cup of coffee, and George told Mary about his daughter.

They talked for hours while he unburdened himself about his life and failures, his cancer and chemo. Facing uncertainty, he wanted to make amends before it was too late. Over the next three months, Mary drove him to treatments, even staying with him after the chemo made him sick and a bond formed between them. She was becoming fond of him. He was the first man she had taken a personal interest in since Charles died ten years earlier. The day before he went to get Lou from the hospital, they had celebrated with lunch after his last treatment. Now, he looked like a whipped dog, and she was worried about him.

George put his suitcase on the chair next to the door, set the wooden box on the floor, and sat on the bed. Though it was mid-afternoon, he felt tired and old. His mind was weary, and his eyes where growing heavy. He drifted off to sleep, letting the rest of his worries wait until tomorrow.

Chapter Seventeen

Lou stopped by the office to ask Brad for Jason's home address and his sister's number for backup, just in case she ran into trouble finding him. Brad didn't seem too keen on her leaving, but he wouldn't have been able to stop her if he wanted to.

After searching through the file David had sent him on Jason, he gave Lou what she wanted, and told her to stay in touch.

Back in the cab, she gripped the handle of her suitcase so tight the skin around her fingers turned white from the pressure. She let go when the cab driver pulled up to the drop-off zone and helped her with her bag. She made it to the station just in time to catch the next bus west. During the bus ride to Portland, she kept running her last conversation with her father through her mind. Her anger returned with a vengeance. She'd trusted him. Now to find out he had been in town for four months before her accident. What had he been doing all that time? It didn't matter—she didn't care anymore.

Lou picked up her tickets at the service counter then made her way through security and to her gate, trying to stay calm. She had been running on adrenalin since her blowup with her dad; her anger had distracted her to even think about what she was doing. She had never flown in her life. She'd never even traveled out of her home state.

Nervous, she leaned back against the seat, grateful she was sitting next to the aisle and struggled with a silent prayer. Lou checked her seatbelt and pulled it tighter over her lap. Her throat felt parched from the stale air in the cabin. She glanced around, worried how flimsy the plastic interior looked, considering that they were about to hurtle through the sky at who-knows-what speed. And what was that loud hum? Panic began to set in, and a gurgling feeling rose through her belly.

"Excuse me", she said to the flight attendant passing her seat.

"Yes. Something I can do for you?"

Lou bit her lip, trying not to show the panic engulfing her.

"Um, this is my first time on a plane. What if I get sick?" Her voice quivered. "What do I do?"

The attendant knelt beside her and took her hand. "Now, honey, you'll be fine. See this little bag in the seat pocket in front of you?" She pointed to the white bag.

Lou bobbed her head, her eyes transfixed on the woman's face.

"If you think you are going to be sick, be sure to use this bag, fold it over, and ring for one of us to come and get it". Then she reached into her pocket and pulled out two stretchy wristbands, handing them to Lou.

"What are these?" Lou took the bands.

"They're for motion sickness. Put them on your wrists".

Lou removed her hand brace, stuffed it into her bag and slid the bands on adjusting them.

"That's it; with the button side down, against your wrist. It's like acupressure and should help calm your stomach. Now, if you need anything else, just push your call light, and I will come check on you. My name is Shirley".

Lou gave her a thankful look, leaned back in her seat, and closed her eyes. She was about to unbuckle her seatbelt and get up when she felt the plane surge backward.

The captain announced they were moving out to the runway and Lou started praying again.

The flight ended without Lou getting sick, though it had been close when the plane hit turbulence. After taking a deep breath, she tried to relax while the plane taxied to the gate.

Lou couldn't believe she'd done it. She'd gotten on a plane and flown across the United States to a place she always dreamed of—New York City. Now she faced a new set of problems. What if he had moved on with someone else?

Fear gripped her, but she had to find out. Once the plane stopped, Lou waited until the passengers had gotten off before retrieving her carry-on from the overhead bin and making her way down the aisle. She stopped to thank the flight attendant for her help and give back the bands.

"Oh, no, you keep them. I carry them for newbies like yourself. Besides you may need them if you fly again".

Lou hugged the woman. "Thanks again for your kindness".

Entering the terminal, its size, and the crowds amazed Lou. Looking around she wondered how she would find her way out, until she noticed the overhead signs saying baggage and ground transportation were straight ahead. Lou followed the throng of people to the nearest taxi stand and hailed a cab. After giving the driver the address, Lou settled into the back seat and less than fifteen minutes later, the cab slowed to a stop. Lou was astonished she had arrived so quickly.

"Here's your stop, Miss. That'll be twenty-five dollars", the cabbie turned in his seat to look at her.

Lou peered out the window at the tall apartment building. She was here.

"Thank you and keep the change". She handed the man thirty dollars and hoped she had tipped him enough as he drove off, leaving her standing in a strange city, on a strange street gazing up at the brownstone. Lou wondered which apartment Jason's was, when a sudden gust of wind gave her the shivers. She pulled her coat closer, picked up her suitcase, and marched up the steps.

Standing in front of the door, she searched the directory until she found Jason's number and pushed the buzzer. She felt like she was back on the plane. Her stomach was doing flip-flops, and her hands shook as she waited for an answer.

Nothing happened.

She pushed the buzzer again.

Silence.

A sinking feeling washed over her. He wasn't home. Lou felt stupid and angry at herself for assuming Jason would sit in his apartment pining for her. *Now, what am I going to do?* She fought the lump in her throat, then remembered she had Jason's sister's phone number and fished out her cell phone.

Joan walked into the kitchen and set her purse on the counter. It had been a long day at the rehab center working with Fred on his balance and strength training and it exhausted her. The heart attack had done more damage than first believed, but he was coming along so well the doctor was hopeful he might come home soon. The thought made her smile.

She knew if it hadn't been for Jason, she wouldn't have been able to get through those first weeks. After a lengthy conversation last night about Lou and he decided he couldn't wait any longer. He took the first flight to Portland this morning and Joan was waiting for him to call. She had just grabbed a bottle of water and was about to take a drink when her cell phone rang.

Joan didn't recognize the number and thought about ignoring it, but saw it was from Oregon.

"Hello?"

"Joan? Is this Joan?"

"Yes, and who are you?"

"I'm sorry to bother you".

"Listen, if you are trying to sell me something, I am not interested, so add me to your do not call list".

"No! I am not trying to sell anything. I'm looking for

Jason".

"Jason? Are you a friend of his?"

"My name is Lou, Lou McClelland".

"From The Dalles?"

"Yes. But how do you know that?"

"Jason told us about you. Where are you calling from?"

"Well, I am standing on his doorstep, but he isn't home". Her voice cracked.

Joan set her water bottle on the counter. "Where did you say you were?"

"I'm at his apartment building, and I don't know what to do".

Was Joan hearing this correctly? Lou was here in New York City?

"Calm down and stay where you are. I'll be over to get you".

"Thank you, Joan. May I call you Joan?" Lou's voice wavered.

Joan could sense the tremor in Lou's voice as it vibrated over the phone. "Yes, and don't worry. I'll be there in ten minutes".

Lou sat on the stoop to wait. The concrete was warm from the sun, but she felt chilled. Darkness was all around her except for the streetlights casting shadows up and down the streets. A pile of leaves stirred along the gutter from the light breeze, and a few three couples strolled by, on an evening walk. Exhaustion crept over her, and her ribs ached. She fell into such a daze; she didn't hear the car pull up on the street and park or a woman climb out.

"Lou?"

"Joan?" Lou stared at the petite woman with blonde hair, standing below on the sidewalk. "Thank you for coming. I didn't know what to do. Jason doesn't answer. This was stupid to just show up— but I had to come and—"

Joan walked up the steps and put her hand up. "Whoa, slow down and tell me what's going on here".

153

"I'm sorry". Lou reached in her coat pocket for a tissue.

"Let's get off this stoop. Jason isn't here".

"Where is he?" Lou looked around, confused.

"Come with me. We can talk about it on the way to my home".

Lou watched out the car window, taking in all the sights as they drove along the streets. She marveled at the high-rise buildings lit up like stars in the sky.

Nothing compared to the stars back home. You only needed to get a few miles from the city to see more stars than you could imagine.

"Lou, would you mind if we stop and get a bite to eat? My stomach is rumbling". Joan asked.

"Sorry. What did you say?"

"I don't know about you, but I'm hungry. Do you like Chinese?"

"Sure", Lou pressed against the seat.

"There's a nice restaurant near to my house. Fred and I go at least twice a month", she said with a hitch in her voice. "I'm sorry. It's been a long day". Joan pulled into the lot and parked.

The scent of fried rice and shrimp hit Lou's nose when they walked in, and her mouth watered.

"Something smells wonderful. I didn't realize how hungry I was until we walked through the door".

Joan half smiled as they sat in a booth next to the window.

"This is my favorite booth. You can sit here and watch the people walking past. Fred and I love to make up stories about what they do for a living, or about their families. It's great fun", she grabbed for a napkin. "Oh, look at me getting all weepy".

"I'm sorry. How is your husband doing? Jason's note said he had a heart attack".

Joan set the napkin down.

"Thank you for asking. He's getting better each day and the doctor says he might come home soon", she stopped in mid-

154

sentence and reached for the menu, changing the conversation. "Would you like to share something? I guess I'm not that hungry".

The two women sat in silence, sipping hot tea while they waited for their food to arrive.

Lou was amazed by the size of the portions and was grateful Joan suggested they share. After a few mouthfuls, they both started to relax and enjoy their meal.

"You said Fred will come home soon?" She took another bite of the sweet and sour chicken with her fork. She had never mastered chopsticks and envied the way Joan used hers. Melancholy washed over her, and she frowned. She realized traveling was harder than she imagined.

"The answer to your question about Fred is yes, he will be home soon. I'm sorry if I got emotional about it". Joan poured more tea.

"No need to apologize. I shouldn't intrude. It's just the reporter side of me, I can't help myself".

Joan nodded. "I don't mean to pry either. But why did you come to talk to Jason?"

Lou took a deep breath, trying to find the words to explain why she had come. Why couldn't Jason have been home?

"I don't know how much you know about me", she began. "Jason and I met working on a story. Things were clicking between us, but then I had a car accident, and he left. I haven't had any communication from him since then. Then I discovered he had left me a note, though I didn't get it until yesterday. After I read it, I realized he's been waiting for me to call. I tried but couldn't get hold of him, so I booked a flight, and here I am."

Lou sat back, exhausted. She hadn't meant to lay it all out, but she couldn't hold it in anymore, and the look on Joan's face worried her.

"Okay, just give it to me straight. He has someone else in his life, and I'm a fool to think he has been waiting for me".

Joan reached over and touched her hand. "That's not it at all. Jason's been waiting for you to call or write. It's been driving him crazy. So much, he couldn't take it anymore. He got on the first plane this morning to go find you".

"He what? But—but—I'm here".

Joan reached for Lou's hand. "How about we call him?" She dialed Jason's new number, but his voice mail picked up instead.

"He didn't answer. Let's go to my house after we finish eating and try to figure out what to do next. Does that sound good to you?"

Lou could only nod.

Chapter Eighteen

Jason landed in Portland on schedule and headed for the rental-car section. This time he made sure he had a car he would be comfortable in before he headed toward I-84 eastbound. More than an hour later he pulled off the freeway toward The Dalles downtown area and The Centennial building. He prayed Lou would be in her office. When he parked his rental, he felt glued to the seat, while his mind screamed at him to get out of the car and go find the woman he loved.

Three minutes later, he stood in front of the receptionist. Jason remembered how rude he had been to her the first time he came to town and regretted his behavior.

"Hi Karol".

Engrossed in her magazine, Karol looked up to the sound of her name. "Oh, it's you. What do you want?"

Jason felt a chill fill the room. "Is Lou back to work?"

"No." Her tone was dismissive.

"Is Brad in his office? I need to talk to him".

"Is he expecting you?"

"No, but I'm sure he would like to see me, please".

Karol looked down at her notepad, then punched two numbers on her phone console.

"Hey, Brad, that Jason Peterson guy is here to see you. Do you want me to send him back?"

"We've talked about this before, Karol. It's Mr. Perkins when you address me".

Karol sat taller in her seat. "Sorry, Bra—I mean Mr. Perkins, he's on his way". She hung up and waved Jason away, then flipped the page on her magazine.

Jason moved down the hall, slowing his pace. Karol said Lou wasn't here, but his first instinct was to go straight to her office. He remembered the first day he walked in, all sure of himself, and found a curly-haired woman with the most delicate cornflower-blue eyes staring at him. Now, he could barely keep himself together as he knocked on her door. He waited, then knocked again. Still no answer.

Karol was telling the truth. Lou wasn't here.

Perspiration formed on his brow as he retreated up the hall and stopped in front of Brad's office. He rapped on the door—he had to find Lou.

"Come in", Brad called out.

Jason opened the door and walked into the office. "Thanks for seeing me, Brad". He offered his hand. Brad shook it, then motioned him to sit.

"Hello, Jason. Nice to see you back. I thought you jumped ship at first, then I received a call from David, who filled me in. It would have been nice to get a phone call from you about your sudden departure and what you were doing with the story". He leaned back in his chair.

Jason tensed. "I'm sorry about that. In my hurry to get home, somewhere between here and New York City I lost my phone and didn't even know for days. When I realized it, I couldn't get my old number back, and I lost all my contacts". Jason saw the look of disbelief on Brad's face. "Swear it's the truth and I know that's no excuse. Ever since Lou's accident, then the problems with my brother-in-law, I'm surprised my head is still on straight".

"How is your brother-in-law doing?"

"Fred's doing well. The doctor says the triple bypass is working, and he's getting his strength back. He should go home soon". Jason tried to let his body relax. He was so tense, his neck muscles felt like vise squeezing his shoulders. "Thanks for asking. But that's not why I am here".

"Are you back to finish the story? You know you put this paper in an awkward position, with Lou out for recovery", Brad said, playing with his pen.

"Sorry, but I had to go, my sister needed me. And Lou was still in the hospital, so I figured I had enough time".

Brad leaned back in his chair again. "But you didn't come back or contact us. Did you know she had planned to return to work today?"

"No, I didn't. I haven't spoken to her since I left. I have to talk to her and explain what happened. How's she doing?"

"From what she told me, the broken ribs gave her the most trouble, though the cast almost drove her nuts. Thank God, her father showed up when he did, or she would have had to go to a rehab center to recover".

Jason's ears perked up at the mention of Lou's father. "I didn't know he was in her life. She never mentioned him. How did that go?"

"He's been taking care of her at her house since the accident. That's all I know. The rest you should ask her".

"The reason I wanted to see you was to get Lou's address. Like I said I have to talk to her".

"That will be difficult now". Brad sat forward in his chair.

"Why, what happened? Did she have a relapse or something?" Jason was getting worried.

"No, that is why I'm surprised to see you. She came in this morning asking for your home address and said there was this confusion about a note. Told her to just call you. She said she had

159

been trying but got no answer. Then she told me she was flying to New York City".

"She did what?" Jason sat forward, searching Brad's face to see if he was joking. "Are you sure?"

"Yes, I am. Like I said, she is determined to talk to you".

Jason shook his head, trying to understand what Brad was telling him. Brad mentioned a note. It must be the one he'd given the nurse for her the night he left. And the number. No wonder she couldn't reach him. What an idiot he was. He should have called her with his new number, instead of thinking she didn't want to talk to him.

Brad sat back and watched Jason adjust to the news. "Anything else I can help you with?"

Jason still couldn't believe Lou had flown to New York. "Would you mind giving me her address?"

"Like I just told you, she's gone".

"I know. I was thinking I could talk to her father before I head back".

Brad found her address and wrote it on a post-a-note.

"Here you go", He handed the paper to Jason. "Good luck. Let me know what happens. I'm still waiting for the story from the two of you".

Jason took the paper and scanned the address. "Thanks, Brad. Appreciate your help and I'll keep you in the loop to what's going on as soon as I find Lou". Jason rose and offered his hand.

Brad shook it, then showed him out the door.

Jason read the address again, put it in his pocket, and went out to his car. What if she's lost in the city? The thought worried him. He needed to call his sister and was reaching for his phone when it buzzed. A wave of dread flooded over him. The call was from Joan. Something must have happened to Fred.

Joan decided tried Jason's number one more time before leaving the restaurant and breathed a sigh of relief when her brother answered the phone.

"Hi, Joan. Did something happen to Fred?"

"Fred is fine. That's not why I called".

"It worried me when I saw your number".

"Jason, I have something to tell you".

"Joan, I know this sounds crazy, but Lou is on her way there. I think she's going to my apartment". Jason got out of the car.

"I know, Jason".

"How do you know that?"

"Lou called me. She was sitting on the front steps of your building".

Silence flooded the line. "Jason? Jason are you still there?" Joan looked at her phone then put it back to her ear. "Are you there?"

"Look, Joan, I just found out she hopped a plane this afternoon. I didn't know she was coming". Jason paced back and forth in the parking lot.

"Jason, listen to me. She's with me now. We just finished eating dinner, then I'm taking her home. How soon can you get back here?"

"Give me a few minutes to call the airlines and see if I can get a flight back tonight".

Joan let out a deep sigh. "Okay, but hurry and call me back".

Joan and Lou walked to her car and sat waiting for his call. They both jumped when the phone buzzed.

"Hey, Sis, it's me. I checked all the airlines. There's a computer glitch, and I can't get a flight until Friday."

"Jason, that's two days away. What am I supposed to do?"

"Don't let her go anywhere!" Desperation filled his voice.

"Jason—I need to go—the poor girl is sitting here exhausted, and I am too. I'll call you later."

"Thanks, Joanie. Love you and Lou." His voice trailing off to a whisper.

"What did he say?" Lou looked like she wanted to grab the phone and talk to him.

Joan didn't repeat the last part of the conversation. She would leave that up to Jason. "He said he can't get back here for two days. I'm to make sure you were safe until then."

"Oh." Was the only word Lou managed to reply.

On the ride to Joan's house, both women sat without talking. Lou looked in shock and just stared out the window. Joan wasn't sure what to do. She pulled into her driveway, hit the garage-door button. Once inside, she closed the door behind them. Lou had dozed off and Joan hated to wake her. She pushed Lou's shoulder.

"Lou. Lou, wake up, we're here."

Lou opened her eyes and looked around. "What? Where are we?"

"We're at my house." Joan unbuckled her seatbelt. "Let's go in the house and talk."

Lou sprang awake, grabbed her suitcase, and followed Joan into the kitchen. She plopped down in the nearest chair, drained from the whole experience.

Joan grabbed two cups from the cupboard and set them on the table. When the coffee finished brewing, she poured them each a cup. "Do you use cream or sugar?"

Lou shook her head. "No, black is fine." She took a sip, and the sweet vanilla flavor reminded her of the first pot of coffee George had made for them. Her eyes teared.

Joan sat down across from her. "Is something wrong?"

"No, the coffee is delicious. It just reminded me of someone at home."

162

Joan got up and retrieved a plate of cookies from the counter and placed them on the table.

"We may as well enjoy a dessert while we talk, don't you think?"

Lou cracked a feeble smile and reached for a cookie. Chocolate chip, her favorite. They reminded her of the ones she ate during Jenny's interview.

"Thanks, Joan. You've been so kind, and you don't even know me."

Joan took a sip of her coffee then set her cup on the table.

"I know a little about you. Jason and I had a long talk before he left. He told me about the story you two were working on, and about your accident. He said he stayed by your side until you woke up from the coma."

Lou looked down at the table and played with her cookie.

"But then he left. I didn't know why. He just disappeared."

It was taking all the strength she could muster to hold it together.

Joan reached out to Lou and patted her hand.

"Jason told me he left a note with the nurse for you to call him. So, when you didn't call, he figured you weren't interested. It didn't dawn on him until today that you wouldn't have been able to reach him. He lost his cell phone and had to get a new number."

"I never got the note. Well, I did, but not until this morning, while I was getting my cast removed. The nurse found it in her pocket. You can imagine how shocked I was. When I tried calling, I only got the message that the number was no longer in service. Then I had a fight with George—my dad. Everything is so messed up now." Lou groaned.

"What happened with your father, if you don't mind my asking?"

Lou tried to compose herself before she launched into another story. When she finished, Joan just shook her head.

"Did you ask him why he waited to come to you?"

Lou looked away. "Well, no, I guess I didn't give him a chance to explain. I said terrible things and told him I never wanted to see him again and stormed out of the house and here I am."

"Do you believe in God, Lou? I think if you give your father a chance to explain with an open mind, God will guide you. From what you told me; it sounds like you were reconnecting with your father until this misunderstanding happened."

Lou wasn't sure how to respond. Did she believe in God? She thought she did as a young girl and remembered the little cross her father gave her the Christmas before he left. But then she thought God was punishing her, so she had yanked the chain from her neck and thrown it from the window of her room. She figured she must have done something wrong to make her mother hate her and her father leave.

Now, she realized she had let her anger get the better of her before knowing all the facts, just like she had done with Jason. She was a reporter, a person who searched for all the facts. Instead she had drawn her own conclusions and brought these problems on herself by being so hardheaded.

"You're right, I walked away. I guess I wanted to hurt him for leaving me." Lou shook her head, ashamed at herself for acting so childish.

"As for the question about believing in God, I'm not sure. I believe in angels. Does that mean the same thing?"

Joan smiled. "Angels, you say. Yes, I believe they are messengers from God. Have you met one?"

Lou told Joan about the others and Joan sat mesmerized while she told her about finding the journal, the accident, and how the angel had saved her.

"What did Jason think of all this?"

Lou sighed. "You know Jason. He can be intense. I think he felt the story was beneath him, and we didn't get along at first."

Lou remembered her own behavior.

"I guess I wasn't nice either. I'd been planning the story before he came along and hoped to use it as my big chance for a promotion. So, I wasn't too keen on sharing with anyone. I was hard on him in the beginning."

Joan laughed. "I'm sorry. I'm not laughing at you. Though I can see the frustration on my brother's face." She chuckled again.

Lou relaxed in her chair. She liked Joan.

"We were getting into a rhythm, even if only for a few days. From reading the files and interviewing the survivors, we both could see a pattern."

Joan got up from the table to retrieve the coffeepot to freshen their cups. "What kind of pattern?"

Lou took a sip before starting again. "Well, at each accident a young woman appeared and helped the victims before anyone else arrived. They always described her the same way. Young, about eighteen or twenty, with a wing-shaped birthmark that covered the side of her face. She wore the same long sleeve white blouse and a calf-length black skirt. It was hard to believe that she was at all the accidents since the first one was in 1948, and then the last one was 2017. But I saw her too."

"Did Jason believe you?"

Lou shook her head. "I don't think so, but when he started to read the journal to me, I think he changed his mind. We figured from the entries that this must be the same person, but before we could finish reading it—he left, taking the journal with him."

Chapter Nineteen

Jason drove around town until he found Lou's house. It was an older looking home in a quiet neighborhood, probably built in the fifties. A big front porch—one where people could sit in two rocking chairs and watch the world go by stretched across the front. The yard was nice, not too big to take care of, but where children could play without the worry of cars rushing past. Shade trees, flowers, the whole package — things he and Annie had wanted.

Grief surfaced for a moment, then a new feeling of hope began to fill the void. He walked to the front door and rang the doorbell.

No one answered, he rang again.

He had hoped Lou's father might be home, so he could talk to him, but the house looked empty and there wasn't a car in the driveway.

"Can I help you?"

Jason turned. "Oh, hello, I'm looking for a George McClelland. Do you know if he's home?" Jason looked past the woman, hoping George was behind her.

"Who are you?" she asked.

"Jason Peterson. I'm a reporter for the New York Post." He held out his hand. When she didn't respond, he dropped it to his side.

Mary recognized the name. So, this was Jason. George had told her about him and about the note.

"Jason Peterson, you say?" She cocked her head to the side.

"Yes. And your name is?"

Mary realized she was being rude by the sound of her voice.

George and Lou were adults, and this wasn't her business. Besides, she had bigger problems. She worried about George. As soon as he'd come back to the boarding house, he didn't look well and wouldn't tell her what happened. When she took him something to eat for dinner and found him running a fever and delirious and had called 911 and George was rushed to the hospital. In his hurry to leave Lou's place, he had forgotten his briefcase with his insurance papers in it. Since Lou had told him not to come back, he had asked Mary to get it for him, using the spare key he had kept just in case.

"I'm sorry. Mary Carpenter. I am a friend of George's—Lou's father." She held out her hand.

"He isn't here."

This young man was wasting her time. She needed to get what she came for then figure out how to get hold of Lou.

Jason shook her hand. "Do you know how I can get in touch with him?"

Mary gave a deep sigh. "Yes, I do, but you won't be able to talk to him right now."

Jason looked confused. "Is something wrong?"

"Would you mind waiting out here? I have to get something from inside the house."

Jason stepped back. "Sure, no problem."

Mary unlocked the front door, disappeared inside, closing it behind her. When she returned, she found him leaning against the post.

"You're still here." She locked the door behind her.
"You asked me to wait."

"Oh, yes, George, Mr. McClelland is in the hospital with a bad infection. I shouldn't be telling you this, but since George has mentioned you, I guess it would be okay. I need to talk to Lou. Do you know how to get hold of her? George never gave me her cell number."

"Does Lou know he's sick?"

Mary set the briefcase on the porch. "No, this just happened. He moved back to my place, where he used to rent a room."

"What happened? If you don't mind my asking."

"George had cancer but finished chemo right before Lou's accident. He was about to tell her, then she needed him. So, he never got around to it. He said he hadn't been feeling well and I asked why he didn't talk to Lou, but he just shrugged and wouldn't answer. He has an infection from where the chemo line was inserted in his chest and he's running a high fever. Lou doesn't know about the cancer."

Jason was shocked. "I'm so sorry. But she needs to know. Is he going to die?"

"I hope not." Mary wanted him to live, wanted them to have a future. "Do you know how I can get in touch with Lou?"

"Yes—she went to New York City looking for me."

Jason checked his watch and realized an hour had passed since he talked to Joan. With nothing else he could do here, he followed Mary to the hospital, then to George's room.

Mary asked him to wait in the hall while she talked to George. When she returned, she told Jason he could speak to George for a few minutes, so he entered the room.

George looked like he was sleeping, and Jason wondered if he should come back later, but he couldn't waste any more time. He stepped closer to the bed and cleared his throat hoping to draw the man's attention.

George opened his eyes.

"You must be Jason." His voice sounded strained. "Lou told me about you—I guess we both messed up bad.:

Jason winced at his words, aware of what he had done, though not sure what George meant.

168

"Yes, sir. I'm Jason." He reached out his hand.

George shook it then laid his hand on the bed. "Nice to meet you, Jason. Care to sit down?"

He motioned toward the chair.

"Pull it over here next to the bed, if you don't mind, so I don't have to talk so loud."

Jason brought the chair next to George's bed and sat.

"Thank you for seeing me, sir."

"Call me George. Sir sounds so formal."

"Thank you, George. This might not be an appropriate time, but I had to talk to you before I head back to New York City and Lou."

George tried to sit up in his bed.

"You're telling me Lou did it?" He crumpled back against the pillow. "That girl must be in love, to get on a plane. Yep, she's fallen hard."

Jason felt like he was floating on thin air. "Something about flying Lou doesn't like?"

George gave a chuckle. "Well, for one, she's never been on a plane, and two, she gets motion sickness from the slightest bumps. She's been that way since she was a child, as I remember. Hopefully, she's outgrown it, or there better be airsick bags on that plane."

Jason didn't know Lou was afraid of flying. He didn't know much about her, but he wanted to learn. Flying had been so natural for him. He couldn't imagine what she went through on the plane.

"I'm sorry about all this, George. It's just one big mess. As soon as I see her and explain, I hope she will give me another chance."

Jason watched the expression on George's face turn to a look of gloom. "Did I say something wrong?"

George shook his head.

"No, it's something I did. I just hope she lets me explain why I did what I did, and I will get one more chance too. Though I probably don't deserve it."

"What happened, if you don't mind me asking?"

"We'd been getting along well since the accident. It was a blessing you had to leave. I'm not saying this to hurt you, but if you'd been here, I don't think she would have given me the time of day but it pushed her into a corner, if she wanted to come home."

Jason nodded in agreement, knowing how stubborn she could be.

"Well, all was going great until this morning. She got her cast off, and the nurse found the note you left for her. Lou realized how wrong she had been about you. We called the airport and got her on the next plane out. Then I remembered I was having dinner with a friend of mine, Mary. You met her."

"I did. I think she's sweet on you." Jason gave him a wink, and George smiled.

"What made Lou so mad?"

"Lou overheard me talking to Mary and asked how I knew her. I wasn't even thinking and blurted out that I'd been staying at Mary's Boarding House the last four months. Lou thought I had returned just before the accident. You can imagine how that upset her."

Jason nodded. "Yes, I can only imagine what she would think."

"When I tried to explain, she wouldn't let me. She blew up, called me a liar, and said she never should have let me back into her life. She told me to get out and never see her again."

Jason felt sorry for George, but if he had been in town for four months, why hadn't he contacted her, instead of waiting until she left the hospital? Then he understood. The cancer.

"I'm sorry, George, but I can see why she might be mad. Your being here all that time and then showing yourself when she was vulnerable would cause her to question your motives. Why did you stay away?"

George turned his head toward the wall for a moment and sighed. "I found out Vivian, Lou's mother, had died and was coming back to town, but I got sick and ended up in the hospital in Boise, Idaho, where I'd been living the last couple years. They diagnosed me with prostate cancer, I had surgery and radiation treatments. The doctors weren't sure if I would make, but they got it under control."

He caught his breath. "What good would it have been to show up in her life if I would only die? The doctors released me on the condition I continued chemo here in The Dalles. Wouldn't have continued with treatments if Mary hadn't encouraged me to fight, hoping for a chance to make things right with Lou."

Jason understood his pain, but Lou should have had that choice. "She doesn't know about the cancer?"

"I never got the chance. I've been doing well. I didn't want her worked up over nothing. Now, I see I was a fool. I should have told her." His voice trailed off to a whisper.

George looked tired.

Jason got up from his chair. "I think I'll go now and let you rest, and I know Mary is eager to visit you."

"Good luck, Son."

"If you don't mind, I'll check on you before I leave town."

George gave him a nod.

Jason walked out the door and Mary hurried past him to be with George.

Exhausted, Jason leaned his head against the wall, still waiting for Joan's call. He tried the airport again to see if he could get an earlier flight, but no luck.

Jason had just hung up when his phone buzzed.

"Hey, Joan, what's going on?" He was trying to sound in control. "Is she with you? Is she okay?"

"Yes, Jason, she's here, and we're doing fine. I have you on speakerphone so we both can hear you. She's tired from the trip and confused, but we're working on that. How about you?"

"I got here fine. Lou? Lou? Can you hear me?"

"Yes, Jason, I'm here. Oh, Jason. I'm so sorry."

"No, Lou, it's my fault. I shouldn't have left you." His voice cracked. "Please forgive me."

The sound of Lou crying cut him deep.

"Jason, she's upset right now so I've taken the phone off speaker. When will you be back?"

Jason was pacing the hall. "As soon as possible. Can Lou stay with you until I get back?"

"Wouldn't want it otherwise. Besides, she'll be good company for me. I like her, Jason."

"Thank you, Joanie. Love you."

"Love you too, Jason."

"Oh, Joan, there's one more thing I need to tell you."

"What's that?"

Jason explained about George and asked if she would break the news to Lou. Joan said she would try her best.

Lou watched Joan's face as she talked to Jason. She'd been waiting so long for the sound of his voice, that all her bottled-up emotions buzzed though her head, making her dizzy. She wondered what they were talking about, as curiosity was getting the better of her.

"I'm sorry, Joan, but what does Jason want you to tell me?"

Joan didn't appear to know where to begin.

"He still can't get a flight until Friday. You will stay here with me until then if that's okay with you. The other thing is about your father."

Lou stiffened in her chair. "What about him?"

"He's in the hospital. From what Jason said, he got an infection

172

from his injection site?"

"What injection site?" Her voice rose higher in pitch. "I don't understand."

"There's no easy way to say this. Your father has prostate cancer. From what Jason said, he had been going through chemo treatments. As I tried to follow the conversation, Jason says that is why your dad didn't contact you when he first came to town."

"That can't be true—he looked just fine." Lou wrestled with the word—cancer. Could this be true?

"Are you sure, Joan? Did Jason check to make sure George wasn't lying?" She regretted how that sounded. "I'm sorry, I shouldn't have said that."

"That's okay, I know you're hurting. With all that's happened in the last few months and today, I can imagine you would question this. To answer your question, yes, Jason checked it out. He talked to your father's friend Mary. She has been helping him through his chemo treatments. He got an infection from the chemo port and was running a fever, so they put him in the hospital to watch him. Jason said he should be fine in a few days and ready to go home."

"What about the cancer? Is he going to die?" Lou forced the lump back down her throat.

"I don't think so. Jason said George had received a clean bill of health before this happened."

Lou walked over to the sink. Why hadn't he told her he had cancer? Why hide it?

She turned to face Joan. "Why didn't he tell me?"

Joan got up, walked over to Lou, put her arms around her, and held her tight. "He was trying to spare you the pain of watching him die. Once he found out he would live, he was making plans to call you. Then the accident happened."

"He should have told me. Trusted me to understand."

"Your father believed he was doing the right thing, Lou. He felt

173

you had too much to manage, to add anymore. I would have done the same thing in his shoes."

Lou looked at her. "You would have?"

"Yes, I would."

"Oh, Joan, what am I supposed to do now? I said I hated him and never wanted to see him again. I even kicked him out of the house. And now I am here, and he needs me." Lou covered her face with her hands.

Joan guided her back to her chair. "All we can do is pray." She held out her hands.

Lou nodded, bowed her head, and joined hands with Joan and hoped she could learn to trust that God knew the way for her.

Joan said amen and gave Lou's hand a gentle squeeze

"How about we get you set up in the guest room? I'm sure you would like to freshen up." Joan stood and stretched her back. "Besides, I'm tired from so sitting."

"Thanks, Joan. Could you show me where the bathroom is? Way too much coffee." Lou chuckled, trying to lighten the mood.

Joan led her down the hall to the guest bathroom.

"You can use this while you are here. Just take your time. I want to call Fred and see how he's doing. I always call before he turns in for the night."

Lou clicked the light on and shut the door. She started to laugh when she saw herself. Her hair had frizzed, and it made her look like a wild woman. Searching her pockets, Lou found a rubber band and corralled her hair in a ponytail.

Even after she washed her face, Lou still felt ragged as she ambled back to the kitchen. Joan was just finishing her call and Lou realized she was crying.

"Is everything all right?" Lou asked, trying not to pry.

Joan wiped her eyes with her napkin.

"Oh, just a small setback. Fred was trying to walk by himself tonight and he fell. He's banged up, but he's okay."

"Do you want to go see him? Please don't think you need to stay here with me."

Joan shook her head. "They gave him a sleeping pill and put him to bed, so no reason to go back tonight, but thank you for asking. It's getting late and I don't know about you but I'm tired."

Joan stifled a yawn. "I think it's time get some sleep. Jason said he would stay at the hospital with your father through the night and will let us know how he's doing in the morning."

"You're right, Joan. Thank you again for all you are doing for me. Did you think your day would turn out like this?"

"Not in a million years." Joan rinsed the cups and put them in the sink. "Today has been full of surprises."

Lou picked up her suitcase and followed Joan down the hall. After she said good night, Lou closed the door and sat on the edge of the bed.

Her mind was on overload, and she was getting a headache, her wrist ached, and so did her ribs, but exhaustion overrode the pain. When she lay back on the bed, she was asleep in seconds.

Jason took turns with Mary sitting beside George's bed. Sometimes George wanted to talk, and other times Jason just sat next to him keeping him company.

During their conversations, he learned about Lou's childhood and began to better grasp her pain and the walls she had put around herself. Jason felt sorry for Lou's mother. Part of him could relate to that feeling. He understood George's need to escape the misery, even though he loved Lou and wanted to protect her.

Jason was seeing there was a grander plan for his life, one bigger than he ever imagined. He hoped Lou would be a large part of it and realized if he hadn't come to do the story, he wouldn't have met her.

And if not for her accident, he would have kept his feelings to himself, wasting the chance to love again. So much had been out of his control. Looking back, he was grateful someone was watching over him.

Jason checked with the airport one last time and they informed him of a red-eye flight that would put him in New York City around 6:00 A.M. Looking at his watch, he figured he could make it to Portland in time to catch the flight.

He worried about leaving but George's fever had broken, and the doctor was sure the infection was under control though they would keep him one more night. Before he left, Jason assured George he would bring Lou home soon and the two men shook hands. Jason left with a lighter step.

Chapter Twenty

The morning light peeked through the curtains and fell across Lou's face. Opening her eyes, she was unsure of her surroundings until she remembered what she had done yesterday and smiled.

She was still reeling from the fact she'd gotten on an airplane.

Lou turned her head towards the clock on the nightstand and shocked to see it was eleven in the morning. She never slept this late.

The sweet scent of cinnamon floating in the air greeted her when she opened the door. Her stomach was hollering for something to eat, and the aroma made her mouth water as she followed it to the kitchen.

Joan was lifting the rolls out of the oven when she saw Lou.

"Good morning, Lou. Did you get some sleep?" She was sliding the pan on top of the stove. "I made us fresh cinnamon rolls; I hope you like them."

Lou moved over to the stove and inhaled the sweet smell.

"Oh my, those smell so delicious. Wish I knew how to make those."

"These are easy. I could teach you if you would like me to sometime."

"Would you? That would be so nice." Lou turned to get the coffee cups and fill them. "Do you bake often?

Lou set the cups on the table.

Joan scooped out the gooey pastry and slid it on a plate.

"Not as much as I would like. You don't bake?"

"No, I never learned how."

177

Her mother never taught her to cook or to bake.

She never taught her anything except how to stay out of her way. Lou could cook the basics. If it came in a box or can. Lou decided this wasn't the time for sorrow.

Today was a new day. She joined Joan at the table

"Any word from Jason?" Lou licked the sweet cinnamon off her fork.

Joan shook her head. "It's early."

"How is Fred this morning after his fall?"

"I called after I got up and Fred's back in the therapy room working as hard as he can. He said he's tired of the place and wants to come home. The doctor has agreed, and Fred can continue his exercises here."

"That's wonderful, Joan. I'm happy for you." Lou finished her cinnamon roll.

Jason's plane ride had been a nightmare. A thunderstorm diverted the plane, and he was four hours late when he landed. Rushing to catch a cab, he didn't bother to call Joan to let her know he was coming—he wanted to surprise the two of them.

On the ride home, he hadn't felt this excited since the day he and Annie rushed to the hospital for Sophia's birth. The memory was bittersweet, but it didn't hurt so much anymore. Within minutes, the cab pulled up outside his sister's house.

As he stood on the front step, he tried to slow his breathing before he rang the bell.

"Would you mind getting that for me, Lou? I have one more batch in the oven."

"Sure, I will." Lou licked her fingers and headed for the front door.

When the door opened Lou was standing in front of him.

Jason pulled her to his chest and felt Lou melt into his arms.

Joan came from the kitchen and saw them hugging. "Jason, you're home!" She hurried toward him.

Jason let go of Lou, reached out, and hugged his sister.

"Hello, Sis. Did I surprise you?"

Joan grabbed his arm and pulled him inside the hallway.

"Let's not stand here with the door wide open." She closed door and ushered them toward the kitchen.

Jason dropped his bag by the door and grabbed Lou's hand in his. "Hey, Joanie, don't be mad at me."

Glancing over his shoulder he gave her his best little boy look.

Joan burst out laughing. "Jason Peterson. Don't you try that look on me. It won't work this time."

"But it used to", he said with a pout on his face.

Joan shook her head and started laughing again.

Lou savored the moment, enjoying the interaction. She wondered if her little brother had lived; would they have acted like that? Now in the kitchen, she took a seat before her legs gave out from the shock of seeing him.

They sat in silence, starring at each other.

Then the questions started.

Joan was first to regain her composure. "Jason, why didn't you call and let us know you were coming?"

"I didn't know myself until late last night."

Lou chewed on her lip. "How is my—I mean, George?"

Jason took her hand in his. "He was doing better before I left. His fever broke, and the doctor is sure everything is under control."

Lou looked away feeling ashamed.

She should have been there for him. The way he had been for her. "Did you talk to him?"

Jason nodded, releasing her hand. "Yes, we had a few lengthy conversations about you."

179

Lou grimaced; afraid Jason knew how terrible she had been toward her father.

Jason slipped her a piece of paper. It had George's number written on it for when she was ready to call him.

"Don't worry, Lou, your dad doesn't blame you for being mad, but he's sorry and hopes you will forgive him."

Jason put his arm around her. "Hope you can forgive me too."

Lou hung her head. "No. You and my father need to forgive me. I don't deserve either of you."

Jason lifted her chin. "Lou, you did nothing wrong. I was a fool for not checking to see if you got the note, instead of assuming. And when you didn't call, I should have realized you couldn't—since I lost my phone. I can just imagine what you must have been thinking after you woke up and I wasn't there. I forgot about the journal, Lou—honest, I did."

"I believe you, Jason." She didn't want to be angry anymore. "What about George and all the terrible things I said to him? And God? Will He forgive me?"

The notion of her father not being in her life again, brought back loneliness of her childhood.

Joan touched her arm.

"God forgives all of us, Lou. All we must do is ask. I believe He brought your father back to you at a time you needed him the most. God will not leave you, as you build this new relationship."

⌒

Jason waited until Lou had left the room to change. "What do you think?"

Jason wondered if God had been with him on this journey. He too had been blaming God for his loss and the heartache. Now he wanted to thank Him for bringing Lou into his life and giving him another chance at love.

Joan smiled. "About what?"

"About Lou? Do you like her?"

"Yes, Jason, I like her". Joan lowered her head.

"What's the matter?"

"I need to call and check on Fred since I didn't go in this morning. I forgot to tell you; he fell".

"What? Did he hurt himself?"

"Not much. He has a few new bumps and bruises. The most important thing, he says he's ready to come home".

"Are you ready, Joan?"

"I think so. I'm worried he might fall again. What if he has another heart attack?" her voice quivered. "Oh, Jason, I am so afraid of losing him".

"Joan, what is it you kept telling me after Annie and Sophia died?"

She looked at him and shook her head. "I don't know. My mind is in such a jumble".

"You kept telling me to trust in God, but I didn't want to believe you. Why would He take Annie and Sophia from me?"

Jason moved his chair closer to her. "Fred could have died that night, but he didn't. He's still here, and ready to come home to his wife. That alone is a miracle, Joan".

"You're right, and I am grateful". Jason held his sister tight

"Lou came into my life at the time I needed hope, and to show me I could love again. And George, he came back hoping for a second chance when Lou was at her lowest".

Jason got up and walked over to the window.

"I don't know why, but I believe everything happens for a reason. Sure, I didn't understand it or want to believe, but deep down I think God has been guiding us".

Joan got up and put her arms around him. "How did you become so wise, little brother?"

"Years of practice". He laughed.

181

"How about we all go to get Fred and bring him home today?"

Lou had been standing in the hall out of sight, listening.

"Hi, I didn't mean to interrupt", she said, trying not to startle them as she entered the room.

Jason turned to look at her. "Not at all. We were just saying it's time to go get Fred, and we want you to come along with us".

"Oh, I don't want to intrude. This is for the family. I can wait here.

"Nonsense, you're like family, and family sticks together", Joan said.

With the mention of family, Lou remembered George.

"Do you mind if I call the hospital first and check on my father before we go? I need to talk to him".

"Sure", they answered at the same time. "How about we give you some privacy?" Joan tugged at Jason's arm.

"Right—right, just take your time. We'll be in the living room until you're ready".

As Jason began to walk past her, he stopped to give her a kiss on the cheek.

Lou savored the moment, then pulled out her cell phone and called the number Jason gave her earlier.

George sat on the edge of the hospital bed, grouchy and wanting to leave. He only had to spend one night and couldn't wait to sleep in a real bed again. One without a nurse waking him up each hour to poke and prod at him.

The doctor said the infection was under control and he would live. He had been thinking about his life and wished he could do it over. He never would have left her and remembered the moment she was born. She had stolen his heart, and she still did

He only hoped, with time, she would forgive him.

At least, he had Mary in his life. She was a good woman, and he cared for her.

The phone beside his bed rang, interrupting his reverie.

"Dad? It's me, Louie".

George's heart almost stopped at the sound of her voice.

"Louie, oh, honey, I'm so sorry".

"It's okay. I'm the one who must apologize to you. I should have given you a chance to explain. I thought you were shutting me out again, so I shut you out first. Can you forgive me? Are you okay? What did the doctor say?"

"Slow down Lou".

"I just want us to be together Dad. Can we do that?"

Lou's words stunned him. She wanted him in her life.

"Yes, I want that more than anything. Thank you, Lou. I love you, and to answer the rest of your questions, I am doing fine. The doctor said I could go home today".

Father and daughter talked for a few more minutes.

"Hey, Dad, I have to go, but I'll call you later, and I'll be home soon. And I hope you will be there". Her voice sounded wistful.

George smiled. "I'll be at the house waiting for you. You take care of yourself and that young man, Lou. I think he's a keeper."

"Thanks, Dad, I will. You take it easy until I get home. Is Mary with you?"

"No, she stepped out to get coffee. She's nice, Lou, and I like her, but we can talk about that later."

Lou was grateful her father had found someone who cared about him. He deserved to be happy.

"Don't worry about it, Dad. Love you."

Lou hadn't realized how long she'd been waiting for those three little words. In the time they had been together, neither one had ventured to say the words out loud. Lou stood for a moment, letting it all sink in, amazed how her life had changed in the last twenty-four hours.

Joan and Jason were deep in conversation when she walked into the living room.

Jason got up to meet her. "How did it go with your father?"

"Good. He's going home today and will be at the house. His friend Mary is watching over him."

Joan grabbed her purse and ushered them to the garage. "Jason, would you mind driving? I'm nervous."

"No problem, Sis." Jason shut her door then went to the other side to help Lou.

"I met Mary. She's a feisty gal, for sure, and wouldn't cut me any slack, after I started asking questions about your father. She's protective of him and of you. Do you know her?"

Lou buckled her seatbelt then turned to Jason. "I met her twice. She runs a boarding house and I did a story on her business. I never thought she would become a part of my life too?" Lou shook her head. "You just never know."

Joan tried to relax on the drive to the rehab center and was glad Jason and Lou were busy talking. It gave her time to calm her thoughts. Why was she so afraid? Fred was still the man she loved. He wasn't a cripple or confined to a bed, but she feared the unknown.

She asked God to give her the strength and guidance she needed, and to accept whatever was to be. She felt calmer and decided to just let things happen as they should and not borrow trouble.

Watching her husband from the doorway of his room, she was excited for the first time that he was coming home and ashamed she ever doubted him.

"Well, hello, handsome," she said, before giving him a long kiss on the lips. Fred looked confused for a minute, then responded, holding her close and kissing her back.

Jason and Lou viewed their exchange from the doorway.

"Okay, old man, enough of your man-handling my sister."

Fred noticed the woman standing by the door.

"So, Jason, you going to just stand there, or are you going to introduce this other pretty woman?" He moved past Jason to greet Lou.

"Hello. You must be Lou."

Lou held out her hand. "And you must be Fred."

Fred cradled her hand in his. "Nice to meet you, Lou."

He winked at Jason.

Jason moved next to Lou.

"Okay, Fred, hands off her. This one is mine." He laughed.

Joan shook her head at the men, grateful for their mutual friendship. She didn't know how she would have gotten through this ordeal without Jason's support. "Okay, you two, enough. Let's get packed so we can go home."

The two men giggled like two schoolboys. Lou and Joan got to the business of clearing the room. Jason grabbed a box, but as Lou reached to get one, he stopped her.

"I don't think you should lift these heavy boxes. You know, with your ribs and arm.

"Don't worry, Jason, I'll carry something light."

Joan stood watching Fred. He had stopped for one last look, then turned and walked out, ready to continue his life.

Fred dozed off halfway home, snoring against Joan's shoulder. The doctor told her Fred would tire and to give him time to build back his strength.

Joan nudged her husband as they pulled into the driveway.

"Fred, honey, wake up, we're home."

185

Fred stirred, then looked at her.

"Thanks, Joan, for believing in me," he whispered in her ear.

Joan gave him a kiss on the cheek.

Jason opened Fred's door and helped him out of the car.

Fred was still unsteady on his feet, so Jason guided him up the steps into the house.

"Thanks, kid."

Jason gave him a pat on the back. "What are brothers for if not to help each other?"

Joan hovered nearby as Fred settled in his favorite recliner.

"Oh, I love this chair." Fred snuggled into the soft fabric and closed his eyes.

Joan decided the boxes could wait. She directed Jason where to put them in her bedroom. She just wanted to spend time with her husband, her brother, and Lou.

When she returned to the living room, she saw Fred had dozed off again and signaled Jason and Lou to come into the kitchen, so they could talk without disturbing him. She got out the cookies and made a pot of coffee before she sat down with them.

"That went well." She picked up a cookie. "I'm glad he's home. I'll fix lunch when he wakes."

Jason grabbed a cookie and broke off a piece then popped it into his mouth. "Wow, these are great. Love your cookies, Joan." He shoved the rest in his mouth.

Lou giggled at Jason.

"What? They're great. Here, have one," he tried to speak without spewing crumbs as he pushed the plate toward Lou.

Lou took a cookie, but just nibbled on hers. "What happens now, Joan?"

Joan shook her head. "I'm not sure. I guess we just take it one day at a time. Fred will go once a month for checkups. And he has exercises to do at home. It will depend how hard he works at getting better."

Jason touched her arm. "You know he will work his butt off to get his strength back. Just give him time, Joan. You'll see."

Joan nodded. "So, Lou, what are you going to do now about your father, if you don't mind my asking?"

Engrossed in Jason's life, Lou almost forgot about her own.

"I guess I need to go home," she said, with a touch of melancholy. She wanted to stay, but Joan and Fred needed their space. Even though she had only been here for a day, it was like she'd known them her whole life.

"Jason, do you have the number for the airlines? I would like to book a flight as soon as possible."

"Don't worry about it, Lou. I'll call and get us booked for the next flight to PDX."

Lou turned to face him.

"Are you sure, Jason? Shouldn't you be here to help Joan?"

Getting on another plane terrified her, but she had to go back.

Joan spoke first. "Lou, I want Jason to go with you. He has spent enough time with me, besides, don't the two of you need to finish a story?"

Lou sat up in her chair. "The story. How could I have forgotten the story? Everything that brought us to this moment began with the story—and—the crosses."

A chill ran down her spine and she tried to shake off the feeling.

"Jason? Do you have the journal with you?"

She hoped he had brought it.

Jason paused for a moment then jumped up from the table and hurried to his bag still sitting by the front door and brought it to the table. He checked the front pocket, but it wasn't there and looked about to panic. He checked inside—still nothing.

When he unzipped the inner pocket and reached in the metal box touched his fingers. Jason let out a sigh of relief as he pulled it out, opening the lid. Inside lay the weathered book. He lifted journal and set it on the table in front of Lou.

She gazed at the worn leather cover. She had feared she would never know what happened to Kelly. Looking up at Jason, she motioned for him to take it.

"Please, Jason."

"Are you sure, Lou? It's yours. You're the one who found it."

He was right. It had been her story until he came into her life and changed it. Lou reached over and pushed it toward him.

"You started reading it to me and I would like you to finish it." She quickly explained Kelly's story to Joan so she could follow along.

Jason found where he left off and began to read.

April 25, 1930

The morning brought the first sounds of laughter in the house since I arrived here eleven days ago. The children complained they were hungry, so Clara made flapjacks — with syrup, no marmalade. Devon was understanding about the preserves, and Clara promised to heed his words the next time he said something didn't taste right.

A wave of sadness comes over me as the time to leave draws closer. I know I must help others, but I have felt so welcome and grateful they didn't shy away from me because of the birthmark on my face. I will leave early in the morning for Maupin and hope that my room is still waiting for me. Devon told me my truck was ready to go. Clara packed a metal tin with lunch and a container of water for me. They want to pay me for my services, but I told them the state pays me.

Clara and the children presented me with a little yellow rosebush that came from the wild roses that grow near their home. Shelly said it would bring sunshine to me always. Such a sweet child. We said our goodbyes, and I tucked the rosebush into the cab next to me. I will cherish it forever and will write more tonight after I reach Maupin.

Jason turned the page, then flipped it back. "That's odd."

"What wrong?" Lou asked.

"I just realized the next entry is five days after her last one." He flipped to the last page.

April 30, 1930

It has been five days since I crashed the truck off the road in a deep ravine. The truck is covered by sagebrush and I don't think anyone can see it from the road. How will anyone find me? Infection has settled into my broken leg and I can't stop it, and breathing has become difficult. I pray each day, asking God to save me, but still no one comes.

Two days ago, I ate the last of my food. I only have a few drops of water left, so today I crawled outside the truck and planted the little yellow rosebush next to the cab and used the last of my water to nourish it. Hope it survives if I don't. My heart hurts as I realize this may be my last night on earth, but I am not afraid; peace has come over me. I am ready to meet God. I only wish I could have stayed longer. I am too tired to get back inside the truck. A warm breeze is blowing, and I will just lie here tonight.

Jason closed the book and set it on the table. The entries had stopped. Jason swallowed before he tried to speak.

"From her last entry about the rosebush, it must have survived and grown so large it covered the truck, hiding it for ninety years. That is—until you found it, Lou."

Lou lowered her head. This young woman dying all alone crushed her. She remembered back to the people they had interviewed. Kelly had helped them after she herself had died—waiting for someone to help her.

Why she had been the one to find the truck and the journal? Why not Jason, or the people who drove that road each day? Why her?

She picked it up and held it close to her chest. She knew what she had to do.

"Jason, we have to go back. We have to finish Kelly's story."

Chapter Twenty-one

The flight to Portland the next morning was easier for Lou with Jason by her side. He kept her mind busy telling her about his flight out the first time. Lou couldn't hold back the laughter when he told her the flight attendant spilled coffee in his lap. They both laughed, remembering her sitting on her office floor, coffee dripping off the desk into her own lap.

With the help of the wristbands; Lou had managed not to get sick and even enjoyed the flight. She was more nervous on the ride to The Dalles. Her stomach felt like she had a meat grinder in it as Jason parked the rental car in the driveway.

"What am I going to say?"

Jason took her hand in his and kissed it. "Just tell him you love him. I'll wait here for you."

"No, Jason, I want you to be with me."

"Are you sure?"

"Yes. From now on we tackle life together."

"I want that more than anything." Jason leaned over and kissed her. "I see we have company." He pointed to the house.

Lou looked up and saw her father and Mary, then blushed like a schoolgirl.

"I guess we do." She laughed. "How about we save this for later?"

"Good idea." He opened his door and got out, then opened hers and offered his hand.

Together they walked up the steps to the open arms of her father. They spent the next few hours talking in the living room and it was like a real family.

"Dad?" She enjoyed the sound of the word. "Are you doing okay? Are you tired? How about something to eat?"

George grinned at her. "I'm fine, Lou. Couldn't be better if I tried."

Lou rose from her chair and put her arms around his shoulders, hugging him tight. "I don't know about you guys, but I'm starving. How about we order Chinese takeout?"

Jason looked over at Mary and George. "Sounds good to me."

By the time they finished dinner, George had agreed to move back to Lou's for the time being. He suggested that Jason stay in his old room at Mary's place.

Jason put up no resistance to George's strong suggestion.

Mary had brought George's belongings over when she drove him home.

Lou watched her father get up gradually with Mary by his side.

"I guess I'm getting tired. Hope you all don't mind if I lie down for a while."

Lou felt like a fool. How could she forget he just got out of the hospital? "I'm sorry, Dad. Here let me help you." Lou moved from where she'd been sitting and stood next to him.

George gave her arm a gentle squeeze. "Don't worry, Lou. I'll be fine after a good night's sleep in a regular bed. You enjoy the evening with Jason. Mary—thank you—and I'll see you tomorrow." George gave Mary a kiss on the cheek before he walked down the hall, then paused.

"And Jason—remember what we agreed on," he said, with a grin on his face.

Lou turned to Jason. "He told you."

Mary smiled. "It's been a long day. I think I'll be going too, and—Jason—George's room is on the second floor. Number 2."

Reaching into her pocket, she pulled out a set of keys. George had given them to her after they came back from dinner.

"If you come in after ten, use the small key to unlock the back door." Mary gave Lou a hug then walked down the steps to her car.

Jason and Lou watched from the porch as she drove away then returned to the living room.

A melancholy mood washed over Lou as the evening sun peeked through the branches of the oak tree, casting shadows through the window. When she closed her eyes, she had visions of Kelly, all alone—waiting—praying for someone to find her. Tears rolled down her cheek. Lou sighed, and Jason put his arm around her, holding her close to him as the sun set behind the hillside.

They talked until midnight before Jason left for Mary's. She couldn't remember the last time she felt this ecstatic. Her life had come full circle, and she couldn't wait to see what would happen next. Tomorrow she would call Brad and let him know she and Jason were back and ready to finish the story. She wasn't sure how to pull it all together without revealing the crash site. Lou feared curious people would start digging around, disturbing the truck if she told where it was. She hoped she would have the answers she needed in the morning.

Lou heard the alarm and hit the off button. She didn't want to get out of bed. She wanted to lie there for once and do nothing. Her sides ached, and she worried if they didn't get better in a day or so, she would have them checked out. Forcing herself to get out of bed, she caught the aroma of brewed coffee coming from the kitchen as she dressed and smiled to herself. George—no, Dad—was home. He was sitting at the table reading the morning paper when she walked into the kitchen.

"Good morning, Dad. How did you sleep?" Lou poured herself a cup of coffee and sat across from him.

George set the paper down and smiled at his daughter.

"Not too bad. It was nice to sleep without the nurse waking me up, just to ask if I was sleeping. Kind of counterproductive if you ask me." He chuckled. "How are you doing? Anything you want to talk about?"

Lou took a sip of her coffee. She loved the vanilla flavoring he added. It brought back fond memories of how they used to share breakfast together when she was young. She remembered how he always had a cup of coffee on the table in front of him while reading the paper. The memory made her smile.

"Nope. Doing okay. Though my ribs are aching. I've probably been doing too much—I'll be fine." Lou picked up a piece of toast and nibbled on it.

"You want to see the doctor?" he asked, concerned.

Lou put up her hand. "Oh—no. I've had enough of doctors. You want to see your doctor?"

He laughed. "See your point. How about we take it easy for a few days? Sound good to you?"

Lou nodded in agreement as she finished her coffee.

"Dad?"

"Yes."

"Do you think there's a cross on Bakeoven Road with my name on it?"

He sat forward in his chair and took Lou's hands in his own.

"I've forgotten about the crosses, with everything that's been happening. Do you want to go look?"

Lou had been thinking about the crosses since the flight back home. She wondered if things would change by telling the world about Kelly. Would she ruin something special?

She frowned "I don't know. Part of me wants to go see. Curiosity—but I just don't know if I'm ready. Besides, I still need to write the story. The problem is—I don't know how to do it without revealing all the details."

Frustrated, Lou knew she needed to talk to Jason. They both

had a stake in the story.

George released her hands and sat back. "I'm sure you'll do the right thing. Just do the story from your heart. You can never go wrong that way."

"You're right. And thanks, Dad. Jason will be here in half an hour, and I'm not even ready." Lou circled the table and gave him a kiss on the cheek before she left the room.

Jason grabbed a cup of coffee and a roll from the kitchen before he headed out the door to pick up Lou. David was counting on him to write a compelling feature article, but how could he, without sharing all the facts about the truck's location and Kelly's identity?

He was still wondering what he should do when Lou opened the door and threw her arms around him before he had time to even say hello.

"Nice to see you too," he said, before covering her mouth with his.

Lou pulled back and grinned. "Good morning, Jason. Did you sleep well?" She took his hand and pulled him towards the kitchen.

Jason followed, trying to catch his breath. "Yes—I—did. Where are we going?"

"Don't you want to say hello to my father?" she tugged at his hand.

George laid aside the newspaper when they came bustling into the kitchen. "Good morning, Jason."

"Morning, George."

"Hear you two have a busy day. Lou says you are going to talk with Brad about the story. I understand Lou has concerns about it. How about you?"

Jason paused. "A few. I guess we'll just work them out at the office. You're looking rested, George. I hope you're feeling better."

"Thank you. After sleeping in a real bed, I am much better."

George rinsed his cup and set it on the counter. "See you later, Lou. I'm going over to Mary's for a while. She'll pick me up, so I can get my car, but I'll be home for dinner, if you two will be here."

Lou gave her father a hug. "Yes, we'll be here if you're up to cooking. You know what my skills are in the kitchen."

George gave a knowing nod. "Yes, I do and yes I'm up to cooking. So, leave everything to me, and let's plan on dinner at seven. I'll ask Mary to come. If that's okay?"

"Mary's always welcome here." She turned Jason. "Will seven work for you?"

Jason shrugged. "I'm not sure." Then took her hand. "If we don't get to the office, we won't be back before midnight."

"Okay. Let's get going." She retrieved her bag. "Off to work we go. See you later, Dad."

Lou buckled her seatbelt and stared out the window.

Jason kept glancing over as they drove in silence. Something was eating at her. He wondered if she was having second thoughts about them. He couldn't imagine his life without her. The emptiness would kill him. He reached over and touched her hand.

Lou turned, gave him a smile, and squeezed his hand back.

"What's wrong Lou? Did I do something to upset you?"

Lou turned in her seat to face him. "I'm sorry, Jason. It's not you. I have so much on my mind. My father—you—the accident, and Kelly. Your boss and mine are looking for a story. I don't know if I can write one."

Jason turned into the parking lot and shut off the car. His heart raced. They had to write a story—his career—was balancing on it.

"I don't understand what you're saying Lou. We'll do the story. David and Brad are counting on us. Besides, this is your big break. Remember? And what about me? I need this story too."

Lou unbuckled her seatbelt.

"Really, Jason? Is that all you care about? What about the

196

people and how it changed their lives? Do we put their stories out there for others to tear apart or do we leave them with the knowledge they all—including me—shared in something amazing? And Kelly? Do we turn her into a novelty, or let the legend stand, giving people hope that something or someone, is watching over that stretch of road?"

Her words stunned him.

"Lou, what's come over you? If we don't do the story, what was all this about?"

Lou opened the door and got out.

"I don't know anymore." She closed the door between them, she leaned toward the open window. "I need to be alone for a while to think. I'm sorry, Jason." She turned and ran to the building, hurrying inside.

Jason's shock morphed to anger. He thought they were in this together. Now she needed time to think. To think about what?

Starting the car, he slammed it in reverse, and peeled out of the parking lot, driving around town. After an hour he returned to Mary's place and slipped into his room unseen and flopped on the bed. Lou wasn't the only one who needed to think. He felt like someone had punched him in the stomach.

Jason picked up his cell and scrolled his favorites for Joan's number.

Joan had just returned from the grocery store and was putting away her items when her cell phone rang.

"Hello, Jason."

"Hey, Joan. How's it going?"

The waver in his voice frightened her. "Jason? Has something happened?"

"It's Lou. I think she's having second thoughts."

"About what, Jason? What are you saying?"

"The story — us—I don't know. She told me she needed to be alone—that she needed to think. She just shut me out. I don't know what to do."

Joan could hear the anguish in his voice. "What do you want to do?"

"I could write the story on my own and ruin any chance we might have together. Or I can give her some time and watch my life and career go down the drain. Either way, I lose."

Joan pulled out a chair and sat down. She was worried. He sounded like he had after losing Annie and Sophia.

"Jason, this might be a dumb idea, but why don't you come home for a while? Give Lou this time to adjust to her new life with her father. I'm sure she will see things clearer in a few weeks. Besides, I'm sure David has other assignments for you. I could still use your help, and Fred misses you."

"Thanks, Joan. You're right. I'll see if I can get a flight back tonight. If not, then in the morning. See you sometime tomorrow. Love you."

They spent a few more minutes talking about Fred, then Jason hung up and called the airlines. There was a red-eye flight, so he booked it. He was thankful he still had the company credit card and David's approval to use it, thought this constant travel was exhausting.

Jason pulled out a sheet of paper, along with an envelope, from the drawer then set about writing Lou a letter. He explained why he was leaving, and this time he made sure she had his correct cell phone number or Joan's number.

He told her he would give her two weeks to decide if she wanted him. If she did, she would have to call this time, otherwise he would never bother her again. He signed it, Love, Jason.

He felt his heart breaking, but knew he had to do this, if they

198

were to have any chance of being together and addressed it to her office. After packing, his first impulse was to talk to Lou.

Without thinking, he dialed her number, but her voice mail answered. Twice more he tried, with the same result. He clicked off without leaving a message.

Mary sat at the front desk as he walked by. "Hello, Jason."

Jason didn't know if he could speak without his voice cracking. "I have to leave, Mary."

"But, Jason, I thought."

"Please, don't ask me questions."

"Okay."

Jason slid the envelope on the desk in front of her. "Will you please see that Lou gets this at her office today? It's important."

Mary took the envelope. "I'll call a messenger to take it right away. Are you sure you don't want give this to her yourself?"

Jason hung his head. "Please, Mary," was all he could manage to say. Turning, he walked out the door, got in his rental car, and headed for Portland. He knew he would have a long wait before his flight home, but he couldn't stay this close to Lou and not want to go to her.

Lou made her way to her office through the back entrance when she ran from Jason. Once inside, she locked the door and drew the blinds. She buzzed Karol and asked her to tell Brad she needed to change their meeting and she would talk to him tomorrow. She clicked off before Karol could ask questions.

She didn't know what had come over her and knew she had hurt Jason, and sure he was mad at her too. He had a right to be, she didn't know why she was pushing him away.

Lou thought about calling Julie, then remembered she never told her about Jason or the accident and didn't want to burden her. even wondered what her mom might say if she were alive. Mom had not been one to spout the virtues of relationships, or emotions. Many times, she told Lou both were a waste of time. That's what bothered her most. Was a relationship with Jason just in her imagination?

Lou had been sitting in her office for more than an hour in the dark with a throbbing headache. She felt her phone buzz several times but ignored it. She didn't want to talk to anyone right now. She knew Jason was counting on this story to help his career, and she had been too, but did she have the right to expose the people who survived by fate, or Kelly's help just in the name of journalism?

So much had happened, she was having trouble processing her own emotions. She didn't want to hurt Jason, but she didn't know how not to hurt him.

Lou laid her head back against the chair and dozed off until a knocking at her door jolted her awake. Looking at the clock on her desk, it shocked her to see it was after six. She'd been sleeping for five hours. Turning on her desk light, she made her way to the door but when she opened it, no one was standing there. Lou stepped into the hall; it was empty.

Turning to go back inside, her eyes caught sight of a letter in her mail slot by the door. Her name was on the front and the return address was Mary's place. Lou opened the letter and scanned the contents. She felt her knees weaken, forcing her to sit in the nearest chair. Now she had done it. She had pushed Jason away.

Lou reached into her pocket and pulled out her cell phone. She had three missed calls from Jason. He had tried to reach her, but she had ignored him. No wonder he left. She was such a fool—and confused. All she had to do was call him. But what would she say?

Nothing had changed yet.

Lou didn't know what to do about the story and wanted to go home and hide. Then she remembered Jason had driven her to the office. Not wanting to explain to her father what had happened, she called a cab and hoped the ride home would give her time to figure out how to explain Jason's leaving.

The cab dropped her off and she hurried up the steps. Why did she have to ruin things instead of just talking with Jason? Would he have agreed with her if she had given him a chance? Her pride and stubbornness were getting her nothing except a major headache.

Lou opened the front door hoping she hadn't alerted Dad she was home, giving her a few minutes to pull herself together before she had to face him.

George checked the roast and thought he'd heard the front door open and close. He glanced out the window but didn't see a car parked in the driveway, so he continued preparing dinner. Looking at the meal he had made, he'd gone a little overboard, but he hoped Lou and Jason and Mary were hungry. He was rinsing the salad greens when the doorbell rang, and he went to answer it.

"Good evening, Mary. Please come in." George could smell her perfume as she glided past him. She looked lovely in her floral dress and he wondered how he could be so lucky to have her in his life.

Mary smiled at George and handed him her shawl.

"Good evening, George." She caught an aroma coming from the kitchen.

"Goodness. Something smells delicious. Are you cooking a roast with garlic and rosemary?"

George nodded. "I wanted to make something special for you—and Lou and Jason. Hope it tastes as good as it smells." He hung her shawl in the closet and turned to face her.

Mary felt his hesitation and kissed his cheek. "Shall we go check on your dinner, George?" Without waiting for an answer, she took his hand in hers and pulled him toward the kitchen.

George followed without saying a word, wearing a big grin on his face.

Lou stood down the hall while her father answered the door and she knew she would have to appear. She heaved a deep sigh, put on her best smile, then headed for the kitchen.

Mary had just sat down as Lou walked in. "Good evening, Lou." She started to rise.

"No, Mary—please sit." Lou motioned with her hand, as she moved closer to her father. "Wow, Dad. That smells so good. You're becoming a great chef." She laughed as she put her arm around him.

George leaned his chin on top of her head. "When did you get home?" He stepped back. "I only saw Mary's car. And where's Jason?" He looked at Mary, who gave him a gentle shrug of her shoulders.

Lou moved to the counter, grabbed a cup, and poured herself coffee. She felt as nervous as a child with her hand in the cookie jar.

"He's not here." She kept her back to them.

"Okay, Lou, spit it out. What's going on with you two?" His chair scraped the floor as he sat by the table.

Lou sipped her coffee, and let the warm liquid slide down her throat, giving her a few more minutes before she tried to explain what a fool she was. "I don't know."

"What do you mean, you don't know? Where is he?" George sounded confused.

Lou stayed where she was, with her back still to them. She didn't want them to see the disappointment on her face. "He left."

"He did what? Lou—turn around and face me."

Lou turned to look at him. "He went home."

"But why? I thought you two worked everything out from the last misunderstanding."

"Oh, Dad," she cried, then plopped down in the chair across from him and Mary. She set her cup down hard, splashing coffee all over the table. "Now looked what I've done," she moaned. She grabbed a napkin from the center of the table and tried to mop it up before in ran on the floor.

George reached over, took her hand, and stopped her. "Lou, what's going on here?"

Lou pulled her hand free and sat back in her chair. "I pushed him away."

"Why would you do that?"

Lou shook her head. "I don't know—I'm just so confused."

"About what? If you don't mind my asking, Lou." Mary's soft voice drew the truth from her.

"It started this morning. I just can't get Kelly out of my mind."

Now Mary looked confused. "Who is Kelly? Is Jason seeing someone else?"

"No, it's not like that. Kelly—she's the person we are writing the story about. She's our angel—I guess that's what you would call her. After all that's happened, I told him I didn't know if I could do the story. I tried to explain that it just didn't seem right, but he got upset, telling me we had to do it. That his career was on the line. I yelled at him, asking if that was all he cared about. Before he could answer, I told him I needed to be alone to think and left him sitting in the car. I sat in my office for hours—thinking—trying to figure out what was the right thing to do. I guess he tried calling, but I ignored my cell phone, not even looking to see if it was him."

George blew out a low whistle. "So—did he leave a message?"

Lou shook her head. "I fell asleep and would still be if I hadn't heard the knocking on my door. I was hoping it was Jason. Instead, I found a letter from him. A messenger must have brought it."

Mary winced.

"What did it say?" Mary and George asked in unison.

Lou looked away, trying to force the lump down her throat. "He said he would give me some time to decide what I want to do. He went home for now."

"Did he say for how long?" George glanced at Mary.

"Two weeks or until I call and ask him to come back."

"Did you call?"

"No."

"Why not? Don't you want to be with Jason?" He looked puzzled by her answers.

"Maybe. Yes, I want to be with him. But what if he only cares because of the story and the accident? How do I know for sure? Maybe he's right and I do need time to get my head on straight."

Lou lowered her head into her hands and rocked back and forth.

"Thinking just gives me a headache."

George rose and put his arms around Lou, holding her close to him. "I'm sorry, Lou. How about we talk about this tomorrow and just enjoy dinner tonight?"

Lou lifted her head. "I'm not hungry. You and Mary eat. I think I'll lie down for a while. My head hurts."

"Can I do anything for you, Lou?" Mary asked.

Lou got up from her chair. "No, but thanks for asking. Please excuse me, and don't worry. Just enjoy your dinner. I'll talk to you in the morning."

If Lou's body could talk, it would be screaming at her by the time she reached her room. Every part of her ached as she crawled into bed. She prayed she would have a clearer idea what to do in the morning. She turned off her lamp and settled against her pillows, hoping to sleep. Two hours later, she still lay staring at the ceiling.

Jason kept waiting, praying for the phone to ring as he drove to Portland, but it didn't. Lou should have the letter by now. Sitting at the airport with his bag tucked between his feet, he tried to take a nap while waiting for his flight but couldn't calm his mind.

He checked his phone once more before boarding the plane—nothing—then turned it off for the trip home. He would give her the two weeks. If she didn't call by then, he would accept she didn't want him in her life and try to move on without her. The thought made his stomach turn as he buckled his seatbelt and laid his head back against the headrest.

The flight home had been quiet. Everyone around him was as tired as he was. The moment he landed, he checked his phone for messages, but nothing. He would have to force himself to wait and see what happened.

Joan insisted on picking him up from the airport. For once he didn't argue and walked off the plane to find his sister. On the ride to his apartment, Jason was grateful Joan didn't ask many questions though she tried to persuade him to stay at her house, but he told her he needed to get back to living by himself and connect with David. Joan agreed to give him a few days but expected him to check in daily with her. Jason kissed her on the check and promised he would keep in touch.

Jason waved as she drove off, then turned and climbed the steps to the front door. He felt he needed to walk off the anger building inside him, so he took the stairs, instead of the elevator. By the time he made it to his floor, sweat covered his body and he felt better. When he entered his apartment; the silence surrounded him turned on his stereo, letting the music of John Denver fill the apartment and his mind. His spirit lifted until the song Denver wrote about his own wife, Annie, came on, causing Jason to flinch. He turned if off deciding silence might be better for now.

205

Chapter Twenty-two

You woke to the buzzing of her alarm, reached over, and hit the off button. It was 7:00 a.m. During the early morning hours; she had fallen asleep but now that she was awake and just wanted to stay hidden in her room. She knew she was being childish, and for the moment, she didn't care. Being an adult was so exhausting.

Throwing the covers back, she swung her legs over the bed and sat on the edge. The smell of coffee brewing propelled her forward, and she knew it was time to talk to her father.

George spent a restless night worrying about Lou. He and Mary talked for hours after Lou retired, but neither of them knew what they could do to help her. George just hoped she wouldn't let her stubborn streak get in the way of her own happiness.

"Morning, Dad," Lou entered the kitchen and headed for the coffeepot.

"Morning, Lou. Did you get any sleep?"

Lou set her mug on the table. "A little. Did you?"

"A little." George saw the dark circles under her eyes. "I'm worried about you."

"I know, but I need to figure this one on my own. But thank you for asking."

George nodded. "Are you hungry? I can fix ham and eggs."

"Sure—I'd like that. And, Dad?"

"Yes, Lou."

"Love you."

"Love you too. Breakfast will be ready soon. How about you

206

make the toast?" George turned and grabbed a frying pan.

After sharing a quiet meal together, Lou promised to talk with him later then suddenly sat erect.

"Dad?"

George saw a frown on her face. "What's wrong?"

"I don't have a car."

"That's right. I forgot all about that. You want me to drive you to work?"

"No. I would like it if you would take me down to the used-car lot." Lou picked up her plate and set it in the sink. "I don't want anything fancy. Just dependable."

George picked up his plate and placed it in the sink next to hers.

"Give me ten minutes to clean up, and I'll drive you."

Lou walked over and gave him a kiss on the cheek.

"What was that for?"

"For not asking a bunch of questions this morning."

"Just remember, Lou, if you need to talk—I'm here for you. Or Mary."

Lou stopped at the doorway. "Thanks, I'll remember that." She felt better while she finished combing her hair and getting her things together for the office. It was becoming so easy for them to talk. He was warming up the car by the time she came out of her room.

Over the next two hours, Lou and George test-drove several cars, until she settled on a 2006 Ford Explorer with only 65,000 miles on it. Lou liked how it handled, and the fact she sat up high like the jeep. After letting George negotiate the price, Lou paid for her new vehicle. It had taken most of her savings, but she at least she didn't need to worry about making payments.

Thankful that was over, she headed for the office. It was time to talk to Brad.

Lou took a deep breath, knocked on the door and entered. Brad was reading the morning addition of the paper.

"Good afternoon, Lou. Nice to see you back at the office."

Lou took a seat in front of him. "Afternoon, Brad. Do you have a few minutes to talk with me?"

Brad set the paper down and leaned forward. "Sure. What's going on with your story?"

Lou didn't know how to explain what she was feeling about the story and Kelly. "I don't know if I can write the story."

"And why is that? This whole story was your idea. What's changed?" He had a concerned look on his face.

Lou stood and walked to the window. Fall was in the air. Few leaves clung to the branches on the trees, and the cool morning had required a coat. Even though she was still wearing hers, she felt a chill run through her body.

"So many things. In the beginning, it was all about the story. And the hope of a promotion. Right before my wreck, I found a crash site and a journal. Jason began to read it to me at the hospital, but then he left and took it with him. I didn't know if it meant anything to the story until I saw Jason again and we finished reading it. It belonged to a nurse named Kelly Turner, and she died out there all alone in 1930. I realized after talking to the people who had survived, hearing their stories and my own accident—something changed; I changed after learning what happened to Kelly."

Brad seemed enchanted at Lou's new insight. "What are you saying, Lou? Doesn't that add depth to the story?"

Lou turned to face him. "I'm not sure. The journalist side of me says yes—write the story—that's my job. But the personal side says, why? Can't we just let her rest in peace?"

Brad relaxed back in his chair. "Sit down, Lou. Let's talk about the pros and cons of the story."

Lou sat down. "What's there to discuss? If we do the story,

maybe readers will see the hope of salvation, in this crazy world we live in today, but they could also know where her wreck happened and could start scavenging the site. I can't let that happen to her. It wouldn't be right. If I don't write the piece, the people, including myself, their stories go untold about this amazing woman. Is that so wrong?" She was speaking with new maturity in her voice. This experience had changed her.

"What about Jason? He's counting on this story to help his own career."

Lou lowered her head. She didn't want Brad to see the hurt in her eyes at the mention of his name. "He's in New York City."

"I know."

Lou lifted her head. "You do? How?"

"He sent me a note explaining his position before he left."

"Did he mention me?"

"He said there was a conflict about the story. Even though he needed it, he would let you decide. He said he was going home to give you time to decide."

Lou chewed on her lip. "He said all that?"

Brad nodded.

She knew she was letting Brad and Jason down if she didn't follow through on the story. "I don't know what to do."

Brad folded the newspaper on his desk and set it aside. "Tell you what, I will hold a slot in November's holiday edition. That's in three weeks. If the story is ready, I want it there. If you decide not to do the story, you will need to supply me with something else. But I hope you understand Lou, stories like this come along once in a lifetime."

Lou knew what he was implying. This was about her career, as well as the story. Rising from her chair, she knew it was time to leave.

"Thanks, Brad. I won't let you down; I promise."

"I'm hoping you don't, Lou." Picking up the paper, he flipped it back open as she left.

Lou returned to her office and checked her phone by habit, then remembered Jason said she had to be the one to call him and set it on her desk. Frustrated, she fired up her computer and immersed herself in her notes on Bakeoven Road.

Jason spent the next day going through his emails. Old friends he had forgotten about were checking to see how he was doing. He realized how much of his life he had put on hold since Annie's and Sophia's deaths. It was time to get back on track with his life and career no matter how things turned out with Lou. Except each time the phone rang, his stomach flipped in hopes it was Lou calling. When it wasn't her on the line, disappointment weighed heavily on his heart.

He checked in with Joan, who told him Fred was working hard on his therapy and she wanted to know when he was coming for dinner, which he promised he would do soon. He felt good considering everything that had happened the last few days. Next, he set up a time to talk to David to discuss the story and see if he had any assignments for him and was ready to jump into work with both feet. Grabbing his bag, he headed out the door with more confidence than he felt in months.

David was finishing a call when Jason plopped down on the chair in front of his desk.

"Hello, Jason. I'm glad you're back." David leaned back in his chair.

"Good to see you too. How have you been?"

"Me? I've been doing well. Anything I need to know?"

Jason cleared his throat. He was sure Brad had kept David up to date on the problem since both papers stood to lose the story.

"I'm sure you've talked to Brad."

"Yes, I did. So, what's going on here, Jason? Are we going to run the story? I'm a patient man, but I'm tired of the drama surrounding this story. From what I am hearing, you told him Lou is having second thoughts about even finishing the story. Is that true?"

Jason squirmed in the chair. He should have called David first and filled him in on the problem before telling Brad. It was too late now but he didn't want to put the blame on Lou.

"Well, sort of."

"What do you mean by sort of Jason? Either Lou agrees or not. Which one is it?"

"I'm sure she'll write it. We'll write it. It's just been very emotional for her after her wreck and all, and she needs more time to sort through her feelings."

"How much time?"

Jason knew David was getting annoyed. "Two weeks, tops. If she doesn't come around—I'll write it alone."

Jason felt like a traitor, but he figured if Lou didn't contact him by then, it would mean she didn't want him in her life. What did he have to lose? The story would be fair game, and he had all the pieces he needed to complete a relevant story.

David seemed to relax by his comment.

"Two weeks, and not a minute more," he said. "In the meantime, I have a few assignments for you to cover. I'll forward all the information to your email. If you have questions, call me."

Jason stood and headed for the door. "Thanks David. I really appreciate it."

David grinned. "Get out of here, and let me work," he said with a chuckle.

Jason signed. He knew his job was secure for now.

The next week flew by and Jason had been out on three

assignments. He was feeling positive about himself and getting back in the swing of things. Though he missed Lou, he had said he would give her two weeks, and he would stick to his word though he had to force himself not to call her.

He was getting himself something to drink from the kitchen when his door buzzer sounded, and a messenger greeted him with a registered letter.

The return address was from a law firm in The Dalles. His pulse quickened as crazy thoughts sprang through his mind. Maybe Lou had sued him for the right to publish the story, then scoffed at the idea and himself, for even thinking such a thing.

Returning to his desk, Jason pulled out his letter opener, slit the envelope open, and pulled out the letter. Inside that letter was another sealed envelope with his name on it too. Jason scanned the first one and sorrow washed over him.

Harold Joner had died, and he had instructed his lawyer to send the enclosed envelope to Jason upon his death. Jason sat for a moment, remembering his conversation with Harold. He hoped the man was at peace and in the company of his loving wife.

Jason lay the first letter aside and opened the second envelope. By the time he finished it; he knew what he had to do.

Lou had spent the last week and a half wrestling with her emotions, and no one was winning. She was crabby at work, and at home. Lou knew if she didn't get her act together soon, her father would move out and Brad would fire her. She couldn't remember how many times she picked up her phone to dial Jason's number, only to stop herself.

Sure, she said she needed her space, but when did anyone listen to her?

Julie called to check on her, but Lou lied and told her everything was going great.

As for the story, she still hadn't decided. Brad expected her to deliver a story by the end of next week and she was still at a loss what to write. Lou would start to type, then delete the words she had written. Her story was going nowhere. She had nothing.

Why did this story have to be so hard?

Lou squeezed the bridge of her nose.

What would Jason do?

Would he still do the story even if she didn't? The idea unnerved her, and she typed for the next two hours, before hitting the save key and closed her laptop.

Since her talk with Brad, Lou had thought long and hard about the story. She felt good about what she had now, but wished Jason were here, telling her she had done the right thing. She hung her head disgusted with herself. She had been the one to push him away, but she didn't have the guts to call and ask him to come back. Her two weeks were almost up and if she didn't make a move soon, she would be living with only her pride for the rest of her life.

Lou glanced up from her computer and groaned when she saw what time it was. She had promised her dad she would be home by five for dinner tonight. She had been skipping dinners to avoid any confrontation with him about Jason by hiding in her office. It was time to stop acting like a child. This was her mess, and she needed to fix it before it was too late.

George wondered if Lou would make it home for dinner like she promised. He had enough of her moping around the house and carrying on like a lovesick hound dog. He had decided they would settle this once and for all tonight. She needed to call Jason, and if she wouldn't, he would dial the number himself.

He glanced at the clock; it was five minutes to five and was about to give up, until he caught sight of her car pull in and park. Relieved, he finished setting the table while he waited for her and was placing the casserole on the table when she entered.

"Hi, Lou, I see you made it home for dinner tonight." He tried not to sound harsh.

Lou smiled then walked over and gave him a kiss on the cheek.

"Hi, Dad. Yes, I did, and it smells delicious. What is it?"

George pulled out his chair, sat down and motioned her to do the same. "Beef and mushroom stew. Hope you like it."

Lou took her place across from him and handed him her bowl.

"Sounds wonderful, and I'm starved."

George couldn't be mad at her and scooped a healthy serving into her bowl. "This will put some meat back on those skinny ribs, young lady."

Lou set her bowl down. After a quick prayer she dug in without another word. "I'm sorry about my behavior."

"You should be. If you were younger, I'd put you over my knee for a good spanking."

Lou laughed. "Yes, I suppose I deserve a spanking or at least a time-out. I don't know where my head's been since Jason left and I appreciate your trying to help."

George set his fork down and gave her a serious look. "Lou, I'm not one to interfere or think I'm an expert on the ins and outs of relationships. Lord knows I messed up with you and your mother, but I would like to think I learned something over the last few years."

"I know. But I…"

"No buts. I've kept quiet while you've been beating yourself up over Jason leaving. Okay, he left, but he was giving you what you wanted. Only this time, you're the one with the power to bring him back with just a phone call. I don't know what you are waiting for, Lou. I know you love him, and I'm sure he loves you, but if you keep putting it off, it will be too late. That's all I will say." He picked up his fork and resumed eating his dinner.

Lou forced down another bite, digesting his words along with her meal. He was right. She would ruin her chance at happiness over a story. A story that most people wouldn't even read. How stupid could she be? Jumping up from the table she ran to get her cell phone and dialed Jason's number.

As she waited for him to answer, she played over in her mind what she wanted to say to him. When he didn't answer it crushed her. Lou returned to the table and sat down, placing the phone next to her.

"Well, what did he say?" George asked.

Lou picked at her dinner. "He didn't answer."

"So. Did you leave him a message?"

Lou shook her head.

"For heaven's sake, Lou, why not?"

"I don't know. I want to talk to him."

"Louise Alice McClelland—you pick up that phone and call that man or I will." George reached for her phone.

Lou grabbed it first. She knew her father was serious, after using her full name. Biting the inside of her mouth, she dialed his number again. The phone rang and she thought she could hear an echo coming from the living room.

While it continued to ring, she got up and followed the sound until she reached the front door and she opened it. Jason was standing in front of her. Lou stood in shock, her phone still to her ear.

"Hello," he said into the phone.

"Hello," she said back to him.

"Who's calling?"

"It's me, Lou."

"Is there something you want to say?" he asked, watching her face.

"Yes. I want—I want you to come back."

"Are you sure?"

"Oh, yes, I'm sure."

"But why?"

Lou let the phone hang in her hand. "Because I love you!"

Jason took her into his arms and covered her mouth with his, kissing her until they had to come up for air.

"I love you too, Lou. What took you so long?"

Lou pulled him close to her. "I'm a fool, Jason and let my pride get hold of me. I almost ruined my chance at happiness."

Then it registered that he was standing on her front steps. "But wait. What are you doing here? Didn't you say you would only come back if I called you?"

"Decided I couldn't take the chance, so here I am." He kissed her again.

Lou swooned at his touch.

He was here. He came back for her. Her wish had come true.

Lou pulled back from his lips

"Jason, what about the story—and your career?"

Jason took her hands in his and kissed them. "My career is fine, Lou, and as for the story—that's up to you. It was always yours to tell. I do have a new piece of information that might interest you before you decide whether to write it."

Lou couldn't imagine what information Jason would have since he left and pulled him toward the kitchen.

"My, my," George said when they entered the kitchen. "You two look cheerful. Something happen?"

Lou and Jason sat down across from him, still holding hands.

"Jason was on the front steps while I was calling him. He came back for me."

Jason squeezed her hand. "I had no choice. Your daughter can be hardheaded sometimes and realized I couldn't leave the fate of our relationship in her hands."

Lou gave him a nudge in his side with her elbow.

"What? I'm right, aren't I?" Jason winked at George

Lou couldn't help but smile. She didn't care who was right anymore. She only knew how loved she felt at this moment. "I called," she whispered.

Jason wrapped his arms around her and held her close. "Yes, you did."

Burying his face in her hair, he calmed any fear she still had. Lou could stay locked in his arms forever, but remembered he said he had something to tell her about their story. "Jason?"

"Yes, Lou."

"Didn't you say you had some information about the story?"

"I did? You're right—I did—I mean I do." Jason released her, leaned back, and pulled the envelope from his inside pocket.

"What's that?" George asked first.

"It's a letter from Harold Joner."

Lou looked puzzled. "Why would Harold send you a letter?"

Jason shook his head. "I'm not sure. I guess he liked me. Harold died last month, and this letter was in his effects. Anyway, it arrived the other day mailed from a law office here in The Dalles."

"I didn't know." Lou turned away. She felt bad she hadn't kept in touch with the people she was writing about.

Jason patted her hand. "It's okay."

"What does the letter say?" George asked.

Jason handed it to Lou. "You should read it first, Lou."

Lou began to read the words Harold had written. Shock, then disbelief rolled through her. Could this be true? If it wasn't for the story about the crosses on Bakeoven Road, would Harold have taken his secret to his grave since he had no reason to tell anyone?

Who would believe him anyway? Lou relaxed against the chair and placed the letter on the table.

"I guess that explains how the journal got under the seat."

"Why is that?" George scratched his head with a confused look on his face. "What does it say?"

Jason took the lead. "The last day Kelly wrote in her journal, she said she was outside the cab that night, sitting under the stars. She said how tired she was, and that she didn't think she would make it much longer. I think by morning she was dead. So, the question was, how did the journal get under the truck seat inside the metal tin?"

Jason picked up the letter and reread the words. "I'm sure Harold was frightened after he stumbled upon the truck along with her scattered bones, two years after his accident. Somehow, she had put the journal inside the metal tin that held her lunch, protecting it from the elements all those years. When he found the book in the tin, he put the pieces together to figure out who his angel was, but who would believe him? That a woman who died in 1930 had saved his life when he rolled his tractor in 1948? Kelly wrote in her journal she grew up at the orphanage and had no family."

Jason folded the letter and slid it back in the envelope. "The way Harold explains it; it all makes sense now. He said he buried her bones next to the truck and put the journal under the seat. From then on, he made it his life's mission to watch over her. Through the years, he made sure the truck stayed hidden, and the roses flourished, until they covered the truck and blanketed the hollow, keeping her safe. He never told what he'd done."

Lou shook her head. "What a burden to carry."

Jason continued with the letter. "Harold says he knows it has to be Kelly who has been helping others, but he doesn't know how to set her free. He said it's haunted him all his life and hoped that since someone was doing a story about the crosses, maybe somehow Kelly would find peace."

George pushed back his chair. "I didn't understand the depth of the story Lou has been working on with you, Jason. She told me about a young woman helping her and I realize now that she hadn't been hallucinating. This angel watched over my daughter. Wish I could thank her for saving you, Lou."

Lou knew she had done justice to the story and Kelly. Tomorrow she would show it to Brad and Jason, but for tonight they had a lot of things to discuss.

George stretched his back and yawned. "I'm sorry. I guess I'm getting tired. Jason, do you have a place to stay tonight?"

Jason shook his head. "Do you think your old room available for the night?"

"I'm not sure, but I can call Mary."

"Thanks, George. If she doesn't, I'm sure I can find a room at Motel 6."

George left the room to call Mary and returned with a smile on his face. "Mary said to tell you she's glad you are back and that my old room is available. She wanted to know if you still have the keys, she gave you?"

Jason fished though his pockets, then pulled out a little key chain holding two keys. "Yep, I've still got them."

"Good." George yawned again. "I think I will go to bed, unless there is anything else you want to discuss?"

Jason hesitated. "No, I don't think so, George, but I would like to talk to you tomorrow for a few minutes."

George grinned. "Night, Lou. Don't stay up too late." After giving her a kiss on the cheek, he left the two of them to continue their conversation as they did the dishes.

Lou yawned. It had been a long and emotional day.

"I'm sorry, Jason. I guess I'm tired too, but I don't want you to leave."

Jason kissed her nose. "Don't you worry. I'll be back in the morning." Then he yawned himself. "Okay, now you're making me do it."

Lou took his hand, guiding him toward the front door. "I love you, Jason."

Jason stopped at the door, then got down on one knee.

"Jason—what are you doing?"

"Lou McClelland, I want you to be my wife, if you will have me. I don't have a ring, but I promise to get you one tomorrow if you say yes. Will you marry me?"

"But, Jason—we hardly know each other—are you sure?"

"Yes, Lou, I've never been surer of anything in my life. Please say you'll marry me."

Lou jumped up and down with joy. "Yes, yes, yes. I'll marry you!"

"That's great. Can you help me up, I have a cramp in my leg?"

Lou reached down to help him, but he teetered off-balance, causing her to knock him over and she fell on top of him.

George came running from his room. "What is going on out here?"

"Sorry, Dad," Lou tried to control her laughter as they lay sprawled on the floor. "Jason just asked me to marry him!"

"What's that got to do with you two on the floor?" He reached out his hands to help them up off the floor.

Lou brushed her hair back with her hand and smoothed her clothes. "He got a cramp in his leg and I was trying to help."

"Did you at least say yes before you trampled him?"

"I said yes!" Dad gave her a hug and shook Jason's hand.

Jason had just asked her to marry him. If this was, she never wanted it to an end.

"Welcome to the family, Jason. But it's time we all got some sleep. So, Lou, tell your fiancé goodnight, then go to bed." He turned and marched down the hall to his room then shut the door.

Lou and Jason burst into laughter again.

"I guess I better go before your father comes back and kicks me to the curb." Jason kissed her again as if his life depended on it.

Lou kissed him back with as much passion as she could, leaving her breathless. "Yes, you better go."

Jason gave her one more kiss, then turned and skipped down the stairs to his rental car.

Lou waved from the steps and was still waving long after he drove away. She couldn't believe what just happened, she was engaged! She wanted to scream it from the top of her lungs but knew she would wake up the neighbors and her father.

With a nervous giggle, she did a jig down the hall to her room and flung herself onto her bed. Lou hugged her pillow and drifted off to sleep dreaming of Jason.

Chapter Twenty-three

George was surprised to find Lou in the kitchen. She had the coffee ready, and it looked like she was trying to make pancakes.

"Morning, I'm cooking breakfast."

He looked around the room. "Where's my daughter, and what did you do with her?"

"Funny." Lou set their plates on the table, sat down, and cut her pancakes into little pieces before covering them in syrup.

"Do you like them?"

He nodded. "They look wonderful, Lou. Thank you for breakfast, but what's the occasion?" He had to chuckle. He knew she didn't like to cook.

When he took a bite, it stirred a vague memory of Lou insisting on making him breakfast for his birthday, and this onetime Vivian had let her—pancakes—and as he remembered—lumpy. He took another bite. He didn't know how someone could mess up pancakes, but he wouldn't complain.

George watched his daughter's face. She wore her emotions on her sleeve, and he hoped Jason stayed true to his word. Lou wouldn't survive another disappointment from him.

Lou grinned at him. "I thought, for once, I would cook you breakfast. You've been so good to me, and sometimes I don't think I tell you how much you mean to me."

George reached over and took her hand. "Don't you worry, Louie girl, I know." With a silly grin on his face, he finished eating the lumpy pancakes in silence.

Jason rose early to shave and shower, grateful Mary stocked the cabinet in his bathroom. In his rush to get back, he hadn't even packed the essentials. And now that he and Lou were engaged, this spur-of-the-moment travel had to stop. Engaged—he liked the sound though there was still the matter of a ring. He wondered if he should let her pick it.

Before leaving for Lou's, Jason called David to let him know what was happening. David congratulated him and told him to take the rest of the week off. Next, he called Joan, who screamed so loud with excitement, he had to hold the phone away from his ear. Once she calmed down, he promised her he would stay in touch.

Leaving his room, he caught the sweet aroma of cinnamon in the air and followed his nose to the kitchen. Mary was pulling a fresh batch of rolls from the oven. Jason stood next to the counter watching as she began spreading icing over the top of the hot rolls, making his mouth water.

"Good morning, Jason. Hope you slept well. Fresh coffee is over by the sink. Why don't you grab a cup while I finish frosting these?"

"Sounds good to me. The cinnamon rolls smell amazing. Are you sharing them, by chance?" He set his cup on the edge of the counter.

Mary smiled. "Take a seat, and I'll bring you one."

Jason pulled out a stool and sat waiting like a hungry puppy.

Mary scooped out a large cinnamon roll, slid it onto the plate, and set it front of him. "So, what's this about an engagement? George sounded excited on the phone this morning, but only gave me the condensed version."

Jason shoved a large piece of the roll in his mouth. Pointing, he chewed as fast as he could.

"Take your time. I don't need you choking."

Jason took a big gulp of coffee to wash down the roll. "Sorry,

Mary. I guess I should take smaller bites. But it's so good."

"Thank you, Jason. Tell me about your engagement if I'm not being too forward."

Jason sat back in his chair.

"It just happened. I didn't even have a ring. Wanted to talk to George first, and ask his permission, but—I don't know—the moment looked right, and I popped the question." Jason nibbled on a smaller piece this time.

Mary tilted her head. "Sometimes you just go with what's in your heart. I assume she said yes?"

"Yep. There I am on bended knee, asking her to be my wife. After she said she would, I got this terrible cramp in my leg. Lou tried to help me up, but we both ended up on the floor in a heap, laughing so hard we couldn't get up, then George came running out of his bedroom, in attack mode. He helped us up—and well— here I am."

Jason tore off another piece of his roll and popped in his mouth, savoring the warm dough and gooey icing.

"That must have been a sight." Mary chuckled to herself. "What are you going to do now?"

"About what?"

"Well, for one, your job. Are you going to be staying out west? And what about the story you have been working on together?"

Jason wiped his mouth. Those were questions he hadn't asked himself yet. He wondered if Lou would consider moving. It was something they would need to discuss.

"I'm not sure. It happened so fast; we haven't worked out the details yet. As for the story, I'm leaving that up to Lou."

Checking his watch, he realized the time. "Thanks again for the delicious roll. My sister, Joan, makes a mean one too." He threw his napkin in the trash and walked out to his car.

Lou and her father had been making small talk during the rest of their breakfast and agreed to talk more that night. Jason would arrive soon to get her. While she dressed, Lou wondered if she dreamed it all. What if Jason hadn't asked her to marry him? She was still fussing when the doorbell rang.

"Good morning, Jason." She searched Jason's face for any sign that last night had been a dream then stepped back and ushered him into the hallway.

Jason stopped inside the door next to her. He dropped to one knee—again.

"What in the world are you doing?"

Jason pulled a ring box from his pocket, opened it, and held it up to her. "Lou McClelland, will you marry me?"

"Yes—oh, yes, Jason—I will marry you. You did ask me that last night—right?"

Jason pulled the ring out and slid it on her left hand.

"Yes, but I didn't have the most important thing—a ring. Figured I would have a do-over. Do you mind?"

Lou lifted her hand and eyed the magnificent diamond ring on her finger. "Oh—my — it's so big."

Jason tried to get up, then crumpled to the floor. "Lou?"

Lou was still admiring her ring. "Huh?"

"Help."

"Oh, Jason." Reaching down to help him up, he pulled her toward him, and they tumbled to the floor in a loud crash, laughing, as they had last night.

George had heard the noise and rushed out of the kitchen.

"What is this? Groundhog Day? Swear I picked you two up off the floor last night." He shook his head and reached out to help them again.

Lou held out her hand. "Look, Dad. Isn't it gorgeous?"

She flashed her hand back and forth in front of his face. He grabbed her hand, then flipped on the hallway light to get a better look.

"Nice job, Jason. Well, congratulations—again. Now if you'll excuse me, I will get ready to visit Mary." He waved his hand as he walked away. "Some of us have a life too."

Lou leaned into Jason's arms still staring at her hand.

"I guess we should go to the office," she said.

She wanted to stay this way forever, but Brad was waiting for them. Together, they had decisions to make about the story, and their future.

Their meeting with Brad turned out well and the story had impressed him, but before she could put the finishing touches on it, Lou knew there was one more thing she had to do. With Jason's help and Brad's approval, they set her plan in motion.

While reconnecting with her father, she had discovered he was a woodcarver. He presented her with a carving of a girl holding a teddy bear. He told her it represented her as a child, and how carving had helped him through the dark times in his recovery. The carving had given her an idea, and together they worked on a plan.

Chapter Twenty-four

One week later, Lou paced around The Centennial's conference room, making sure everything was ready. She had sent the invitations and would have to wait to see if her guests would come. She was still fussing with the table, arranging the vase of yellow roses, when Jason came up from behind and put his arms around her.

"Just take a breath, Lou. The room looks fine." He kissed the top of her head.

Lou leaned back into his arms. "Are you sure? I want this to be perfect."

Jason turned her around to face him. "It's perfect, just like you. Now try to relax before your guests arrive."

Lou frowned. "What if they don't come?"

"You don't have to worry. Look behind you."

Lou turned and saw the people she was waiting for coming through the door. Bill, Brandon, Linda, Caroline, and Jenny were all here. The only one not present was Harold.

This was the first meeting of the Bakeoven Road survivors. Lou decided this should be a private affair, along with Jason and her father.

After introductions, each person, including Lou, told their story about the angel who helped them after their accidents, and Jason shared Harold's. They reminisced about how their lives had changed since then, and Lou knew she had done the right thing by bringing them all together. Rising from her chair she addressed the group.

"Thank you for sharing. You're all aware of the newspaper story that Jason and I are writing, but before I send it in to my editor, I wanted to get us all together. I left out a few things, but I felt it was important to share them with all of you. I know from my experience how emotional it has been tonight. Being here together is a miracle of its own, though we are missing one person. You know that Harold died before I finished the story, but I'm sure he would have loved meeting everyone. Let us raise our glasses in his honor."

"To Harold. The first to get a cross," Caroline said. The rest joined in the toast.

"What is it you want to tell us?" Linda asked.

Lou set her glass down and motioned to Jason and George to come forward. They both carried hand-carved wooden boxes, the size of a cigar-box, and set them on the table, one in front of each person.

"As a special gift to my new friends, my father, George McClelland, has made something for you." Lou choked back her emotions as she picked up the box.

"Look close and you will see a cross, the symbol of eternal life carved into the top, your name, along with the date of your accident. Under that, is the inscription from your cross." Lou gave out a deep sigh. "Okay, open your boxes."

One-by-one the tops of each box came off to sounds of delight. Inside lay a wooden angel. Her skirt had been painted black, and her blouse was white with her dark-brown hair tied back with a blue ribbon. In her hands, she held a yellow rose. Lou watched as each of them lifted the little angel from her resting place to admire the splendid carving George had done for them.

"This is your angel. Her name is Kelly Turner. She was traveling to Maupin across Bakeoven Road in 1930 to start her tenure as a circuit nurse for Wasco County. She never made it. She ran off the road and perished alone. Why she remained along that road is a mystery. Perhaps, she was waiting for the right time."

"What's the yellow rose for?" Brandon was the first to ask.

"What does it mean?" Jenny questioned, glancing at the others.

Lou felt the energy filling the room and smiled.

"That's the part of the story I left out and why I asked you here tonight, and to come alone. You probably wonder how I had enough information to write the whole story."

Caroline gently touched the carving. "I've been wondering that myself."

Lou cleared her throat. "It happened right before my accident. I was coming back from Shaniko and approaching the location where the large yellow rosebush covers the ravine. I don't know if any of you have seen it. I nearly drove by, when a reflection caught my eye and I stopped to see what it could be. It was a long climb down to the bottom and I could barely see the road from where I was standing. I wanted to turn and run back to my jeep, but something was pulling at me to stay. The blossoms were long gone, but the branches were thick with thorns, so I found an old tree limb and started poking around the bush. It was so hot, and the air was silent. I was about to give up, when I lifted a vine and saw the fender of an old truck."

Brandon let out a low whistle. "Bet that freaked you out. Know I would have been."

"Yes, at first. Then my curiosity took over. It took a while, but I moved enough of the vines on the driver's side, to look inside the cab."

"What did you see? Was there? No—don't tell me," Linda said.

Lou smiled. "No, Linda, there were no bones inside, if that's what you were thinking, though it crossed my mind too. The truck was empty. Sage rats had torn the seats apart and the glove box was laying open giving up hope of finding who it may belong to. Then I spied the edge of a metal tin wedged under the seat. It took me a few minutes, but I got it out. When I opened it and found a journal, I was sure it must belong to the driver of the truck and was on my way back when a tire blew out and I wrecked my jeep."

A collective sigh came from the group. "When did you get to read it?" Jenny asked.

Lou glanced over at Jason and reached her hand out to him. Jason moved to stand next to her. "Jason was the one to read it to me in the hospital. That's a story for another time. The point is, the book was Kelly's. It covered the day before she left the orphanage where she had lived all her life until the day she died." Lou reached down and picked up five manila envelopes and passed them around the table.

"Inside these envelopes are copies of the journal and a letter from Harold. I felt you each deserved the whole story. You can tell your family or loved ones about Kelly, but I ask you never to tell anyone what Harold's letter has to say."

The group looked confused until they scanned the final page and gasped. Only those who held the boxes, along with Jason and George knew what the yellow rose meant. In a show of solidarity, everyone swore never to divulge its secret.

Lou replaced her angel and closed the lid before sitting in her chair. One by one, the others did the same.

The room was silent until Bill stood. "I hope I can speak for the others thanking you for bringing us together tonight, Lou. Ever since that day I've wondered what her name was. Now, with this lovely gift, I will hold her in my heart even tighter."

Bill reached for his glass and held it high. "I propose a toast to Lou, a fellow cross-holder and dear friend. And to Kelly, may she rest in peace."

The rest of the table stood, glasses in hand, and toasted Lou and Kelly, then the evening was over. After heartfelt goodbyes, everyone promised to stay in touch.

Tonight, had been perfect. Lou asked her father if he would leave with the others so she could spend a few moments alone with Jason while they cleaned the room.

"Thank you, Jason," she said, as she cleared the tables.

"For what?" He was tossing the cups in the trash.

Lou walked over and took his hands in hers. "For believing in Kelly's story, in me—in us. Tomorrow the world will know all about this special person."

Brad glanced at the clock on his desk and watched the seconds tick by. If Lou didn't show up in five minutes, he would have to pull her slot and run something else in its place. He didn't want to, but it would leave him with no choice, if he wanted to get the paper out on time. He was about to call the copy room when a knock sounded on his door.

"Come in," he called out. A sigh of relief washed over him as Lou and Jason entered. "You were worrying me, Lou." Brad motioned them to close the door and take a seat. "Hello, Jason, good to see you too."

Lou grinned and slid the papers onto his desk before sitting.

"Here's the story. We hope you like it."

Brad looked at Jason, who nodded in agreement, then picked it up and began reading. By the time he'd finished, he was smiling, with a hint of a tear in his eye. "This is good, Lou, fantastic job. Though it's different from what I expected."

Lou relaxed into the chair. "Thanks, Brad, that means so much to me. I couldn't have done this without Jason's help. The story is ours."

Jason reached for her hand. "The story is yours, Lou. It always has been. I've just been along for the ride, and it's been a wild one, for sure."

Lou huffed and smacked him on the arm. "What's that

supposed to mean?" She gave him a sly smile.

Jason grinned back.

Brad shook his head at the two of them and laughed.

"Okay, enough with you two. I have a paper to get out, and you, Lou, are holding up production. Is this on your computer ready to file?"

Lou straightened in her chair. "Yes, it's ready to go. I was waiting for your approval to send it."

"Well, you have it. Now get to your office and file this story. The whole production team waiting."

Brad rose and came around his desk. "Good job, Lou. I think this might be your best work—so far, from my new investigative reporter."

Lou gasped. "Are you sure? What about Chris?"

Brad nodded and gave her a hug.

"Yes, Lou. The job is yours. Chris left the paper for a job in Seattle. Though I had been leaning towards you from the beginning. And you too, Jason. If you ever want a job, let me know. It's not as fancy as New York City, but it's a good place to work."

Jason was speechless.

"Ah, thanks, Brad, I'll take that under consideration. For now, let's get Lou's story published."

Jason shook Brad's hand and ushered Lou out the door.

"Come on, Lou, don't you have a story to send?"

Still reeling from Brad's declaration, Lou followed Jason back to her office and sent the story. Now it was time to relax. The hard part was over. Thinking about the story, Lou realized it had become bigger than all of them.

She hadn't told Jason while he was in New York City; she drove out to Bakeoven Road to see if a cross stood with her name on it.

Twice on the way out, she had almost turned back afraid there wouldn't be one for her since she was the one to discover Kelly.

What if she had ruined the mystery?

Lou's heart had raced in her chest when she approached the spot of her accident and white cross stood in all its glory, and a smile flooded her face.

The mystery continued.

Lou had pulled over and got out of her car. It took her a few minutes to gather the courage to walk over to it and when she finally did, thoughts of Kelly crossed her mind, and she understood the words in front of her

It said, "Lou McClelland, saved to let go of the past and embrace the future. August 25, 2018." It was then she understood the words and how she wanted to finish the story.

Jason watched Lou and wondered what she was thinking. His own thoughts were in such a jumble he was having a tough time making them fit together. What would be next for them now that they finished the story? He had almost given up on the chance for happiness with her, and now he was letting doubt cloud his mind once again. He loved Lou, and she loved him. The rest would work itself out.

Lou's story proved to be an enormous success. The paper sold out each day, and Brad was into his third printing. Letters and phone calls to the editor flooded the paper. People wanted to congratulate Lou and the paper on their inspirational story about hope and love, and most of all, believing in the magic of miracles. Lou told the stories of the six crosses and what the survivors had done with their lives after their chance meeting, with what Lou could only call an angel.

She wrote about a young woman's a short journey until her untimely death somewhere on Bakeoven Road. But she left out the part about the rosebush to protect Kelly's final resting place. She wrote of the loss of Harold Joner, the first cross-holder, and of her own experience after her wreck. How she too believed she had met an angel that day, and how it forever changed her life.

As for the crosses, she wanted people to form their own opinions why they appeared. More than anything, she hoped readers would remember someone was watching over that small country road, protecting those who traveled it.

Lou called Julie knowing she would see the story and filled her in on what had happened since she left. Though upset with Lou, Julie said she understood, but made Lou promise never to leave her in the dark again. And, even though Lou and Jason hadn't set a date, they agreed to get together soon to plan Lou's wedding.

Six months had passed since the story was published, and life had settled down for both of them. Jason had gone back to New York City to continue working for his paper and Lou was busy researching her next story—hunting for Kelly's family—while she and Jason navigated their long-distance relationship.

Each month they would trade-off a weekend. Fred was getting stronger, and Joan had become like a sister whenever Lou visited. When Jason was in The Dalles, he and her father would talk for hours, and Lou welcomed Mary's encouragement.

Lou found out Julie was expecting her first baby and she wanted Lou to be the Godmother. Lou was honored and terrified at the same time and promised to do her best. She had also been thinking about Kelly and realized there was one final thing she needed to do to wrap up the story. Lou knew she could have gone by herself, but she wanted to share this major decision with Jason.

Chapter Twenty-five

It was the end of May, and spring flourished on the high desert. The afternoon sun heated the early afternoon air as Jason and Lou drove across Bakeoven Road and a soft breeze swayed the wildflowers dotting the landscape, with bursts of purple and pinks among the green of the sagebrush and junipers.

They were enjoying the drive until they rounded the corner and came up out of the curves and approached Lou's cross. Jason stopped for a moment, then continued without saying a word.

It was still hard for her to imagine she had almost died there.

Lou squeezed his hand and sighed. As they drove closer to where she knew the truck lay hidden, Lou felt the energy pulling at her. She motioned for Jason to pull over and park. Carefully, she got out on the side of the road and waited for Jason to join her.

The wild rosebush displayed its full bloom now, billowing in the wind like a buttery yellow ocean.

"Is the truck down there?" Jason looked at the blanket of yellow roses.

Lou nodded, glancing around the road. "Maybe we should park up the road then walk back. Just in case someone comes along and wonders what we're doing."

"That's a good idea. You stay here, and I'll move the car." Jason drove the car up to the next pull-out section and parked, then he jogged back to where Lou stood.

"Are you ready?"

"As much as I will ever be." Lou stepped off the edge of the road. The hillside looked steeper to her this time as they worked their way down to the bottom of the ravine. Being mindful of the loose rocks and gravel they used the sagebrush to hang onto to keep from sliding and landing in the thorns.

Once they reached the bottom, Lou's pulse pounded with excitement the closer she got. She still couldn't believe she had been the one to find it and searched the ground until she found the branch she had used before. Lifting a large clump of yellow roses, she exposed the front bumper.

Jason whistled low. "You're right. No one would have found her, even after the flowers faded, hidden under the vines."

Lou lowered the flowers and backed away as if she had disturbed a gravesite. Then remembered Harold's letter and felt a deep sorrow. "I believe it was just luck when I saw the reflection that day." She stepped back next to him. "Think of all the years people have traveled this road, and no one ever saw the truck except Harold. Why me?"

Lou was still having trouble realizing that Kelly had died in this very spot, all alone, so many years ago.

Jason put his arm around her, pulling her close. "I'm not sure, Lou. Maybe it's God's way of setting the universe right again."

Lou leaned into his chest. Maybe it was.

"Jason, I don't want anyone down here looking for Kelly. It would tear me apart."

"I agree. But we need to honor her." He began searching the ground until he found two old pieces of a wood fence, then pulled a piece of string from his pocket. He tied the two pieces together to fashion a cross. Next, he took out his pocketknife and carved Kelly's name into the wood.

Lou watched in awe. It was perfect, then she frowned.

"You know we can't put it up on the road. Think what people would do if they saw it."

"Your right. Scavengers would destroy this place. I've got an

236

idea. Get that branch you were using. Harold said he had buried her close to the truck. We can put it next to the bumper then cover it with the roses."

Lou grabbed her branch and with both hands, held up the rose clump. Jason pushed the makeshift cross into the ground. Before setting the rose vine over it, she said a silent prayer, hoping God would answer her. Lou felt the silence again, giving her a chill and slide her hands in her pockets, then remembered what they came to do.

Pulling the metal tin from her pocket, she held it up to Jason.

"There's one more thing." Lou made her way to the side of the wild rosebush where the truck door lay hidden. "Jason, can you lift this vine?"

Jason picked up the branch Lou had been using and struggled with the vine. "Hurry, Lou, this thing is heavy."

Lou reached her arm in through the door, just enough to slip the metal tin back under the seat where it belonged. She pushed as hard as she could and closed the door before she stepped back.

"Okay, Jason, you can let go."

Jason began to lower the vine when the branch cracked, then broke in half, dropping the vine over the door, hiding it from all. It was a fitting end as he tossed the rest of the branch to the ground.

"I guess that does it." He moved next to Lou.

Lou slipped her arm in his, surveying the roses. "Do you think it's covered well enough?"

"We could put a few more branches to be sure," he said.

A single cloud covered the sun, casting shadows across the roses as if agreeing with him, then moved on, leaving them in the hot, sticky air as they each took a side of the truck, working to fill any open spot they could find.

Jason was surveying their work when a gust of wind blew by him, stirring up the dust as it traveled up the hill to the road. He looked up the embankment, shading his eyes with his hand and was sure he saw someone standing at the edge of the road looking down at them. The hairs on the back of his neck stood on end as he strained his eyes for a closer look.

That's when he saw her—Kelly!

She appeared just like Harold and the others had described, dressed in a black skirt and white blouse. Suddenly the wind caught her long dark hair, arching it into the shape of wings behind her.

Time stood still and silence surrounded him.

He tried to call out to Lou, but nothing came from his mouth. Frightened, he closed his eyes, but forced himself to open them again. This time he saw Annie standing next to Kelly, holding their baby, Sophia. A bright light shone around them. He lifted his hand to wave, but the light dimmed, and they disappeared.

Jason dropped to his knees. Had he seen his wife and daughter with Kelly, or was his mind playing tricks on him? A soft breeze swept over him bringing the sweet scent of lilac, Annie's favorite flower and he was sure he felt someone or something, brush against his cheek.

Lou finished covering her side of the truck and turned around to find Jason kneeling on the ground. Rushing to his side, she knelt next to him.

"What's wrong, Jason? Are you hurt?"

"They were here." His voice quivered.

"Who was here? I didn't see anyone."

"Kelly. It was her." He pulled Lou close to him. "Annie and Sophia were with her."

"Are you sure?" She had felt the energy that surrounded them and hoped Kelly might show herself.

Jason nodded. "Yes. It was them. They were just the way I

238

remembered—happy. My greatest fear has always been that they were in pain. Now, I can let go and start a new life—with you, Lou."

Lou bit her lip. She was ready to begin their lives together and tackle the next part of the story. Finding Kelly's family. Most of all, Lou believed God had answered her prayer.

Kelly was still the angel on Bakeoven Road.

The story continues…

Return to Bakeoven Road

Reporter Lou McClelland is still amazed by the power of hope and second chances that resonated with her readers. It began as a story of survival but turned into so much more for the survivors and Lou herself, when her feature story was published about the crosses on Bakeoven Road. Lou still wondered if it had been plain luck or divine intervention when she found the wrecked truck, and the journal of a young women named Kelly.

The one thing she did know, she believed in angels.

So much had happened since Jason Peterson arrived that summer day a year ago, throwing her life into chaos. He was a man, with a broken heart, but while working together they realized life offered them a second chance at love. Now as Lou attempts to navigate their long-distance engagement, she works on her new assignment to unravel the mystery surrounding Kelly's birth and try to find her family.

Intrigued by what she hopes to find, Lou decides to search for her own family's history, exposing secrets she isn't prepared for or how they will change her life forever. When Lou's new-found faith is tested after receiving devastating news about Jason, she draws upon that strength and returns to Bakeoven Road where it all began, praying there's still an angel standing on it.

Coming Spring 2020
Pre-order now at
www.SandyCereghino.com